“Your skin. It’s...” Dev looked down at their hands, where the live current seemed to dance between them.

“Electrifying?” Ione drew him to the couch. “Not bragging. You have the same effect on me. I think Kur’s blood has mixed with your own and it responds to the Lilith blood in mine. As mine does to yours.”

He sat beside her, bemused.

“I’m not sure what it means, but I’m not going to bother trying to figure it out right now. Suffice it to say, you’re the last person I should be attracted to. You’ve been sent to take everything away from me.”

“That’s not exactly—”

“And yet I find you irresistible.”

Dev ran his tongue along his bottom lip. “Well, I know this isn’t necessarily the wisest thing,” he said, rising and sweeping her up. He hiked up her skirt as she wrapped her legs around him. “But it is definitely what I need.”

BEWITCHING THE DRAGON

JANE KINDRED

First Published in Great Britain 2017
By Mills & Boon, an imprint of HarperCollins*Publishers*
1 London Bridge Street, London, SE1 9GF

ISBN: 978-0-263-93007-8

89-0517

Our policy is to use papers that are natural, renewable and recyclable products and made from wood grown in sustainable forests. The logging and manufacturing processes conform to the legal environmental regulations of the country of origin.

Printed and bound in Spain
by CPI, Barcelona

Jane Kindred is the author of the Demons of Elysium series of M/M erotic fantasy romance, the Looking Glass Gods dark fantasy tetralogy and the gothic paranormal romance *The Lost Coast*. Jane spent her formative years ruining her eyes reading romance novels in the Tucson sun and watching *Star Trek* marathons in the dark. She now writes to the sound of San Francisco foghorns while two cats slowly but surely edge her off the side of the bed.

Jane is represented by Sara Megibow of KT Literary.

For my big sisters, who may not always get why I write what I write but have always encouraged me to write it.

Chapter 1

There was another dead crow on her doorstep this morning. A piece of red thread encircled its neck, not as though it had been the instrument of the crow's death but as a macabre decoration, tied into a neat bow. After finding the dead birds three days in a row, Ione had come out to get the paper this morning armed with a pair of disposable latex gloves and a small paper sack.

Given the time of year, she might have assumed this was some practical joke from a neighborhood kid, maybe someone who knew she was a high priestess in the Craft. A setup, in poor taste, for a Halloween trick of which Ione was the punch line.

But it was no mystery who was behind this. This was a message from her ex. Carter Hanson Hamilton was up to his old tricks.

With the crow carefully deposited into the paper bag, she carried it around the side of the house to the outdoor altar—which did double duty as a brick-enclosed barbecue pit—and performed the Dispersal of Energy ritual to nullify whatever magical influence Carter might have in mind with these little gifts. The smell of smoke from the small blaze in the pit wouldn't be completely out of season. Though the air was sharp and crisp this morning, it hadn't quite gotten cool enough for a fire, but it was only a little late for a barbecue.

"Go in peace," Ione murmured as she finished the ritual. She wasn't sure if birds had spirits, but it couldn't hurt to commend this one's to a better rest.

The "Gladys Kravitz" of the Village of Oak Creek was watching her through the blinds of the house across the street as Ione came back around to the front. Ione gave her an exaggerated wave from the porch in her bathrobe and slippers. The blinds snapped shut. Maybe Ione had watched too much *Bewitched* on TV Land, but that woman was a dead ringer for Samantha Stevens's nosy neighbor.

The phone was ringing when Ione stepped inside and she managed to catch it before it rolled over to the answering machine. Her younger sister Phoebe gave her endless amounts of crap about that machine, as if Ione were the last person in the world to still have a landline.

"Ione? Sorry to bother you at home. Um, oh—it's Cal. Sorry. This is Calvin." The tentative, apologetic tone was typical of Calvin Yee. The elderly Asian gentleman had been Covent kin for years, far longer than Ione had even been a member of the Sedona coven, but he still treated her as if she were his boss or a school professor.

Ione smiled into the phone. "Not a problem, Cal. What's up?"

"Uh…the others thought I should let you know—*we* should let you know. I, uh, volunteered to be the one to let you know."

Ione's heart dropped into her stomach. It was finally happening. The coven had voted to boot her out on her butt. After weeks of walking around on eggshells, they'd finally decided they couldn't work with a high priestess who'd been stupid enough to fall for a psychotic necromancer like Carter Hamilton.

With a deep breath, she gathered her courage. "To let me know what, Cal?"

"We've received a summons. All of us. Each of us."

"A summons?" She let out the held breath cautiously. "From the Superior Court?" She'd thought this business with Carter was done. He'd confessed and was sitting in prison awaiting sentencing.

"No, somebody from the Covent leadership. We've been ordered to appear at the temple tomorrow morning at ten."

"I see." *Crap.* Maybe she *was* being ousted, just not by her personal coven members.

Calvin cleared his throat a few times with a couple of false starts before he continued. "You didn't get one, I take it."

"No, I didn't. Thanks, Cal. I really appreciate you letting me know."

Ione tried not to speculate about the possible intentions of the Covent's pending action, but it was hard not to see a summons of her coven members that excluded her as anything but a kick in the teeth. She'd worked hard to be accepted into the Covent on her own skill and merit, and even harder to prove herself worthy of leadership. At twenty-nine, she'd become the youngest high priestess in the history of the Sedona Coventry. But at thirty, thanks to being dumb enough to fall for Carter, everything was falling apart.

One thing was for certain, there was no way she was going to sit at home and wait for someone else to decide her fate. She would be at the temple in the morning, whether the Covent leadership wanted her there or not.

In the meantime she had work to do. Carter might be safely behind bars but the creeps who'd patronized his little sideline business—paying for a shade possession called a "ride-along" for the ultimate in nonconsensual sexual thrills—were still out there. One of the call girls who'd participated as a living host before dying under suspicious circumstances and ending up on the other side of the equation had implicated cops, businessmen, even lawyers and judges. And none of them had been held accountable. After Carter's arrest, they'd scurried away like roaches into their cracks and crevices of respectability. Ione was determined to find out where they'd gone into hiding and bring them out into the light.

Sedona's nightlife was hardly that, but Ione had followed the rumor mill to a dive bar near Oak Creek Canyon that was unusually lively and catered to the kind of clientele Carter's side business had thrived on. The mixture of college students and favorite sons plus a steady, inevitable stream of tourists provided a wealth of potential clients—as well as plenty of unwary young women to exploit. It wasn't really the sort of place Ione Carlisle looked at home in. But she wasn't Ione Carlisle tonight.

Magic, she'd learned, was merely a matter of perception. Change the perception of a thing and you might change the thing itself. With a simple spell that amounted to little more than magical cosmetics and dressing the part, Ione had remade her image into the one she wished to project. She still had her favorite clothes from her aborted year at college before becoming insta-mom to a teenager and twin ten-year-olds after the death of her parents. With a pair of leather pants and a black tank, a red, zip-up leather jacket and a slick of bright cherry lipstick that pulled the look together, Ione had invoked a shadow glamour.

The pert-nosed, blue-eyed blonde with loose waves

around her shoulders—nothing like Ione's gray-green eyes and straight midnight-brown and bronze ombré mane that hung down her back—was attractive in a generic way and utterly forgettable. It was a spell she'd perfected as a teenager when she'd needed an alter ego to channel the impulses of youth she hadn't known how to deal with. Even in adulthood, however, it had its uses.

The bartenders at Bitters knew her as Kylie when she came in with this face—she'd been on the prowl enough that the bartenders knew her by name. And knew her drink, Balcones, which arrived almost as soon as she sat at the bar.

Ione set her motorcycle helmet on the stool beside her. It kept guys from hitting on her unless she wanted them to. Sitting at the end of the bar took care of the other side. She could have used a repelling spell, but too much magic in one night made her feel even worse than drinking too much.

"Is that your Nighthawk outside?" The cultured, Hugh Grant–esque British accent sent a tingling vibration through her that completely missed her spine and went straight for the genitals. God, was she really this hard up that a fancy accent was all it took?

Maintaining cool disinterest in the man standing beside her helmet's stool, Ione took a sip of her drink before turning her head slightly in his direction. Giving him the once-over out of the corner of her eye did nothing to dispel the disconcerting vibration. A pair of golden-brown eyes to match her glass of Balcones looked back at her, pieces of tiger's-eye quartz rimmed in dark lashes against the warm teakwood hue of his skin. Thick black hair, impeccably styled, with a charming streak of gray at the temples, completed the picture. And the expensive suit said business tourist—but the kind of business that didn't require sitting behind a desk in an office.

She was a sucker for a sharp-dressed man. And a posh

accent, apparently. But ogling hot guys in expensive suits wasn't what she was here for. She tried to assess whether he could be part of the network of what one of Phoebe's clients in the Public Defender's Office had referred to as "a bunch of power-tripping dicks."

Ione realized he was waiting for her answer. "Maybe."

"Sorry, that wasn't a line." He leaned against the bar as if he had no intention of moving on and gave her a crooked smile that made the tiger's eyes shimmer. "I just haven't seen one of those in a while. You've kept it in excellent shape."

Ione gave him a dismissive shrug. "You never know what's under the chassis. Maybe I just keep it looking pretty and ride it into the ground." She went back to her drink, deciding he seemed a bit too straitlaced to fit the profile she was looking for, but he didn't take the hint.

"I doubt that. The bike shows signs of being well loved." He moved to the open seat beside the helmet and ordered a beer.

"Do you ride?" Ione hadn't intended to talk to him, but her vibrating pussy apparently had a different agenda.

He shook his head. "I've ridden on the back of a friend's bike, but my parents would never let me ride myself."

The corner of Ione's mouth twitched. "You live with your parents?"

"What?" Her companion choked a bit on his beer and set the bottle down. "Oh. No, no. You've misunderstood me. I meant growing up. Of course, even now, my mum would probably kill me before I could get myself killed on one if I even so much as…" His voice trailed off and he looked chagrined. "I just made it worse, didn't I? Let me try this again. I'm Dev." He held out his hand and Ione stared at it for a moment before he let it fall. "I'm just in town for a few days. Don't really know anyone here—and I am *really* sounding like an arse."

A little smile slipped out before she caught herself.

The bartender threw Dev a challenging look. "This guy bothering you, Kylie?"

Ione shrugged. "Nah, he's fine. Thanks, Gus. I think maybe he just needs something a little…stiffer." She tipped her glass toward him. "Get him one of these."

"I'm really quite fine with the beer, actually."

"Are you?" Ione looked him up and down. "Quite?"

His dark brows drew together. "Sorry…are you making fun of my speech?"

"Absolutely not. There is absolutely nothing funny about your speech."

Gus brought the Balcones and Dev started to object, but Ione interrupted. "It's on me."

With a shrug, Dev lifted his glass to Ione and nodded before taking a drink. "So, do you come here often?" He grimaced as the words left his mouth. "God, that sounded like another line. I mean *a* line. The first one wasn't a line. Neither was this—I mean…there were no lines. Oh, hell." He concentrated on the drink and Ione laughed and shook her head. "What I meant," said Dev, "was that it seems you come here often enough for the bartender to know you." He paused for a moment as if he'd just heard himself and rolled his eyes. "I seem to be determined to keep digging this hole deeper." Downing his drink, he slipped off the stool and straightened his suit. "It was lovely meeting you, Kylie. Thank you so much for the beverage."

Ione strangled the urge to laugh at the word "beverage." "You don't get out much, do you?"

Dev paused in the act of turning away. "Sorry, do you mean me?"

She threw him a sidelong glance. "I'm pretty sure Gus's

job gives him plenty of opportunities to hit on women. So, yes, I meant you."

The warm hue of his skin became even warmer. "I really wasn't hitting on you—"

Ione turned on her stool and leaned back with her elbows propped against the bar. "My God, you're adorably awkward—Dev, was it? Do they make them all like you across the pond?"

She seemed to have rendered him speechless.

Dev glanced around as if trying to find the actual person she was talking to before laughing at himself and shaking his head, the tension of his stiff posture finally easing. "I don't think they make any more like me anywhere, thankfully. I am rather dreadful at this, aren't I?"

Ione gave him a wry smile. "So you admit you were hitting on me."

Dev looked down at his feet with a smile, rubbing the back of his neck. "I might have done. Just a bit." That little vibration inside her began to quiver once more, like a tuning fork buzzing with a faint, pleasant note.

Ione swiveled around toward the bar and raised a finger as Gus glanced in her direction from the other end where he was ringing someone up. "One more over here, Gus, when you get the chance." She looked back at Dev, still standing there regarding her with a quizzical smile. Those eyes were really unfair. No one needed eyes that incredible. "Well? You in?"

Dev eased himself back onto the stool and smoothed back the gray curls at his temples with a grin. "I'm not sure what I'm in *for*, precisely, but I believe that I am, in fact, 'in.'"

Ione finished off her Balcones. "The ride, of course."

Dev paused with his hand on the glass Gus had set in

front of him. “I’m not sure it’s the wisest idea to be riding a motorbike after imbibing alcohol.”

She rolled her eyes and Dev’s cheeks went scarlet. He lowered his head over his drink and paid great attention to it as he sipped. With her elbow on the bar and her chin propped in her hand, Ione studied him. It probably wasn’t the wisest idea to be contemplating what she was contemplating, either. He was *not* what she was here for. But that vibration was only getting stronger.

She couldn’t take him home, though. She’d nursed her drink over the course of an hour and she had a sobriety elixir that allowed her to ride safely regardless, but she couldn’t exactly explain the elixir to this charming, awkward stranger who had her halfway to climaxing without even touching her. Or even knowing he was doing it. Which was what made her want to get to the other half so damn bad. She had a feeling his witting participation in getting to that goal would be toe-curlingly, ass-numbingly incredible.

“Do you have a car?” She’d blurted the words before her non-lizard brain could stop her. And of course he had a car. Did she think he’d walked all the way here?

Dev wiped sweat from his upper lip with a sensual gesture he probably wasn’t even conscious of as he glanced up at her. “I probably shouldn’t be driving at the moment, either.”

“You’re assuming I’d even let you drive.” Ione picked an ice cube out of her emptied glass and sucked on it. It was now or never. She crunched the ice between her teeth and slipped off the stool, pulling out her wallet to leave Gus a generous tip. “It’s kind of loud in here. I thought we could talk outside.”

She headed for the door without waiting to see what his reaction was. If he didn’t follow, she’d just take the sobriety elixir and get the hell out of there. And if he did, well…

Chapter 2

Dev twirled his glass in the ring of condensation on the bar, avoiding looking toward the door. He'd behaved recklessly, for reasons he couldn't explain. Kylie wasn't even his type. And, type or no type, he didn't make a habit of hitting on women. As if that hadn't been painfully obvious. He was here to gather information for his employer, not to snog strangers in pubs.

Although maybe it was a perfectly reasonable response to the pressure he was under. It was his first solo assignment, and if he didn't get this thing right, he could lose everything he'd worked for. He supposed the inclination to let off a little steam before he got down to business was to be expected. Or maybe he was just letting Kur get to him.

It was the name he'd given the thing that coiled at the base of his brain—or more likely the base of his cock.

Simply put, Kur was a demon. It had been part of Dev since his first disastrous attempt at conjuring. The demon had been caged by Dev's mentor, the first witch he'd been apprenticed to. Though, Simon, it turned out, had been something more than a witch. By all appearances a kindly white-haired elder, Simon had indulged in arcane arts that would have horrified most conventional practitioners. He'd trusted Dev with his secrets and Dev, in turn, had trusted him implicitly. But dabbling with the dark arcane and believing one could control such forces was a fool's errand. Simon had lost his life trying to tame Kur—and Dev had lost his soul.

Dev had only been nineteen when the demon had fused with him because of his foolish attempt to call it as Simon lay bleeding from the wounds Kur had inflicted on him. He'd tried to put it back in its cage—and had woken in hospital three days later, his back shredded and his memory of that morning gone. It was only months later that he realized the marks on his back were where the demon had clawed its way in to take up permanent residence inside him.

Dev set down the glass with a decisive thump against the bar. Kur wasn't in control of him.

He headed out to his rental car, keys in hand. He would politely decline if Kylie was actually out there waiting for him. Which he sincerely doubted she would be. She'd probably just been having a laugh at his expense. Either way, he'd have to take a chance on driving back to the hotel with a couple of drinks under his belt. It was a straight shot down the highway, which had been mostly empty when he'd come this way. And he was fairly certain that if he lingered at the bar any longer to make sure his blood alcohol level was sufficiently lowered, it would end up becoming much higher instead. Kur never let him off that easy.

Outside in the parking lot under the solenoid lamps, the red-leather-clad blonde was leaning against the passenger door—no, the driver's door—of his rental, arms folded across her chest. She'd unzipped the red coat. *Bollocks.*

"I'm afraid I need to make an early night of it" was what he'd intended to say as he approached the car. Instead he leaned one shoulder against the door beside her and said, "Hey."

Kylie gave him a sly smile. "Thought you'd changed your mind."

"Well, I haven't really *made* up my mind—about anything in particular."

"Haven't you?" She wasn't giving an inch, this one.

Dev tried to talk himself out of it. This really was the worst idea. Instead he found he'd leaned closer to her. He contemplated the cherry-bomb red of her lips for a moment before they both moved together in unison, his palm sliding behind her neck and her fingers slipping around his and into the hair at his nape. And then a blazing spark of desire shot up from the base of his spine and skittered along his skin like fire as their lips came together.

Dev rolled across her, his body pressing her into the cold metal, and Kylie moaned into his mouth, making his cock granite, her hands sending shivers through him as they roamed over his back beneath the suit jacket. Those hands were coming dangerously close to the ugly knot of scar tissue above his sacrum, and Dev reached behind his back and grabbed her wrists, pinning them beside her against the car. The aquamarine eyes almost seemed to flash green with warning, and Dev let go as Kylie stiffened against him.

He thought he'd blown it, and he drew back, but her hands had gone to the buckle of his belt, yanking it open, and she'd unzipped his pants before he could recover himself and grab for her hands once more. "We can't do this here."

Kylie was breathing hard, her rising chest drawing his gaze to the tight peaks of her nipples beneath the cotton vest. “Then open the door.”

Dev let out a soft groan as she reached into his pocket and pulled out the keys, dangling them in front of him. He hadn’t done it in a car since he was a teenager.

Kylie raised a questioning eyebrow and, when he didn’t object, hit the unlock button on the fob and climbed into the backseat.

Some small part of him was still trying to be rational, but the leather hugging that perfect arse smothered the last of his rational thought. Kylie turned and pulled him inside, and Dev felt light-headed and intoxicated as he fell against her, but it had nothing to do with the alcohol he’d drunk. There was something about her skin against his that seemed to send little electric shocks along the surface, further incensing his baser impulses. Her hands were at his fly once more, and Dev groaned more loudly as she slipped in her hand and took hold of him, wrapping her fingers around the almost painful heat of his shaft.

He lowered his mouth to her breast, sucking the hard nipple right through the fabric, and Kylie breathed in sharply, her hand tightening on his cock, letting her breath out in a soft, plaintive moan. After sliding the strap of the shirt down her arm until he’d drawn the collar below her breast, Dev closed his mouth once more over the black lace of the bra and sucked her in, thrusting involuntarily into her hand at the taste of her skin through the rough lace. Kylie’s legs wrapped around his hips as she moaned and squirmed, pressing herself up into his mouth, her tight grip sliding against the head of his cock.

Dev groaned, rocking into her hand. The damn bra had to go. He prodded at the lace, higher brain function completely gone, and tore it open, freeing the sodden nipple so he could get his mouth around it without interference. The high-pitched noise Kylie made, along with the rapid motions of her hand, brought him dangerously close to the edge.

He put a hand on her wrist, pulling his mouth from her breast with a slick *pop.* "You have to stop," he gasped. "I'm going to come."

Kylie's fingers unclenched. "Have you got a condom?"

"Condom?" Dev tried to make his brain work. "I don't think so." He needed his mouth on her skin.

Kylie made a growling noise of frustration in her throat. Tightening her legs around his hips, she swiveled suddenly, flipping him onto his back on the seat cushion.

Dev reached for her damp nipple, but she shoved him back and shimmied downward, swallowing his cock before he could do more than groan in surprise. Surprise was quickly supplanted by even deeper groans of pleasure as he rocked into her mouth, feeling the slippery heat of her lips and tongue sliding over him, and he came swiftly, gripping the seatback beside him with a shout as she swallowed it all.

As he lay back, his entire body going limp with release, Kylie zipped up her jacket, swinging her feet through the door he realized he hadn't even latched, and climbed out.

Dev struggled to sit up, hampered by his state of undress and the fuzzy post-ejaculatory brain cloud. "Kylie?" The door swung shut. Dev scrambled to put himself together and crawled across the seat to open it just in time to see her fasten her helmet and swing her leg over the Nighthawk, kick-start the engine and drive away.

Halfway down Highway 89A, Ione realized she hadn't taken the sobriety elixir. She pulled off to the side of the road and took the little vial out of her pocket, popping the cork and downing it swiftly. As soon as she had, the post-magical hangover kicked in, along with a dose of mortifying reality. *Mother of God.* Ione groaned into her gloved hands. What had she been thinking? At least he was only passing through and there was no chance she'd run into him again around town. Not that he'd know her if she did, but it would be awkward enough even if she was the only one aware of what they'd done together.

Mortification aside, she was no closer to exposing Carter's sick friends. If Dev was in town to hook up with a call girl—even one of the nonmetaphysical variety—he hadn't acted like it. She should have ignored her out-of-control hormones and stuck to the script she'd written for herself, keeping her eye out for one of the club patrons who fit the bill.

She shook off the glamour as soon as she got home, anxious to get out of her sweaty clothes and into a hot bath. Undressing while the tub filled, she paused for a moment at the sight of the ruined bra in the mirror as she drew the top over her head. The memory of how it had gotten that way sent that frisson of vibration through her once more. The touch of his mouth on hers had been like a narcotic rush, but when she'd felt his tongue on her breast, she'd nearly climaxed. And, God, what a climax that would have been. She could feel it just out of reach even now and she moaned involuntarily.

Ione touched her fingertips to her lipstick-smeared lips. She wasn't used to seeing herself like this. Usually she cleaned up before dismissing the glamour, because it was a bit unsettling to see the remnants of another face on her *actual* face. It was dishonest and a sort of dissociative game she wasn't proud of, but it was a defense mechanism she'd learned long before she'd started hunting Carter's accomplices. Sometimes she needed the freedom to be someone else. Because Ione Carlisle did not behave like this. Couldn't behave like this. She had to keep things together. So she'd split herself apart.

After washing off the makeup, she tossed the bra in the trash with a little growl of disappointment. It had been her favorite. *Do* not *think about how it got that way again.* But she was already thinking it as she wound her hair up into a loose bun and stepped into the fragrant, foaming bath. The water was a bit too hot, but the sting of it felt good. She closed her eyes and leaned back against the built-in headrest, Dev's charming accent murmuring in her head. Her fingers slipped down between her legs and she indulged in a little mental replay, the stroke of her own hand making up for what he'd neglected, while hot water and patchouli-rose bubbles sloshed against her nipples as a stand-in for Dev's sensuous mouth.

The climax made her cry out and she nearly swallowed a mouthful of bathwater and bubble bath as she slipped down the edge of the tub with the release of the tension she'd been holding in her legs. Not nearly as satisfying as actually having that sweet cock inside her, but still one heck of an orgasm.

Ione opened her eyes with a sigh and made a mental note to always carry her own condoms when she went out on a glamour bender. Even if she wasn't planning on having sex, it was only smart.

The bath and the orgasm had made her nicely sleepy, and Ione fell into bed later without bothering to dress, snuggling under the down comforter while the light patter of autumn rain played against the roof. She fell asleep almost as soon as her head hit the pillow and, for the first time in weeks, managed not to have a single nightmare about Carter Hamilton.

Chapter 3

The chime of her calendar notification in the morning reminding her of the Covent summonses brought her temporarily forgotten troubles crashing back. Time to face the music.

She tried to tell herself she was just being paranoid as she stroked her razor over her legs a bit aggressively as a proxy for the source of her frustration. Though it wasn't really paranoia when a necromancer had gone to such elaborate lengths to inveigle his way into the Covent's midst. Carter had spent years on his deception, becoming a respected member of the Phoenix branch of the Covent. He'd come to Sedona as part of a convention of the Regional Conclave to deal with the sudden rash of lingering shades of the recent dead in the area—shades, it turned out, that Carter himself had been trapping here.

Ione let out a sharp exclamation as the razor bit into the tender flesh at her ankle. Blood dripped onto the white marble tile like garnet beads scattering from a broken rosary—blood from the veins of a demon.

That was the crux of it. Carter had targeted her because of something she hadn't even known she possessed. She had been the last to know and the last to believe that she was a descendant of the most ancient of demons. She was a daughter of Lilith. And the Lilith blood was what Carter had coveted, the magic ingredient that would give him the power to command the dead. Phoebe had been his ultimate target, but he'd used Ione to set her up.

Despite the way they'd found out about it, Phoebe had seemed to take the news of their heritage in stride. Unlike Ione, she hadn't spent years struggling to reconcile the practice of magic with a belief in God. But everything was easy for Phoebe. She'd walked away from the church and embraced her gift years ago without a backward glance. If you could call being a way station for the recently deceased a gift.

Ione touched her finger to one of the drops of blood on her ankle, holding the tiny red orb on her fingertip under the cool white glow of the LED bulbs around the mirror. She concentrated on the drop until nothing else existed, the convex surface glistening like a miniature crystal ball in crimson in which her reflection was inverted. An angel on the head of a pin. Or a demon.

With a murmured incantation, she set the ruby bead floating above her fingertip. It was a simple trick, one of the first she'd learned. A trick for slumber parties when she was a girl. *Light as a feather, stiff as a board.* She'd thought then it was her own affinity for magic that had made it come so easily to her. It was because of that affinity that she'd started on the path that had led her to the Covent.

She'd come to believe in magic as a gift, and an art to be learned, not some kind of transgressive aberration. But this tainted blood was where her magical aptitude had come from, not hours of practice and months of apprenticeship; not innate talent. Not a gift from God.

Even so, it had allowed her to do what she loved. And if the Covent was going to take that away from her, she intended to walk into the temple as Ione Carlisle, high priestess of the Sedona Coventry, with her head held high.

She dressed in a crisp, white blouse and slim-cut black pants fresh from the dry cleaner's, topped with a black, flared, knee-length frock coat with delicate gray pinstripes. Presenting a confident, authoritative air was crucial in maintaining the respect of her coven, and Ione never left the house without making sure she was representing the office of high priestess with the utmost solemnity—when she left in her own face, at any rate. A light layer of foundation, a pale smudge of blush, a swipe of mascara across her bottom lashes and a dab of clear, matte gloss across her lips conveyed both professionalism and a certain understated grace.

The parking lot of Covent Temple was full when she arrived. As Calvin had implied, every member of the Sedona Coventry must have received a summons. Yet the Covent hadn't seen fit to inform their high priestess. Tears slammed against the backs of her eyes as she paused inside the atrium, and she dug her fingernails into her palms to keep them from going any farther. This was it. She was going to lose everything. Carter Hamilton had kneecapped her from behind bars without even trying.

Ione deepened her breath and exhaled the frailty of ego. She'd been elected to serve the needs of the magical community, not as some kind of merit badge or status symbol. If what the coven needed to heal from Carter's betrayal was for Ione to step down as high priestess, she would do it graciously. Even if it meant collapsing into a quivering heap on her bathroom floor when she got home and sobbing until she was sick. And then picking herself up and getting a job in the real world.

When she entered the temple, the rest of the coven members were seated on the comfortable benches that lined the aisles. The temple had been built with much the same design as a Catholic church—the Covent's origins steeped in the religion from which it had emerged—but its pews were for comfort not worship. So maybe this wasn't a ritual defrocking, after all; if they meant to perform any kind of ceremony, they'd be gathered in a formal circle at the altar.

All eyes turned to her as she came up the aisle—including a pair that were a glittering tiger's-eye golden brown.

Ione stopped still, blood rushing to her cheeks as well as to other more inconvenient and intimate places. It was impossible, but there he was, seated among them, just a little apart from the rest: last night's epic bad judgment. When he rose, the others rose with him.

The golden-brown eyes widened slightly at the sight of her, and she was certain for a mortifying instant that he'd somehow seen through the glamour last night. He knew exactly who she was. But the expression was gone just as quickly with no hint of recognition in his eyes, only grim determination.

"Dione Carlisle?" He'd pronounced her given name as "Dee-ohn"—which was the reason she'd changed it.

She willed herself to behave like someone who hadn't just run smack into the man she'd sucked off in a parking lot the night before while wearing another woman's face. "I go by Ione, actually. But I don't believe I've had the pleasure." Her cheeks throbbed at the unfortunate word choice, and he studied her with a peculiar expression.

With a slight, formal bow, he held out his hand.

"Dharamdev Gideon. The Leadership Council sent me."
Ione's heart sank. So this was her replacement, after all.

His skin tingled with magical energy as she shook his hand. She should have recognized it last night, the vibrational hum his proximity—and his touch—had set off inside her. It was magic—ordinary magical ability and not the pulsing tremor of some karmic sexual connection. She tried to ignore how the warm vibration of his skin touched off that answering warmth inside her that was decidedly more carnal than spiritual. And to ignore the enticing scent of his skin.

Realizing she'd held his hand a moment longer than necessary, Ione released it.

His expression masked, Dev clasped his hands behind his back, his deep-charcoal suit obviously tailored, as it accommodated his movements with perfect ease. "I'm the Covent assayer. I assume they told you I was coming."

Ione tried to make sense of the words. She'd thought for sure he was the new interim high priest. But maybe he was just some kind of number-cruncher or efficiency expert. Maybe the world wasn't ending.

"No, I'm afraid they didn't, Mr. Gideon. Assayer...what is that, exactly?"

Dev cleared his throat and drew himself up tall as he straightened his raw silk tie in dark teal, his face expressing disapproval—and a touch of what looked suspiciously like disgust. "The Covent seeks to determine what role you may have played in the infiltration of the necromancer Carter Hamilton. I'm here to evaluate your failure of leadership, Miss Carlisle, and to decide on an appropriate punishment." His cheeks seemed to color, but only for an instant. "Penalty."

The furious heat in Ione's cheeks was undoubtedly far more obvious. The Covent leaders apparently intended to treat her like a naughty child. The sense of resignation and grief at what she'd believed she was about to lose was quickly giving way to umbrage.

"I see." Ione put her hands in the pockets of her coat to keep the angry tremble from showing. "I take it my account of the events is in question. I suppose that's not entirely a surprise, given that none of the Council members was here to witness what happened. But the police accepted my account, Mr. Gideon. And Mr. Hamilton himself confessed that he alone was responsible for his actions. I'm sure any of the members of my coven can tell you what an act he put on, how he fooled us all."

She glanced at her fellow coven members to be sure they were still on her side. A few looked embarrassed but no one was avoiding her gaze.

"I'm not proud of being fooled, and I'll accept whatever censure the Covent deems fit to mete out for that failing, but I can assure you, Mr. Gideon, that I did nothing unethical."

Dev gave her a condescending smile. "I will, of course, be interviewing every member of the coven at length. But by your own account, your actions were anything but ethical. You used unauthorized magical influence on a Covent member—"

"A Covent member who happened to be a *necromancer*, Mr. Gideon. Who was in the act of attempting to murder my sister and another member of my coven."

"*Unauthorized* influence." The gemstone eyes seemed to crackle with intensity. "There are no exceptions to this rule. Rafael Diamante subdued him with the very necromancy of which you've accused Hamilton, and it appears from your account that you helped Diamante do it."

Ione's mouth dropped open and she had to work to get her jaw to function normally. And to respond without screaming. "You're not actually suggesting Carter Hamilton is *innocent*?"

"I'm not suggesting anything, Miss Carlisle. I'm merely explaining to you, since you seem to be having difficulty with the concept, that you took actions that are greatly frowned upon by the Covent. And a full investigation is more than warranted to determine exactly what happened here and who is culpable." Whatever trick of the light had made him seem so damnably attractive a moment before, his smug condescension had managed to shake Ione loose of it. Now he just looked like a pompous jerk.

He glanced around at the others as if just remembering their presence and let out a sigh. "I trust that you'll all cooperate fully with my investigation. I'd like to begin with brief, preliminary interviews with each of you, no more than ten or fifteen minutes, before Miss Carlisle and I sit down to discuss her account at length." Dev turned back to Ione. "I hadn't expected you to attend this preliminary session." His frown expressed disapproval of whoever had leaked the news. "Since I may be a few hours, it might be best if you leave and return later." He took out his phone, poised to make an entry. "If you'd give me your mobile number, I'll call you when the interviews are completed."

"I don't have a 'mobile' number." She couldn't help echoing his British pronunciation. Ione fixed her gaze on him as he looked up, daring him to mock her for being a Luddite. She actually did have a cell phone—for *emergencies*—but she was rather proud of the fact that she hadn't succumbed to the pressure to carry the phone about with her. "I don't need to reach anyone that urgently and anyone who needs me knows to reach me at my home number."

She took a book from her bag and turned to take a seat beneath one of the stained-glass windows. "I'll just sit and read while I wait." The glass depicted the tongue-thrusting goddess Kali. Ione hadn't chosen it on accident.

"Miss Carlisle." Dev hadn't moved, his brows drawn together in consternation when she glanced up from her bench. "I'd prefer not to have any…undue influence on the accounts of the others."

Ione glared daggers of ice at him. "I beg your pardon?"

Dev seemed to blanch as if only now aware of his choice of words. "I mean, it would be better if none of the coven members were to discuss their versions of the events with you prior to our interviews."

She let out an astonished and offended laugh. "You think I'm going to coach them, Mr. Gideon? You don't know a thing about me or my coven if you imagine for one moment that I'd tell anyone here to lie for me—or that any of them would."

Chatoyant eyes glittered dangerously in the candlelight. "Well, that's just it, isn't it? I *don't* know anything about you or your coven. That's what I'm here to assess. There's a process and protocol that must be followed."

Ione shrugged and opened her book. "Then follow it. I pledge a solemn oath before Kali beside me, Mr. Gideon, that I will sit here quietly and read and not 'influence' anyone in any way."

He was still staring at her. She could feel the indignation radiating from him in waves as she continued to ignore him until he finally sighed his disapproval and gestured to one of the coven members to accompany him to the vestry behind the altar.

Self-satisfied prick didn't know whom he was dealing with. She'd sit here all day if she felt like it—even if he didn't deign to talk to her at all.

A beam of sunlight through the window dappled the pages of her book with vivid reds and golds. Not the best reading light, but she was reading the same four or five words over and over again anyway, unable to make English out of them, her heart still pounding with anger—and more than a little anxiety.

"Is this seat taken?"

Ione glanced up to find the newest member of the coven smiling at her. Fresh and eager, Margot had apprenticed to an elderly member who'd decided to retire a few months ago. Ione hadn't gotten to know her yet. Not that Ione ever really got to know anyone. Once she'd been anointed as high priestess, it seemed wiser to keep her personal and coven lives separate. As the disaster of dating Carter had proved.

Ione smiled back, grateful for the overture. "It isn't, but aren't you afraid I'll accidentally influence you?"

Margot sat beside her, crossing her ankles beneath a pair of multicolored paisley leggings peeking through a sheer black skirt. Her relaxed, fun sense of personal style was the polar opposite of Ione's carefully conservative attire. Besides the responsibility of representing the coven as its high priestess, Ione had always feared being judged as perpetuating some kind of metaphysical trend. Sedona had a reputation for being a little out there, and, while many of the merchants were perfectly genuine, some of the more touristy businesses exploited that reputation for maximum effect.

Margot crossed her arms over her ample bosom. "Don't worry about Chauncey in there. Maybe he just can't let go of that stick up his butt because it's so damn tight." She grinned as Ione nearly strangled on the startled burst of laughter she was trying to suppress. "Man, you didn't see that thing walking away, did you?" Margot fanned herself. "Kinda makes you wish we could bring back the Great Rite."

Now *that* was something Ione didn't need to be thinking about. The image of rolling about on the floor in front of the altar with a stripped-down Dev Gideon was a little more than she could handle. Not that the Great Rite was really about rolling around on the floor having an uninhibited orgy, per se—God, she really needed to get laid more often. Ione shuddered, realizing the last time had been with Carter. And she did *not* find Dev Gideon attractive, she reminded herself. His personality had ruined it.

"And speaking of Rafe Diamante..." Margot winked. "How's your sister Phoebe doing?"

Ione couldn't hold back the laugh this time. "Yeah, my little sister pretty much hit the jackpot with that one, didn't she?"

"Not that I was trying to get into that boy's pants or anything, but I know quite a few women who are quietly weeping about not getting into those pants." Margot shook her head ruefully. "All joking aside, do you think he'll be coming back to the Covent?"

Ione closed her book. "No, I think he's had enough of organized practice." She was careful not to mention that, thanks to Phoebe's demon blood awakening his inner Quetzalcoatl, Rafe now had a tendency to sprout wings and get a bit scaly when he practiced ritual. Not that Phoebe seemed to mind that this, apparently, also included the raising of sexual energy.

Ione knew just a little too much about her sister's sex life these days. Not so much because they'd gotten particularly closer since the Carter incident, but mostly because the twins were busybodies and couldn't resist sharing juicy tidbits with Ione after calling Phoebe to pester her for details. To hear Rhea and Theia tell it, Phoebe hadn't left her house in weeks—because she was having trouble walking.

"Well, if you talk to him, let him know we all miss

him. And not just because of his pants." Margot smiled, putting a hand on Ione's shoulder. "And, seriously, don't worry about this investigation. We all know you didn't do anything wrong. We've got your back."

"Thanks." Unexpectedly, Ione had to work not to tear up. It was nice to have a vote of confidence. "That means more than you know."

She felt Dev's approach without looking up, as haughty, self-righteous energy filled the aisle of the nave. "I thought you were going to read quietly, Miss Carlisle."

Margot jumped up. "Sorry. My fault. I was getting a little antsy sitting around. But don't worry. I didn't let her give me the whammy."

Ione choked back another laugh and had to pretend to be focusing on her book once more, unable to look either of them in the eye.

Dev tried to vibe her with a folded-arm stance of paternal disapproval that she pretended not to see from the corner of her eye until he gave up. "And what is your name, Miss…?"

"Margot Kelley."

"Miss Kelley, why don't you accompany me to the vestry and we'll have a little chat."

Ione rolled her eyes. What was he, a headmaster in his day job?

The first interviewee, Calvin, passed her with a nod and an encouraging smile on the way out. That was two votes of confidence, anyway.

As she started to make an actual effort to put the proceedings out of her mind and read her book, a strangled cry of alarm came from the antechamber, and Calvin came stumbling back inside.

Ione was on her feet in an instant. "Calvin? What is it?

What happened?" She stepped into the aisle and put an arm around his shuddering shoulders.

"On the door," he choked out, looking ill.

Dev Gideon had come swiftly at the noise and he marched past them with determined steps, Margot following, bemused. Calvin had sunk onto one of the benches, too horrified by whatever he'd seen to articulate it.

Ione started toward the doors just as Margot hurried back inside. "What is it? What's going on?"

"You don't want to see it." Margot shuddered, blinking back tears. "Somebody—some sicko nailed a dead cat to the door."

Chapter 4

She was still high priestess of this coven, and it was her duty to protect it. Ione squeezed Margot's hand before ignoring her advice and heading into the atrium. Dev stood in the doorway, his body framed in sunlight, looking down at the paper in his hand.

He turned as Ione neared the door and shook his head. "There's no need to look. Someone was obviously going for shock value, and we don't all need nightmares."

"This is my coven, Mr. Gideon, and I'm not some delicate flower."

Dev caught her arm as she tried to pass him and the surge of vibrational energy struck her once more—not sexual this time, thank heaven, but a powerful bolt like a warning that stopped her in her tracks.

"Let go of me."

"Sorry." Dev released her, looking shaken. "I'm just trying to spare you any more trauma than is necessary."

"Necessary?" Exactly what kind of trauma would be necessary?

Dev held out the note. "I believe you were the target of this little act of terrorism."

Ione took it, unable to resist one last glance beyond him to the mangled thing that lay on the stone walkway. She looked swiftly away. Maybe he was right about this. Whatever the aim, she had no doubt this was an escalation of the message that had been intended with the dead birds left on her porch every morning for the past week. She'd been so focused on the summonses she hadn't even noticed the absence of this morning's "gift."

Her head swam as she tried to concentrate on the words written on a piece of parchment in the careful, talented hand of a calligrapher—in what appeared to be blood.

"It's ink." Dev guessed at her assumption. "They obviously wanted it to look like blood, but it's ink."

Ione breathed a little more easily and read the note aloud. "'Out of love for the truth and from desire to elucidate it, I, Nemesis, intend to defend the following statements.'" She glanced up at Dev. "This nut is doing Martin Luther's 95 Theses?"

Dev nodded grimly. "Just ten, but they're what I believe Americans would call 'doozies.'"

Ione continued. "'One. When the Covent was established in the Canton du Valais in the Swiss Confederation in 1533, its aim was to illuminate the arcane as a complement to the glory of God, not to profane it.

"'Two. The practice of the Sacred Craft within the tenets of the Covent is the antithesis of the practice of evil.

"'Three. The thirteen founding families believed in purity of heart, purity of mind, purity of body, and purity of soul.

"'"Four. There is therefore no place in the Covent for those who harbor evil within them.

"'"Five. The high priestess of this coven has brought the stain of impure blood onto this body.'"

Ione's voice trailed off. The remaining theses were more than she could bring herself to read aloud.

6. High Priestess Ione Carlisle, being of one of the venerable Covent families, has hidden the shameful secret that kept the Carlisle family from the ranks of the Covent for nearly four centuries: that she is of the blood of the accursed demoness Lilith.
7. Impure blood cannot be tolerated, and the body of the Covent must be cleansed.
8. Let her who pollutes the purity of the Covent be anathema and accursed.
9. To allow Ione Carlisle to continue as the high priestess of the Sedona Coventry is an act of heresy against the Covent.

The parchment shook in Ione's hands.

10. She who brings evil into the halls of the Covent shall be admitted only into the halls of death and hell.

Dev quietly took it from her. "The writer of these words is obviously mentally unhinged, and the Covent doesn't tolerate such harassment. But you'll forgive me if I ask… is there any truth to the accusation?"

Glancing up, expecting judgment and derision in his eyes, Ione was surprised to see compassion and concern instead. "That I carry the blood of a demon in my veins?" The weight of every self-recriminatory thought she'd been having for weeks pressed down on her. Every fear she'd had of losing everything was coming true. And she deserved it. She was tainted. "If my sister Theia's research is to be believed, I'm afraid the answer is yes."

She felt deflated and empty after holding the secret inside for so long. Spoken aloud, it seemed commonplace, something that couldn't possibly mean the end of everything she'd known. But it was.

Ione drew back her shoulders. "I'll save you the time and bother, Mr. Gideon. I just need to collect a few things before I go. If you want to have someone accompany me to make sure I'm not stealing any Covent property, I'll understand."

"Collect a few things?" Dev frowned. "Where are you going?"

Ione wrinkled her nose at him. "I—home, Mr. Gideon. I'd rather go quietly without a public spectacle. My coven deserves better, even if I don't."

Dev lifted an eyebrow. "Miss Carlisle, you seem to be operating under the misapprehension that I endorse the agenda of this deranged person or persons calling themselves Nemesis and defiling the sacred grounds of this temple. I have no intention of asking you to step down. Not for this.

"Depending on the outcome of my investigation, once concluded, if my recommendations to the Covent administration include electing a new high priest or priestess, it will be because of your involvement with the necromancer. Not because of some antiquated notion of impure blood."

Where had the smug prick gone? Was he actually being nice?

"I'm confused. What this 'Nemesis' nut says is true—my ancestor was found guilty of having demon blood, and when a member of my family was discovered to have married one of her descendants, the Carlisles were expelled from the Covent. Doesn't the Covent frown on dark magic?"

Dev's eyes were piercing. "Do you practice dark magic?"

"If you're asking about necromancy, of course not. But my affinity for magic clearly isn't born of goodness and light. It's…demonic." The word felt bitter on her tongue.

"There's a world of difference between demon ancestry and what modern religion defines as demonic. It so happens that demonology was my area of focus at university. What we call a 'demon' these days is more accurately a malevolent energy. Anyone can cultivate such negative energy. One doesn't have to be 'possessed' by some ancient spirit. In fact, it's rather racist to suggest that what's in a person's blood should make them inherently evil, don't you think?"

"I…hadn't given it much thought." She'd given it a lot of thought, actually. She'd thought of nothing else since Theia and Rhea had broken the news to her. But the way Dev was looking at her with those luminous eyes was making her feel as though she'd said something inappropriate and offensive.

"Don't get me wrong, Miss Carlisle. There may still be consequences for withholding this information from the Covent leadership. I am obligated to report it, after all. The Leadership Council may not all be quite as enlightened on the subject, and not disclosing this information when you learned of it may be viewed as a breach of faith." He carefully rolled up the parchment and made a gesture toward the remains. "Look, why don't I clean this up? And then you and I can talk at length—if you don't mind sticking around for a bit. I can interview the rest of the coven members at another time."

This was exactly the opposite of the reaction she'd expected from him. A few minutes ago he'd all but accused her of making up the accusations of necromancy against Carter and practicing it herself. And now he was trying to reassure her that her demon blood didn't make her evil?

Dev glanced around. "Do you keep any rubbish bags on the premises? Preferably dark, heavy-duty? I'd rather not carry that about in something transparent and have the others seeing it."

Ione studied him and nodded with an intake of breath. "I think there are some gardening supplies in the basement." Though she didn't exactly relish going down there. It was where one of Carter's victims had been stowed, and the smell had been impossible to get out completely no matter how much ventilation they'd given it. "I'll have someone go downstairs and scare something up."

Her conscience needled her for being a coward, but Margot was waiting inside the atrium, eager to do something to help. Ione sent her down to get the bags before reassuring the others that someone had just pulled a rather nasty prank and it was being taken care of.

On the bench farthest from the doors, Calvin sat, looking gray. Ione popped into the back office to get him a bottle of water and returned to slip onto the bench beside him.

"Hey." She handed him the water. "Mr. Gideon's going to clean up and then the rest of you can go home. Are you okay to drive or do you want someone to give you a ride?"

Calvin took the water gratefully and shook his head as he took a sip. "I can manage. I just…don't want to see that again, you know?"

"I know. I'm sorry you had to be the one to find it."

"Do you think it's…was it the necromancer?"

"Carter Hamilton?" Ione shook her head decisively. "He's behind bars and he's been stripped of his power. He can't do anything to hurt us. This is just some disturbed individual who's focused on me because of everything that's happened. Just trying to rattle me."

Calvin huffed. "Well, it sure as hell rattled me." He glanced up at her, brow wrinkled with concern beneath his receding hairline. "About that night—you needed our help—*Rafe* needed our help—and the coven let you both down."

Ione squeezed his forearm. "You couldn't have known how far gone Hamilton was. None of us knew. It all turned out all right in the end, anyway, so please don't give it another moment's thought."

"But we're not going to let you down again. I just wanted you to know that. We're all standing with you."

Ione smiled. "Thanks. I appreciate it."

Dev returned from washing his hands and dismissed the others, promising to contact them for their interviews at a later time. With the temple empty except for the two of them, there was no more putting off a one-on-one discussion.

But for the love of all that's holy, do not *think about your last one-on-one.*

From the moment Ione Carlisle entered the temple, Dev had felt the ground wobbling beneath him, refusing to stabilize, as if some kind of psychic fracking operation had disrupted his equilibrium. There was something painfully familiar about her, like someone he'd met in a dream or another life, his mythical counterpart split off by a vengeful Zeus. Which was preposterous. At best, she had to be grossly incompetent as a high priestess and, at worst, she was in league with a necromancer and guilty of malfeasance. Never mind the fact that he didn't believe in such nonsense as soul mates.

Her eyes, a grayish green, like the color of lichen or pale

jade, were the most uncannily familiar part of her. When they fixed on him, he felt as if he had something on the tip of his tongue he meant to say but couldn't quite recall it. And worse, Kur seemed to stir inside him at the sight of her as if he knew her.

"Have a seat, Miss Carlisle." Dev sat behind the desk he realized was most likely her own, but it was important to maintain the symbolic position of authority. He couldn't very well take her to task from the guest chair while she sat behind the large oak desk herself.

She took the empty chair without any sign of resentment. "Ms."

"Sorry?"

"*Ms.* Carlisle. You keep calling me 'miss.' That's considered a bit sexist and archaic here."

"Oh. I beg your pardon. Ms. Carlisle—"

"And, frankly, that seems unnecessarily formal. Just call me Ione."

He chose to ignore the fact that this pleased him unreasonably. "I *am* here in a formal capacity, but as you wish. Ione. Now that the others are gone, I wanted to get your thoughts on who amongst your coven might have reason for any kind of resentment or grudge against you."

Her perfectly sculpted brows drew together in disapproval as she uncrossed and recrossed her legs. "Among my coven? You think one of them did *that*? Absolutely not. Even if they did have a grudge against me, none of them would do anything like that. I know them. It's impossible."

"The cat wasn't killed by whoever put it there. At least, not directly. It was road kill, and a day or two old by the look of it." Not to mention the smell.

"I don't care. None of them did this."

Dev clasped his hands on the desk. "Do any of them know of your ancestry?"

She shook her head. "Not that I'm aware of."

"Who does?"

"My sisters. Rafe Diamante..." She paused, coloring. "And Carter Hamilton."

"You shared that with him?"

Ione's mouth was set in a hard line. Foolishly, he regretted being the one to provoke such displeasure on that otherwise lovely mouth.

"Shared it? I used it against him, Mr. Gideon. It's how we managed to bind him."

Dev hadn't heard this detail before. "How do you mean?"

"As my report states, I tried to gather a quorum of coven members to perform the necessary ritual, but without proof of Hamilton's necromancy, they were reluctant to interfere, particularly on the word of an outsider and in defense of a warlock."

He nodded impatiently. "So you helped Mr. Diamante use his necromantic abilities against Mr. Hamilton. I've read all this."

Her green eyes darkened. "We did not use necromancy. If you repeat that slander one more time, Mr. Gideon, I may be sorely tempted to violate the Covent doctrine against using magic for spite."

Dev had to work not to smile. Those eyes were really wreaking havoc with his poise. "You may as well call me Dev—in the interest of not being unnecessarily formal. But I suppose I can refrain from making such judgments until my investigation is complete. Please continue."

Ione's expression said she thought he was full of shite. "Given that my sister Phoebe's life hung in the balance, I reluctantly agreed to attempt to share magical energy with my younger sisters, who had just revealed their theory to me about our...enhanced blood. Despite the fact that neither of them is trained in witchcraft, I managed to raise sufficient energy with them to project a binding spell upon Carter Hamilton's magic from several miles away. We arrived at the Diamante family home just in time to see Rafe recover his nagual from Hamilton as the result of our binding. At which time, a spirit Hamilton had enslaved entered him—*of its own accord*—and bound him physically, as well."

"Nagual?" Dev wrote the unfamiliar word on the pad of paper he'd been using for his interviews. "And what is that?"

"I don't fully understand it myself, but as Rafe explained it, it's a sort of spirit animal representing the god Quetzalcoatl, whom Rafe claims to be descended from. He can project it outside himself in various forms—or he can take on its form himself."

Dev glanced up from the notepad. "He transforms physically? Into what?"

Ione shifted in her chair. "He calls himself 'quetzal.' He retains a mostly human form, except the tattoo of Quetzalcoatl on his back becomes an extension of him physically."

"I'm not following you. Quetzalcoatl is represented in Aztec art as a feathered serpent. You're saying he transforms into a feathered serpent in human form? Exactly how does that work?"

"I haven't examined him personally. It seemed a bit awkward."

"Then how do you know he actually did it?"

Ione cleared her throat and shifted her legs again. "Because he had wings. Iridescent blue-green-and-violet-tipped wings with an eight-foot span. Couldn't really miss them."

The pen slipped from Dev's fingers. "That—wasn't in the report."

"No." Ione shrugged—a vulnerable, feminine gesture that Dev found endearing. "It didn't seem relevant. The facts were that Carter appropriated Rafe's power through necromancy, my sisters and I bound Carter's magic and Rafe got the power back. I understand you're determined to make me out to be the villain of this piece because I was briefly involved with Carter Hamilton, but the fact is that he did what he did on his own and I was just stupid enough to fall for his act."

There was a weariness in her eyes that couldn't be faked. He wanted to believe she was telling the truth. But Dev had to be objective. He couldn't afford to let his basest instincts color his opinions in this investigation. He had a responsibility to the Covent. Several members of the Leadership Council had been against his appointment, and they were watching him like hawks, just waiting for him to screw up. Dev wasn't about to give them the satisfaction. And he would not be ruled by the demon. Tales of winged reptiles notwithstanding. Though he was going to have to interview this Diamante fellow for more than just his version of the facts of that night.

"I appreciate your candor, Miss—Ms.—Ione. So if I understand correctly, Carter Hamilton was made aware of your unique bloodline because he felt the power you and your sisters were able to project?"

Ione's gaze slid away from his. "Not exactly. I mean, I'm sure he must have felt it. But evidently he targeted me because he'd researched our family. He knew my sister's blood would fulfill the requirement necessary to awaken Rafe's quetzal power so he could steal it from him. He referred to Phoebe as a divine scion, as Rafe himself claims to be. In Carter's mind, I suppose, Lilith is a goddess and not a demoness."

Dev inclined his head. "If you subscribe to certain

pagan theories and academic speculation, Lilith may be equated with a number of ancient Semitic deities. It's a matter of perspective, I suppose. One man's demon is another man's divine. Or woman's." He cleared his throat. "Be that as it may, this additional information about Carter Hamilton is significant. If he has an obsession with your ancestry, I think it's quite likely he's behind this morning's act of terrorism."

Ione didn't seem surprised. "You think he's orchestrating this from behind bars?"

"He seems the obvious suspect and the only one with evident motive to want to harm you. This Nemesis may be an alias he's using or it could be the alias of someone he's convinced to act on his behalf. He can't use magic against you from prison because of the Covent's binding, but, from what you've told me, it seems he's rather persuasive."

Ione's cheeks flushed pink. "Most psychopaths are."

"Indeed." Dev made a note to look into how to get a record of Hamilton's visitors and correspondence. "In the meantime, this seems most likely to be harassment and not a threat. But you should probably take some extra precautions. Perhaps you could stay with one of your sisters for a bit?"

"I'm quite sure I can take care of myself, Mr. Gideon."

He gave her a wry smile. "Dev."

Ione's jade green eyes flickered with an expression he couldn't interpret. "*Dev.* I assure you, I'm perfectly capable."

"I don't doubt it. As for your ancestry, let me assure you that I haven't come here to dig up reasons to malign you before the Leadership Council. My job is to determine your fitness to serve as high priestess by assessing the facts of the events surrounding Carter Hamilton's crimes. I strongly suggest, however, that *you* tell them before someone else does."

She nodded stiffly as she rose. "I'll take that under advisement."

Dev stood to shake her hand. As before, he felt a bit of a shock jump between her hand and his as their skin touched—just as he'd noticed with Kylie. What was this, some new idiotic tic of the demon's to prod him into further mischief? Whatever the demon wanted, he would not be a slave to his desires.

"Thank you for cooperating in this matter. I understand that this is all very awkward and unpleasant, but I appreciate your professionalism." Despite his annoyance with himself at his reaction to her, when Ione withdrew her hand, he felt childishly disappointed at the absence of it.

As she buttoned her coat, something about the motion reminded Dev of the way Kylie had zipped up her leather jacket before riding away last night, leaving him in the backseat of his rental car with his prick out—well satisfied though it may have been.

"I take my position as a high priestess of the Covent extremely seriously," she was saying.

He was barely listening to her, the prospect of her disappearing into a world he wasn't familiar with suddenly as frustrating as the disappearance of Kylie. "You said you don't have a mobile number. How can I reach you if I need to?"

Ione picked up his pen and paper from the desk and wrote a number. "My landline. I have a machine."

Chapter 5

The disquieting flicker of energy that emanated from Dev Gideon's skin hadn't dissipated until Ione was beyond the temple. There was something odd about a witch who seemed to project a magical aura even when he was simply sitting still. Maybe he *was* glamoured. It would account for how unfairly attractive he was. But even Carter hadn't emanated such ceaseless power. Dev was like a live wire emitting a warning hum.

The light was blinking on her answering machine when she arrived upstairs, and her insides gave a stupid little jump of anticipation, as if the message might be from Dev. Why on earth would she care if he called her? If he did, it would only be to tell her she was being removed from her position. Or worse.

She played the message as she undressed. It was from Phoebe. Funny. Phoebe hadn't even been speaking to her for months—maybe years, if one wanted to get technical—

before this mess had thrown them together. Ione had been the one leaving unanswered messages.

"Ione, I know you don't want to be bothered right now, but something's happened."

She paused in pulling on her yoga pants.

"I don't like talking on a machine. Could you please call me? This is serious. I'm kind of freaking out over here."

Images of Theia and Rhea lying mangled on the freeway like the bodies of their parents eleven years ago seized her, and Ione sucked in her breath as if someone had punched her in the gut. *No. No, please. Don't let it be one of the twins.*

She grabbed the phone and hit Phoebe's number on speed dial. Her sister picked up immediately.

"Phoebe, it's me. What is it? What's happened? Are they okay?"

"They?"

"The twins. You said something happened."

"Oh, God, no. Nothing like that. They're fine. I mean, as far as I know. I haven't talked to them. I wanted to talk to you first."

The pressure squeezing her heart and lungs eased. "What, then? You said it was serious."

"I've been over at Rafe's for a few days. We brought Puddleglum with us. Thank goodness."

Ione rolled her eyes. Phoebe treated that cat like it was her baby.

"When I got home this afternoon, there was—someone left—something…on my porch."

Ione's stomach clenched. "A dead cat."

"Damn. You, too?"

"At the temple this morning. There was a note."

"Yeah, I got a note, too. 'Righteousness will not dwell in an unclean temple.' I don't even know what that means."

"Was it signed 'Nemesis'?"

"Maybe. The handwriting was so stylized. I think it's written in blood. I thought it said Genesis." A rustling sound followed before Phoebe spoke again. "Yeah, I think that's it, after all. Nemesis. Who's Nemesis?"

Ione sighed. "I don't know, but the note I got was a little more detailed. Nemesis laid out a disputation in ten theses explaining why my impure blood was polluting the Covent, promising to purify the temple."

"Oh, hell. I'm sorry."

"Whoever he or she is, I think Nemesis is working with Carter."

Phoebe made a sharp noise of disapproval. "Goddamn him. I thought we were done with his sorry ass."

"Whose sorry ass?" Rafe's deep, baritone voice came from the background.

Phoebe snorted. "One guess, babe. I'm putting you on speaker, Di." Only her sisters got to call her that. Anyone else would find themselves on the receiving end of a palm-heel strike to the sternum.

Rafe's voice became clearer. "You think this is Hamilton's doing?"

Ione shrugged at the phone. "Nemesis brought up the 'Lilith gene.' Who else knows about it besides us? You haven't told anyone else, have you, Phoebe?"

"Oh, *shoot*. You know, I did take out that full-page, coming-out ad in the *Sedona Demon Times*. Should I not have done that?"

Ione was used to pretending her little sister hadn't spoken. "Besides the five of us, Carter's the only one who knows." She sighed. Might as well tell them about the birds. "This wasn't the first dead animal I was gifted with, either. I've been finding dead crows on my doorstep."

"Crows." The symbolism seemed significant to Phoebe.

"Why, does that mean something?"

"That's one of Rafe's naguals."

This was news to Ione. "You have more than one nagual?"

Rafe cleared his throat as though Phoebe had mentioned something indelicate. "I transformed into a crow early in the quetzal's awakening. I believe it was a subconscious response to Hamilton using his necromantic powers to become the coyote when he was appropriating the authority of Quetzalcoatl's nemesis, Tezcatlipoca."

Nemesis. There was that word again.

"It does seem like Hamilton's MO." Rafe paused. "Why were you at the temple on a Saturday morning?"

"They sent a Covent assayer to investigate me—sort of a magical insurance claim adjuster—and he was there, along with the entire coven, when we discovered the cat."

"No." Phoebe managed to give that one little monosyllabic word the weight of an entire sentence.

Rafe was subdued. "I'm so sorry about all this, Ione."

"I suppose it was inevitable. And this is *not* your fault, Rafe. I just wish they'd sent an actual licensed investigator so we could find out how Carter's doing this. If he's communicating with someone on the outside, I don't think we have a legal right to know." She paused. "There must be some private investigators you work with through the Public Defender's Office, Phoebe. Maybe there's someone you can recommend?"

"Um, yeah, about that…"

"You might as well tell her, babe."

Ione's entire body went tense, like it used to when Phoebe's high school would call to tell her legal guardian about her latest trip to the principal's office. "Tell me what?"

"I don't work for the PD's office anymore. I quit my job to apprentice as a private investigator."

Ione's blood pressure shot through the roof. "You *quit* your job? You spent three years getting that law degree, Phoebe. Not to mention all the time you've spent putting in your dues. What are you thinking?"

"I'm thinking practicing law while having shades jump in and out of me at random is never going to stop being a conflict of interest. Not to mention awkward in the courtroom."

"Can't you just forbid the shades to bother you?"

"That's not exactly how it works. And I happen to like helping them. We've been over this a hundred times. I'm not giving it up. Even if I could keep them out, I won't."

"I didn't mean you shouldn't help at all. It's just…you're a really good lawyer, Phoebe."

Phoebe was silent for a moment, as if Ione had shocked her. "You've never said that before."

"You already know you're good at it. Why do I have to tell you?"

Phoebe sighed. "Anyway, I can always return to practicing law if this doesn't work out. But right now I'd say it's damn lucky I have my investigator's license, because I have access to the prison visitor and communication logs at the Florence State Prison."

"Oh." Ione smiled reluctantly. "I guess that *is* lucky, then."

"I'll take a drive down there and see what I can find out."

"I've strengthened the protection spell around Phoebe and around the house," Rafe reassured Ione before she could object. "I can come over and ward the perimeter at your place, too, if you like. My wards have a little extra kick these days with the quetzal magic."

"Why not?" A little extra protection couldn't hurt.

Dev was starting to think certain members of the Council had given him this assignment on purpose to smoke him out. Rumors had surrounded his mentor Simon's death and Dev's part in it. There was no question that something unnatural had attacked them both, but no one had quite been willing to say "demon." At least not aloud. And now some anonymous person was making accusations about demon blood and cleansing the Covent—and Dev was right in the middle of it.

He tried to shake off the disturbing events of the day as he headed back to his hotel. Documenting the impressions he'd gathered from the day's interviews—and the peculiar turn of events that had cut them short, he'd ended up staying at the temple much later than he'd planned.

The temple itself was a curious combination of enchanting and repelling. The temporal and spatial glamour around it to keep the general public from prying was exceptional. He hadn't even noticed the property as he'd approached this morning—though he'd been mesmerized by the landscape, which he supposed was part of the magic the glamour merely needed to draw from—until the white neo-Gothic spires had risen from among the damp rocks looking utterly out of place.

Despite the incongruous beauty of it, he'd felt the unpleasant residue of necromancy hanging in the air about the temple as he'd followed the twisting road to the small courtyard at the center of the labyrinth. No amount of stark, unearthly white stone had been able to mask what seemed like an almost visible muddy-gray pall. He'd thought then it was the negative influence of the necromancer and his high-priestess girlfriend, but now that he'd met Ione, Dev wasn't so sure. Perhaps the person who'd left the note and the dead cat had been hiding somewhere on the property at the time. That might have accounted for it.

But he was done thinking about those gruesome images for today. There was ordinary enchantment all around him.

He'd thought the view spectacular this morning, but he'd been preoccupied with the case. Or maybe it was simply more stunning this direction. Light rain fell like an afterthought on the pillars and domes of rock lining the highway. Their fantastic orangey-red hues struck a breathtaking contrast with the cerulean sky melting into a blend of indigo and violet—like the juice of a pomegranate running into the horizon. It was as if he'd driven off the highway into the land of the Fae, otherworldly and impossibly beautiful in a way he couldn't even articulate.

Much like his impression of Ione Carlisle.

Dev groaned. Best to nip that kind of thinking in the bud. She was the subject of his investigation and nothing more.

He tried to steer his thoughts toward a safer target—the image of Kylie driving away on her motorbike last night, leather pants supple against the shapely arse on the seat—the arse he'd let slip away because he hadn't been adequately prepared. He'd had no business starting something with her in the first place when it came to that. He'd gone to the pub to experience the local color, playing tourist before he had to face the drudgery of his assignment. But, despite the fact that she hadn't been his type, he couldn't get over the odd intensity of his response to her.

He felt like he'd taken the tiniest bite of enchanted Turkish delight before losing sight of the sleigh on which the White Witch of Narnia had ridden away, only to realize he'd die without another taste of that unearthly sweet.

Dev laughed. That sugary metaphor was Kur's influence for certain. "All right, you miserable sod. Let's go look for the White Witch." At least it would get his mind off Ione Carlisle.

Chapter 6

Ione had hit pay dirt. She rarely put on the glamour two nights in a row, as the magic could be both exhausting and addicting, but with Carter's campaign against her escalating from petty harassment to disturbing threats, she was more determined than ever to find out who was helping him. Rafe had finished giving the wards around her place a final infusion of quetzal magic just before dusk, giving her just enough time to perform the glamour before heading to Bitters once more.

As soon as she'd arrived she'd struck up a conversation at the bar with an off-duty cop who bragged of connections with "certain important people in the community." He'd promised to put Kylie in touch with "an interesting crowd" looking for fun girls like herself for the parties they hosted. The braggadocio, combined with his aggressively sexual behavior, seemed promising in terms of the sort of dirtball she was looking for. She'd even dropped a few names herself, mentioning how sad she'd been when her friends Barbie Fisher and Monique Hernandez—two of Carter's unfortunate victims—had died this past summer.

As she flirted with him, however, a familiar deep vibration—like the hum of machinery buried miles underground, the beating heart of Fritz Lang's *Metropolis*—struck Ione to the core. Without glancing up, she knew Dev Gideon had entered the club. *Dammit.* What was he doing here again? The answer, of course, was looking for Kylie. She had to admit, she'd probably made a hell of an impression.

"Fancy meeting you here." The cultured British accent behind her sent a delicious shiver up her spine. Which was so not cool.

She turned, prepared to make some sort of smart remark about his natty, out-of-place suit, but the sight of the white T-shirt stretched over his pecs and tucked into a pair of jeans that drew her eyes straight to his crotch left her with her mouth hanging open.

Ione closed it carefully and let her gaze travel back up to his face and the amused luster in the golden-brown eyes. "I see you got into something a little more comfortable."

He cocked an eyebrow. "I'd like to." Damn, this boy learned fast. But Ione wasn't going to succumb to her inappropriately pumping blood. This was the Covent's assayer and, now that she knew it, she wasn't about to let her pussy lead her around on a leash and do something foolish.

"Mind if I sit?"

Yes, you mind, dumbass. Do not encourage him. "Actually, I was just..." Her voice trailed off as she glanced at the seat to her left and saw that "Officer Paul" had moved on to hit on a group of giggling undergrads—probably drinking on fake IDs—at the next table. She wanted to jump up and tell them they were being creeped on by a predator, but they would only think she was trying to badmouth him because she was jealous that he'd switched his attention to them. And it would have blown any chance she had of getting closer to the ringleaders.

Dev had already slid onto the stool on her right, his arm so close to hers that little pulses of static electricity seemed to be flowing between them. And he smelled delicious. Without meaning to, she'd moved her arm closer.

"What are you drinking?"

For a moment she thought he'd said, "What are you thinking?" Which was a very good question.

Ione tamped down her runaway libido. "Water."

"Keeping safety in mind, then?"

She swiveled on her stool and rested her elbow on the bar to study him. "Why? Did you come prepared to ride?" She groaned internally, her sensible self watching her speak as if it was just an observer. Her libido was threatening mutiny. This was *not* going to happen tonight.

Dev's cocky smile widened into a grin. "Even brought my own helmet."

"Is that a metaphor?" Why was she still talking?

"Do you want it to be?"

It was like she had a pulse in her pussy. Ione's rational mind made one last, desperate attempt to rein herself in. She was going to regret this. It was one thing fooling around with some stranger in a parking lot. But this was someone she was absolutely guaranteed to see again, and not in a pleasant capacity. It wasn't a matter of right or wrong, even. Just a matter of not being stupid. She absolutely could not do this.

Ione swung off the stool. "Well, let's see how you sit a saddle, then, cowboy." She was going to hell.

Dev gave Kylie's waist the tiniest tug to set her hips squarely against his thighs as she started up the bike after he'd climbed on behind her. She'd been highly amused when he got the helmet from his rental. He hadn't wanted to give her any opportunity to ride off and leave his arse in the dust again. He wasn't averse to screwing in the backseat of an automobile, but it wasn't his first choice, and he imagined it wasn't hers, either. He'd been perfectly prepared to offer to drive to his hotel, but he'd been hoping she'd opt for her place.

He hadn't been on a bike in years. Kur seemed quite taken with it. He could swear the little bastard was purring inside him. Lord knew, Dev felt like purring.

Kylie's waist was warm against his palms as he held her lightly beneath her jacket while they sped through the now cloudless night. The stars were rather spectacular out here, unimpeded by bright city lights. No wonder Percival Lowell had built his observatory in the mountains near this desert. They were heading down the highway in the same direction as the temple, turning just a bit south of it onto a twisting road among the spectacular rock formations.

Another half mile up into the hills, Kylie pulled into the driveway of a white, split-level stucco. The garage door opened, admitting them smoothly and closing automatically as Kylie came to a stop and shut off the engine. She took off her helmet, shaking out her blond waves, and Dev swung off the bike behind her and followed suit—sans hair swinging.

Kylie didn't speak as they went through a side door into the interior, but before she opened the inner door, Dev curled his arm around her waist and stopped her in her tracks to kiss down the back of her neck. She tilted her head to the side, just a slight acknowledgment that gave him greater access, letting him work his way toward the front. He wrapped his arms around her from behind and unzipped the jacket as he traced his tongue along her jawline, slipping his hands inside the leather to cup her breasts.

Kylie leaned back against him with a soft moan that made his stiffening cock spring completely to attention. As tightly as he was holding her, there was no way for her to miss it.

She chuckled softly in her throat. "This is the laundry room, in case you hadn't noticed. Do you maybe want to see the rest of the house or were you planning on bending me over the washing machine?"

He hadn't been, but now that she'd mentioned it…

Kylie turned in his arms, blue eyes sparkling like the stars over the desert. "You got that helmet?"

Stupidly, he almost answered that he'd left it on the bike before realizing they were doing metaphor again. He grinned, unbuckling his belt and opening his trousers.

Kylie's eyes were amused as he shifted his hands from his trousers to hers. "I take it that's a yes?"

"Yes." He kissed her as he yanked her belt from the loops, and she gasped into his mouth. He hadn't meant to take the belt clean out, but there it was in his hands. He wrapped it lightly, teasingly, around her wrists as he let go of her mouth, giving her plenty of opportunity to slip her hands out. Instead she wove her fingers together, breath quickening as she held his gaze.

Dev slid the belt through the loop and buckled it, pulling it just a notch tighter than he needed to. He unfastened Kylie's pants and slipped his fingers inside, breaching the lace, inching downward and finding the warm hood of her clit. Kylie moaned, blue eyes lidded with desire, pressing herself against his fingers.

"You'd better not be a psychopath," she said breathlessly.

Dev smirked. "A bit of a pervert, perhaps, but definitely

not a psychopath." He drew his hand out, making her moan again, this time with disappointment. "Before we go any further, I just want to get a verbal—"

"*Yes*. For God's sake, yes."

He stopped wasting time and yanked the leather trousers and lacy pants down her hips in one go, then picked her up with his hands on either side of her waist and sat her firmly on top of the washer. The brushed steel had to be freezing but she didn't complain. The legs of her trousers were too narrow to get over the heels of her boots so he stepped into the circle of her knees instead of bothering with tugging off all the leather.

Dev kissed her once more, enjoying the way she trembled at his touch while hooking her ankles behind his arse and tugging him closer. She had a way of being in control and ceding just the right amount of it at the same time. But he wanted a little more of it just at the moment. He lifted her arms above her head and slid the belt buckle onto a hook on the underside of the shelf overhead meant for hanging clothes. The slight stretch raised up her cotton shirt on her waist. He pushed it higher, letting his thumbs drag over the hard points of her nipples through the lace of the bra as he lifted the shirt to sit above it.

Kylie squirmed on the washer lid, suddenly making kitten noises instead of deep moans. This was where he wanted her, so soaked with desire that she didn't care how she sounded. He tugged the bra down and lowered his head to her breasts, sucking each nipple in turn while she writhed and made more insistent mewling sounds.

He dug in his pocket for the condom, not finding it for a horrible moment, and enduring a look of disbelief from Kylie that promised coming wrath, just before his fingers closed over it. Dev presented it in triumph and grinned as he opened the foil packet. She rewarded him with a dig of her heels into his thighs like she was urging a horse to full speed, and Dev complied, unrolling the condom onto his cock and driving forward to meet her as she bucked against him.

The washer was already slick with her arousal and the unimpeded motion joined them together like a freight car coupling with a train. Dev held her face between his hands, marveling that her sparkling eyes now seemed more green than blue, and groaned appreciatively as she rocked against him with a circular motion of her pelvis. Kylie turned her head and sucked his thumb into her mouth—the thumb he'd dragged against the slickness on the metal as he'd pulled her in close. She moaned at her own taste and closed her eyes, and Dev braced his free hand against the washer and began pumping his hips, thrusting inside her with all the grace of a wild animal taken over by the instinctive drive to procreate.

His thumb slipped from her mouth and Kylie threw her head back, moaning loudly in tempo with his vigorous thrusts. Determined to make her miss a beat, he picked up speed, driving her to a stuttering staccato, and Kylie let her legs fall open, arching her back and making the most insanely hot keening wail he'd ever heard in his life. The sound dropped into a sort of mournfully sexy moan as her head hung forward, and it was only then he realized he'd already made her come.

The look she gave him as he unbuckled the belt around her wrists was somewhat dazed. Dev draped her arms over his shoulders and lifted her off the washer, supporting her with her buttocks cupped in his hands.

"Where's your bed?"

Kylie tightened her arms around his neck. "Through the door and up the stairs."

She clung to him while he let go with one hand to turn

the doorknob, and then he rebalanced her weight against him and stepped up into the utility closet off the kitchen. The stairs were to the left. Dev had to draw on the demon's strength to mount the stairs without losing his grip on Kylie—in more ways than one.

"Second door on the left," Kylie gasped as he reached the landing overhanging the living room below. A decorative iron railing was the only thing between them and a ten-foot drop.

Dev managed to swing Kylie through the bedroom door and onto the bed without a mishap. He wanted to hear her make more noise. A lot of it. He pulled out, careful not to let the condom slip, and Kylie protested, trying to hook him in place with her boot heels.

"There'll be plenty of time for that," he said patiently. "I'm not done with you yet." He had to duck down and sidle backward to get out of her grip, and he had the feeling he would have failed if the leather trousers weren't so difficult for her to maneuver in. Dev worked her boots off and tossed them aside, and Kylie watched him as he slid the leather over her ankles one at a time. The look in her eyes made him wish he'd kept her belt a little longer. Of course, he did have his own.

Her eyes fixed on his hands as he began to work his belt out of the loops. "What are you doing?"

"I left yours downstairs."

She raised an eyebrow but didn't stop him when he slipped her arms from the leather jacket and trussed her wrists a second time. "You'd better make this worth my while."

"Count on it." He winked and rolled her over onto her stomach before she could protest, slipping the belt through the headboard and tying it off.

Kylie turned her head. "That yes I gave you wasn't an

irrevocable free pass to the entire amusement park. Certain rides take extra tickets."

Dev laughed as he climbed onto the bed and stretched himself along her length. "Don't worry." He kissed the back of her neck, breathing in her scent. "I intend to earn every ticket I plan to use." He unhooked her bra, glad to see it was the kind with adjustable straps that crossed in back. All he had to do was slip the little hooks at the end out of the tabs and he was able to draw the entire garment out from under her. Otherwise, he'd have had to resort to his pocket knife.

Unfettered, Kylie wiggled to reposition herself against the bedspread. "Nice trick."

"I know a few." He kissed his way down her back, drawing a contented hum from her when he placed one at the top of her bum. He wasn't going for contented hums. His tongue slipping along her crack made her shiver and let out a little gasp. Still not what he was going for.

Dev spread her cheeks with his thumbs and made his slow, steady way over every little bump and ridge of flesh while she moaned into the pillow until he reached what he was after and thrust his tongue against the swollen flesh between her legs. Kylie made those kitten noises again as he tasted her, drawing the flat of his tongue from bottom to top, from his perspective, like the first, gluttonous lick of an ice cream cone.

The kitteny sounds got louder as he stroked again, spreading her open. Lifting her hips a little to give himself better access, Dev buried his face in her heat, his mouth locked on the prize.

Kylie's moans were loud and unabashed as she shook under his attentions, rolling her hips in his hands, shuddering and gasping until she was almost crying. When he was sure he'd made her climax, he straddled her legs and leaned down to her ear. It was wet with tears. She really was crying.

Dev laid a hand on her back. "You okay, darling?" He thought for a moment she was sobbing but realized she'd begun laughing uncontrollably.

"Am I okay?" she gasped between the laughter. "Holy Mother of God. If you want to kill me that way, it's fine with me, but if you're planning to fuck me, I think you'd better do it quick before you render me unconscious with that damn tongue."

Dev wasn't about to waste any time. He yanked off his boots, stripped off his clothes, and drew Kylie up onto her knees and entered her once more while she pulled back on the belt that held her wrists and rocked into him to meet his thrusts. Feeling light-headed as he pounded toward climax, he dismissed it as the natural effect of his pent-up desire.

He put his mouth close to her ear. "Do you want me to come inside you?"

Kylie moaned and gyrated her hips. "God, yes."

"Tell me. Tell me to do it."

She turned her head toward him and he leaned in to snatch her mouth with his so that the words were moaned against his lips. "I want you to come. Come for me."

Dev jolted inside her with a roar of pleasure, biting her lip a bit harder than he'd meant to and tasting a drop of blood as the ejaculation shot out of him. He felt as if every muscle he had was releasing simultaneously with it, and he clutched her waist to his as he collapsed onto his side against the bed with an almost giddy sense of lightness.

"That was—" He tried to catch his breath, licking the salty taste of blood from his lip. "That was—" He pulled out swiftly with a cry of surprise as the scar tissue at his back felt like it had caught fire.

“Dev?” Kylie tried to turn her head toward him. “What’s wrong? Are you okay?”

He was on fire, every inch of him crawling with agonizing heat. Dev looked down at his chest. His skin looked like it was boiling. No…it looked like it was—

“Kurrrrr!” The word, hurled from his tongue, was the last coherent thought in his head before he leaped from the bed and stumbled backward on the floor with a sound coming out of his throat that wasn’t his own.

Chapter 7

In place of the constant tingle that had been animating her skin since Dev's first touch, an icy column of fear gripped her spine. That growl had not been human.

Scrabbling noises of something large and lumbering thudded along the wood floor. The bed shook with the impact.

"Dev?" Ione realized she'd squeezed her eyes shut and she opened them with effort. She was still facedown against the pillow, tethered to the headboard. She took a deep breath and turned her head. At the periphery of her vision, a dark shape hulked. A dark shape that was making heavy breathing sounds—and seemingly emitting steam. *Oh, God.*

She held her breath and grabbed the belt with one hand just above the spot where it was buckled while folding her other hand almost in two, the pad of her thumb against the outer edge and fingers tented tightly together, and tugged. Dev hadn't strapped the belt tightly this time and, with a little effort, she freed the hand. She quickly undid the buckle to free the other. Ione sat up on her knees and took another breath before turning around.

An expletive she'd only uttered once or twice in her life burst out of her as she scrambled back against the headboard. Covered in vivid green scales, like poison personified, the creature hulked inside her doorway on all fours, its massive bulk tight and compact, as if ready to pounce. Tension quivered in its thick, muscular limbs, while fiery gold eyes glared out at her from a narrow, reptilian face beneath a bumpy, ridged forehead that sloped back into hornlike protrusions. The bumps on its head continued in a bisecting ridge of the bony substance that traveled down the creature's body and all the way to the end of the long tail stretching out the door.

The hottest sex she'd ever had and the guy had to get eaten by a monster. And she was about to be the second course.

Her mind was processing this, assessing the situation, as though hulking monsters in one's bedroom were an ordinary occurrence.

The creature breathed out a huff of steam and made a deep growling noise in its throat that seemed to set the whole house rumbling. Ione considered going for the gun she kept loaded in the nightstand. Her eyes flicked toward it. Depending on how fast this thing moved—the thing moved, and instinct kicked in. *Change the perception of a thing and you might change the thing itself.*

Ione flung out her hand toward the creature with a sort of battle cry, pushing against air with a move she'd learned in krav maga. The monster flipped backward, cracking the doorframe as it tore through it, a look of surprise in its fiery eyes as it righted itself and skidded along the landing. Ione was almost as surprised as it seemed to be. She'd imagined the force of air throwing it backward, but she hadn't really expected it to work. It crouched on the landing, tail switching and taking out a row of the railing behind it. Before she could lose her nerve and allow logic to surface, she made the gesture and shouted again, this time with words.

"In the name of God and the Goddess, get *out*!"

The creature tumbled backward over the railing, bat-like wings at awkward angles as if it had forgotten how to use them, and landed on its back on her living room floor with enough force to shake the building. She prepared for an attack, this time going for the gun, and ran out onto the landing with the weapon in both hands, aimed at the thing's skull. She'd taken shooting lessons to be sure she'd know how to use it if the time ever came, but she'd never actually had to fire at anything but a shooting-range target.

Ione squeezed the trigger, realizing too late she'd also squeezed her eyes shut. The bullet struck the window behind the thing's head.

Instead of lunging for her, the creature got to its feet and turned to barrel into the wide pane of plate glass that extended across the far wall. The thick glass shattered and the beast clambered through it only to let out a roar of surprise as it struck an invisible barrier inside the walled garden. *Rafe's wards.*

"Oh, crap." She hadn't expected to need anything to get out; they were fashioned to keep unwanted magic from getting in. If they'd been her own, she could have unlocked them, but these were Rafe's arcane Aztec symbols.

Ione stepped onto the landing, the gun still aimed at the creature in her backyard. If the place was warded so well that this thing couldn't get out…how the hell had it gotten in? The golden eyes blinked at her like huge tiger's-eye gemstones.

"No…effing…way."

Steam huffed gently from its nostrils as it contemplated her from where it sprawled in the blanket of shattered glass. Ione was still holding a gun on it, threatening a creature she'd effectively cornered. And she was standing naked on her landing. She lowered the gun. The creature didn't move. Ione stepped into the bedroom to grab her robe from the door. There were Dev's pants and boots in a heap at the foot of the bed. She stepped back out, wrapping the robe around her. The creature hadn't moved except to sit back on its haunches like a dog waiting for its master.

Ione descended the spiral staircase that led to the second floor from the front entryway, gun still clutched in her hand, and slowly approached the broken window. The creature breathed out a soft plume of smoke and lowered itself to the ground, settling its bumpy muzzle against its front feet.

With her finger poised on the trigger, Ione studied the glittering eyes from her closer vantage point. "What the hell, Dev?"

The creature let out a sigh, its ridged back gently rising and falling.

She took a step closer. "If that's really you...why can't you change back?" Eustace Scrubb had woken up similarly transformed in *The Voyage of the Dawn Treader* after falling asleep in a dragon's lair coveting its hoard. What had Dev coveted? Ione? Well, Kylie, anyway. She glanced up at her reflection in what remained of the window. *Crap.* Ione. When had she lost the glamour? Not that it mattered now. The Covent assayer sent to end her career had screwed her brains out and turned into a dragon. Because, seriously, this was a *dragon* she was looking at.

"Did I do this to you? My Lilith blood?" The dragon didn't seem to have the answer to that.

Someone was going to walk by and see this thing from

the side path. "Come in here. It's all right. I won't shoot you." She set the gun aside and opened her palms to show they were empty in case the dragon couldn't understand human speech.

The creature raised its head, tilting it.

"Come on." She pointed inside the house.

The dragon rose a bit clumsily and she saw why as it started forward. Blood dripped from its left foreleg. She hadn't entirely missed it, after all.

Ione backed out of the way as the dragon limped through the gap in the wall and hovered just inside. Whether or not it had Dev's consciousness in there, it definitely wasn't trying to hurt her.

Watching her, it settled onto the floor, favoring the leg she'd struck, and curled its tail around its body, again resembling an obedient dog. Except this "dog" was taking up half her living room—and would take up all of it if it stood and stretched its wings.

She took a tentative step toward it. "Can I look at your leg?" When it didn't move to stop her, she came closer and crouched beside it to try to determine how badly she'd injured it. She'd heard the bullet hit the window, so it must have gone clean through. Ione could only see one wound. Perhaps she'd just clipped it. Even so, the dragon was losing a fair amount of blood.

"Stay here." Ione went for the first-aid kit in the downstairs bathroom opposite the laundry where Dev had—*Christ.*

With the little kit in hand, she realized what she had wasn't exactly made for dragon proportions. Or dragon flesh. She brought a towel with her to clean the wound and ended up tying it in place around the upper foreleg. The gauze and bandages were useless. The dragon put up with it patiently.

"Sorry." She glanced up at the glowing gold eyes. "It's a good thing I'm not a better shot."

The dragon made a soft rumble in its throat that might have been a growl or a murmur of agreement. Ione's stomach answered with a growl of its own. She hadn't eaten anything since a cup of cottage cheese and a pear before going to the club. Dev probably hadn't eaten dinner, either. Which meant the dragon was probably hungry. What did dragons eat? It was sort of like a dinosaur, which was a sort of lizard, right? What did lizards eat? Smaller lizards? Ione was on a vegetarian kick, so the only animal proteins in the house were eggs and cheese. Maybe lizards were herbivores.

She compromised and scrambled some eggs with spinach, mushrooms and peppers and crumbled some sharp cheddar and seitan sausage substitute into it. After dishing it up—the largest portion in a big serving bowl—she grabbed the rest of the bag of spinach and tossed it into a separate bowl with some cucumbers and tomatoes, just to give the dragon some options.

"I wasn't sure if you were hungry," she said coming back from the kitchen with the food. "I'm always starving after s—" She swallowed the word, heat rushing to her face. The dragon probably had no idea what she was saying, but it didn't seem right to discuss having been intimate with someone who was no longer in human form. "I don't know if you're a grazer or a hunter. I'm guessing hunter, but this is all new to me…so, here—take your pick." She set the bowls in front of the dragon, but it merely gave them a disinterested sniff.

"Suit yourself." Ione sat to eat on the one chair that hadn't been knocked over in the chaos.

By the time she'd finished eating, the towel she'd tied around the dragon's wound was soaked through. Ione got another from the laundry room and this time wrapped it around a smaller towel folded into a square and pressed against the wound. She could swear as she finished that the dragon was purring.

She tucked her robe around herself as she stood, realizing she'd probably been flashing it. Not that Dev hadn't seen it all, but this wasn't exactly Dev. Ione pinched the bridge of her nose and realized how tired she was. The events of the night had worn her out—some more pleasantly than others. Maybe she'd be able to come up with some way of dealing with the dragon in the morning if she just got some sleep.

Damp wind was still blowing through the gaping hole that had been her living room wall. Ione pulled the heavy curtains across it, which helped a little. Between Rafe's wards and the alarm system—and the fact that a freaking dragon was camped out in her living room—she'd probably be safe enough. She pocketed the Glock just in case.

"Okay, I'm going up to bed. Will you be all right down here?" Like he was going to answer. "Okay," she said again. "Good night."

She figured she'd probably just lie there on the bed no matter how tired she was. How could she possibly sleep with a dragon in her living room? But she was out like a light, only waking early in the morning to a loud thudding and clattering on the stairs.

Ione grabbed the gun and jumped up, launching herself into the hall to find the dragon clumsily attempting to climb the spiral staircase, its tail coiling through the railing.

"Mother of God. What are you doing?"

The dragon's claws slipped on the open wooden stairs and it tumbled backward before flinging its wings out instinctively to catch itself, apparently finally remembering it could fly. It circled the open-plan area beneath the vaulted ceiling, sweeping pictures off the wall and onto the living room floor—with every other item it had knocked over on its way to the stairs—finally settling on the landing, puffing steam like the "Little Engine That Could" and looking rather smug.

Ione tucked the pistol into her waistband at the back of her cotton pajamas. "You're pretty pleased with yourself, I see. What do you want, a treat?" The dragon tilted its head. Ione yawned. Judging from the pale glow from the skylight, it was about six in the morning. "I'm going back to bed. If you're hungry, you're going to have to wait until a reasonable hour."

After climbing back under the covers, she heard the dragon lumber into the room, just barely clearing the door frame, and settle onto the floor by the bed. Ione opened one eye as the dragon curled its tail over itself like a cat for warmth. How a dragon could be cold with steam coming out of it, she wasn't sure, but it certainly made for a comfortable room for a human.

She woke again a few hours later to find the dragon gone, but a curious lapping sound was coming from the bathroom down the hall. "Oh, God." She'd forgotten to give it water. This was why she didn't have pets. Among other reasons.

Ione kept her eyes closed and pretended not to hear it, stirring only as the dragon thumped back into the room. She opened her eyes, a bit disappointed that the dragon's transformation hadn't simply reversed given a few hours. Was he going to be stuck like this? Blood was dripping down the creature's foreleg, the makeshift bandage soaked through.

She got up and got another set of towels to replace the sodden ones, trying not to think about the state of her pale wood floors and the cream-colored carpet in the living room as she rebandaged the wound.

But by the time she'd cleaned up and gone to the bathroom, blood was already seeping through the towel. Shouldn't the bleeding have stopped? Maybe dragons had different circulation systems. What the hell was she going to do? It wasn't like she could dial 9-1-1 and get a paramedic over here to treat a dragon. She needed a vet.

It occurred to her that Theia had worked as a veterinary assistant while studying for her degree in zoology. God, she couldn't bring Theia into this.

The dragon's warm breath seemed to be more rapid than it had been. She had to do something.

Theia answered on the first ring. "Hey, Di. Guess you must have felt me dreaming about you, huh?"

"Uh, no. Not exactly." Before learning about the Lilith blood, she'd never taken her baby sister's prophetic dreams seriously. "What have you been dreaming?"

"Mostly just vague dreams about power—your magic growing stronger."

Ione didn't know about that, unless her magical abilities had been responsible for what had happened to Dev.

"I also dreamed you got a dog. Which is hilarious, because you hate animals."

"I do not hate animals. I just don't like having to clean up after them. I did enough cleaning up after you guys." She bit her tongue. "I didn't mean that the way it sounded."

"You did, but that's okay. I know it couldn't have been easy having to take care of a bunch of snot-nosed kids when you were barely more than a kid yourself. And we love you for it. You know that."

Ione's eyes were smarting and she pinched her arm. She couldn't afford to be sentimental right now.

"Actually, that's what I'm calling about. Animals. Do

you know anything about…reptiles?" God, was it a reptile? Were dragons reptiles?

"Some. Why?"

"I thought I heard a prowler last night and I ended up shooting this poor lizard. Just winged him, but it's bleeding a lot and I can't figure out how to stop it."

"You…*shot*…a lizard. With a gun."

"Yeah."

"You have a gun?"

"Obviously. Can you give me some advice on how to treat it? I can't exactly put a Band-Aid on it."

"You're trying to treat a lizard. That you shot."

"Yes."

Theia was quiet for a moment. "Wouldn't a bullet just—rip the poor guy in half? How big is this lizard?"

Ione tried to keep her voice calm. "It's big. Some kind of Gila monster maybe."

"You know those are venomous."

"I'm not getting too close to it. Anyway, it seems to understand that I'm trying to help."

"How are you planning to treat a Gila monster without getting too close to it? Don't mess around with that thing. You should call Animal Control."

"Theia, just tell me what I need to do." She'd slipped into her "stern mom" voice.

Theia was quiet for a moment. "Di? We're not actually talking about a lizard here, are we?"

"Of course we're talking about a lizard. Stop quizzing me and tell me what to do!"

"This is an actual reptile."

"*Yes*, it… I don't know. I think it's a reptile. Shit." She was losing it. Ione tried to steady her breathing and get things back under control.

"I'm on my way over there."

"*No.* Theia, do not drive all the way down here. Don't you have a class this morning?" It was over an hour's drive from Flagstaff where Theia had just started graduate school and was a teaching assistant for undergrad biology classes at Northern Arizona University. "Theia?" Ione realized she'd hung up.

She put the phone back in the base and glanced at the dragon. "You hungry? I still don't know what to feed you."

Slipping her gun back into the waistband of her pajama pants, she headed downstairs. When she reached the bottom, the dragon coasted down from the landing and took up its place in the corner of the living room. Ione made eggs again, which the dragon again showed no interest in. It also turned its head away with a steamy sigh at oatmeal and fruit, though it eagerly drank an entire dishpan full of water when Ione remembered to offer some after recalling the bathroom incident.

After opening the heavy curtains to let some light in, leaving the sheer inner ones rippling in the breeze through the empty pane, Ione righted the overturned couch and sat watching the dragon drink, chin in her hands and elbows on her knees.

"I don't know what to do. Usually when I bring a guy home he leaves right after. Not that I bring a lot of guys home… Anyway, they most certainly don't turn into dragons and take up residence in my living room. Not that I'm blaming you. I'm sure you'd rather not be here, either. And I'm not saying I don't want you here, I…" Ione rolled her eyes at herself. "I don't even know you, is the thing. And it seems like, lately, every time I get involved with someone, he turns into something crazy, so I was absolutely not planning to get involved with you or anyone else. Not that last night wasn't absolutely amazing—"

The doorbell rang and Ione nearly vaulted to open it,

relieved not to have to be alone with the dragon and her unstoppable mouth. Instead of Theia's dark, chin-length bob, Rhea's shock of bleached-blond hair met her on the doorstep.

Rhea grinned, bouncing from toe to toe. "Where is it? Where's the dragon? I *have* to see the dragon." She bounced past Ione into the house before Ione could stop her, while Theia, having made a slightly more sedate exit from the car parked in the drive, arrived at the door. At least Rhea had remembered to slip off her shoes in the entryway before she'd barged in.

Ione frowned and grabbed Theia's arm to pull her inside. "Who said anything about a dragon? And why did you drag Rhea into this?"

Theia slipped off her skimmers and took the pair of socks Ione handed her from the basket by the door. "She has some kind of tattoo convention in Flagstaff and decided to surprise me for breakfast. I couldn't exactly keep her from finding out where I was going. Or why." She folded her arms. "And if you try to tell me it's a Gila monster one more time—"

"Oh. My. God." Rhea's awed voice echoed from the living room.

Ione found her sitting on her heels on the carpet, barely a foot from the creature. "Rhea!" The dragon's tail was uncoiling slowly, its eyes fixed on Rhea with mistrust. "Get back! It doesn't know you."

Rhea reluctantly let her twin pull her to her feet and drag her away. "How does it know *you*?" Rhea turned with her hands on her hips. "Why do you get a dragon?"

"I don't *get* a dragon. I just—happen to have one at the moment."

Despite having pulled Rhea away, Theia was now crouching in front of the creature with her hand outstretched. "Hello, there. I'm not going to hurt you. I just want to look at your wound. Can I look?" With her head slightly bowed, she reached tentatively for the bloody towel, one eye peering out from under the short curtain of her hair to gauge the dragon's receptivity.

"Theia…" Ione took a step toward her, her chest tight, but the dragon merely lowered its head back onto its paws.

"What happened to the window?" Rhea had just noticed the gaping hole in the room.

"What do you think happened to the window?" Ione tried to keep one eye on Theia to make sure the dragon wasn't going to change its mind as she undid Ione's make-shift dressing. Being pulled between both twins felt familiar. They'd been like twin dervishes as children, one finding more trouble to get into while Ione tried to clean up whatever mess the other had made.

Rhea's gaze fell on the butt of the Glock tucked into Ione's pajama pants and she fixed Ione with a furious glare. "Jesus, Di. Did you shoot that poor thing? What is the matter with you? And why do you have a gun?"

Ione sighed and untucked her white cotton tank to cover the piece. "It's for protection." The house was a bit isolated, at least from the back, and even with the alarm, the full-length window was an easy target. Ione wanted to be prepared if she needed to defend herself or her property before the sheriff's department could respond to the alarm. "And I shot it because I thought it was about to kill me."

Rhea looked back at the dragon, her eyes wide with admiration. She'd always had a fondness for the mythological version—which, until now, Ione had assumed was the only version. "Where did it come from?"

Theia saved her from answering. "The bleeding really should have stopped by now. It's not that deep a wound.

Maybe there's something preventing it from clotting, like a charm designed to ward against it, or a spell."

"Rafe came by earlier and put quetzal wards all around the property. Maybe that's affecting it."

Rhea paused in pushing a chunk of glass around at the base of the window with her stockinged foot and looked up. "If there are wards around the property, how did the dragon get in?" She glanced back at the glass. "The window's broken from the inside."

Nothing ever got past Rhea. "It was already inside before it…transformed."

Rhea turned to study the dragon. "That's a person?"

"It was."

"Who?" Theia's eyes were on her now.

Ione sighed. "Dev Gideon. He's the Covent assayer. They sent him to investigate me because they think I was in league with Carter Hamilton. I'm pretty sure he came to get rid of me."

"And he came to the house?" Rhea's brows drew together. "You said this happened last night."

There was no way Ione could keep the heat out of her cheeks under Rhea's scrutiny. She could feel it spreading across her face like fire.

"Oh. My. *God*." Rhea gaped at her before raising her hand to meet her twin's high-five without even looking. "I owe you fifty bucks, Thei."

Ione scowled. "For what, exactly?"

Theia grinned. "I bet her you weren't as tightly wound as you like to seem. That you were secretly getting way more action than the rest of us."

Ione turned to Rhea, catching her in a little dance that she immediately stopped. "And you bet I was an uptight prude."

"Uh, no…" Rhea looked at her twin and grinned sheepishly. "Okay, yeah."

"Nice. The both of you are terrors."

"We try."

"So what's he look like in his human form?" Rhea eyed the dragon appreciatively. "Is he hot? Tell me your new boyfriend's not a stick-up-his-butt doofus like Carter Hamilton."

"He is *nothing* like Carter Hamilton." The words had come out a little more violently than she'd meant them to. "And he's not my boyfriend. Can we not talk about this in front of the dragon?" Stupidly, she'd lowered her voice only on the word "dragon," as though that was the one thing she didn't want Dev to hear. "I have no idea whether his consciousness is still in there."

The dragon had raised its head and was watching them curiously.

Rhea's expression changed as she studied it. "Does he have a tattoo?"

"I…" She wasn't about to admit that she hadn't seen Dev naked except out of the corner of her eye as he was face-deep between her thighs while she was tied to the headboard. "I don't think so."

"I see something patterned." Rhea went closer, crouching to peer at the dragon's breast. "It's a pentagram. Could that be the ward? Maybe it's there to keep him from transforming into the dragon. Until something triggered it and now the tattoo is working against him."

Theia nodded thoughtfully. "So what triggered it?"

Without saying anything else to each other, the two of them seemed to come to some conclusion simultaneously and they both turned and fixed their eyes on Ione, speaking as one. "Lilith blood."

Chapter 8

Ione quickly steered the conversation away from the inevitable question. "I don't care how it got this way. I want to know what to do about it. I can't even get it to eat anything. It drank some water but I've offered everything I've got in the house and it isn't interested."

Rhea headed toward the kitchen. "Have you tried raw meat?"

"I don't keep meat in the house."

"For crying out loud. You can't just give him carrots and apples like some pet horse."

"I didn't give him—*it*—carrots and apples." She wasn't about to start ascribing gender to the dragon as if it really was Dev. For all she knew, he was gone for good. "I made eggs with cheese and meat substitute. And I gave it a bowl of salad just in case."

The twins burst out laughing and Ione glared, about to tell them off. But the tension she'd been trying to contain finally broke and she sank onto the couch and laughed until she cried.

After the three of them had gotten it out of their systems, Rhea took her keys from her pocket and headed for the door, shoving her feet into her sandals as she opened it. "I'll go to the store and pick up some steaks. And then maybe we can put our heads together and try to figure out how to reverse the transformation."

Theia sat in the one chair by the window that hadn't been knocked over. "So…exactly how did he get this way?"

"How do I know? He just—transformed out of the blue."

"What were you doing at the time?" Theia's eyes widened when Ione didn't answer right away. "You weren't actually *doing* it when he shifted?"

"No! For God's sake, no." Ione swallowed. "It was right after."

"So just after he—?"

"Yes."

"Was there, um…fluid exchange?"

"We used a condom. And I am *really* uncomfortable talking about this with you. And in front of the dragon. Not that it seems to be able to understand me."

"So how did the two of you get together? You and—what was his name?"

"Dev Gideon. And, yes, he's hot, if you must know—because I know you're going to report back to your partner in crime."

Theia grinned, and Ione couldn't help elaborating just a bit.

"Really, it's almost cruel how hot he is. You have no idea." She sighed wistfully. "But we didn't exactly get together. Honestly, I'm pretty sure he loathes the sight of me, so this is going to be pretty awkward if and when we manage to get him back."

"Why would he sleep with you if he loathes the sight of you?"

Ione sighed again, this time loathing herself. "He didn't know he was sleeping with me. Exactly."

"Wait, what?"

Ione buried her face in her hands and spoke to her palms. "I went out in a glamour and picked him up at a bar."

"What?" Theia sounded baffled and incredulous at the same time. Ione wasn't sure if it was what she'd said or the fact that she'd mumbled it into her hands.

She moved her hands into her hair, combing her fingers through it, annoyed to find knots. She probably looked like hell.

"I used a glamour. It's a spell to change your physical appearance."

"I know what a glamour is. I've seen *The Craft*."

Ione pulled her hair back and tied it in a knot at her nape as she looked up. "You know that movie was total crap. That's not how any of it works. There's no 'Manon.'"

"Yeah, yeah. Go back to the part where you went to a bar pretending to be someone else to get the Covent assayer into bed with you."

"That is *not* how it happened."

Rhea threw the door open, back with the steaks. The explanation would have to wait.

"I bought ten pounds of top sirloin. That should tide us over if it takes a few days to figure this out."

"It *cannot* take a few days." Ione rose and took the bag of steaks to the kitchen. "What am I supposed to tell the Leadership Council?" She opened the butcher paper, grimacing at the sight of animal flesh, and got out a frying pan while she spoke. "You shouldn't have gone to so much trouble. This had to be expensive."

Rhea leaned against the doorway of the kitchen. "Yeah, well, it was your card." She handed Ione the credit card she'd apparently swiped on her way out without Ione even noticing. "You don't need the pan. He'll want it raw."

"How do you know?"

"He's a *dragon*." Rhea tossed one of the thick cuts onto a plate and took it back to the living room to set it on the carpet.

Ione's mouth dropped open as the creature flicked out its sizable tongue and devoured the raw meat like a chameleon scooping a bug from a leaf.

Rhea grinned. "So that was an appetizer, I guess." She went back to the kitchen and piled on a few more steaks, which the dragon made short work of in the same horrifying manner.

"He looks a little better now." Theia stroked the dragon's muzzle. "But he feels warm."

"Maybe that's just the temperature a dragon is supposed to be." Ione shuddered as Rhea tossed the last of the steaks in front of it and they disappeared into the somewhat toothier mouth than she'd been imagining.

"I don't know. He's still losing a steady supply of blood."

"That's all I've got, big guy." Rhea opened her hands to show they were empty when the dragon sniffed the air with a hopeful look. "We'll get you some more later."

Ione frowned. "There can't be a later. We have to do something."

"I could read the tattoo like I did with Phoebe to find Rafe when Carter abducted him."

"I thought that only worked if you were the one who'd done the tattoo."

"For the shared visions, yes. But, recently, I discovered I could get something from other tattoos. The images aren't the same as the sort of visions I get with my own work.

They're just…sort of impressions. I found out while I was giving a guy a touch-up. Unfortunately."

Ione picked up the plate to take it to the kitchen. "Why unfortunately?"

"The image was of what he was picturing doing to me. I hadn't even started yet. I was just assessing it and, *boom*, creepy guy being creepy on display in my head. And he wasn't aware of it at all. No shared vision. I just got a front-row seat to what was going on in his head. Needless to say, he did not get his touch-up."

Ione shuddered. "I guess it's worth a try. But be careful."

Rhea crouched in front of the dragon, extending her hand and placing it gently on the scaly chest over the vague pentagram shape. She closed her eyes and her brows drew together in concentration.

"Anything?"

"Shh." Rhea's eyes moved back and forth behind her eyelids as though she was watching something intently. "There's something, but I can't quite… Kur."

"Kur?" Ione and Theia repeated it together.

Rhea was quiet for a moment, still concentrating, and then opened her eyes and dropped her hand. "That's the dragon's name. Kur. I could sense the man inside, but I couldn't get any images from him, except that he was… caged, I think?" She glanced up. "But Kur seems to like you, Di. I think he'd prefer to stay, but he seems to know that whatever magic is acting on him is harmful to him in this form. I got another image of a cage from Kur himself, and an older man he called the Sorcerer binding him inside it." Rhea frowned as she stood, putting her hands on her hips. "I think this other guy bound Kur and your Dev together. And it seemed to involve a lot of…" Rhea grimaced. "*Torture* is the only word I can think of."

"Torture?" Ione glanced at Kur, who didn't seem to be taking much notice of their conversation.

"Beatings, and burning and 'sharp' things. Those were Kur's mental images. Along with him apparently tearing the guy's throat out as a thank-you."

Ione swallowed. How close had she come to having her own throat torn out? "So if the magic is harming him, how do we stop it?"

"Well, you seem to have started it." Rhea took a step back when Ione whirled on her. "I'm just saying."

Theia looked thoughtful. "Maybe Rafe will know what to do. He's used to shifting between human and quetzal form."

There were enough people in her living room. Ione was putting her foot down.

"We're not bringing Phoebe and Rafe into this. Everyone in the world doesn't need to know I picked a guy up at a bar and accidentally screwed him into being a dragon."

"You picked him up at a bar?" Rhea looked impressed. "What else are you hiding?"

"I'm not hiding anything—" Ione paused as the doorbell rang insistently, looking from the door to Rhea.

"Yeah, that's Phoebes. I already called them while I was out getting steaks."

"Rhea!" Ione clenched her fists at her sides and counted to ten in her head before she went to the door. Phoebe and Rafe looked like they'd just climbed out of bed. But not from sleeping in it. Both of them wore hastily tied ponytails, Phoebe's clipped from the underside and fanning out in a perky waterfall and Rafe's dark curls poking out messily from the short stub.

Ione shook her head as she held the door wide. "Come on in. Everybody else has."

Phoebe stepped through the entryway onto the cream

carpet without taking off her shoes. At least Rafe was observant, taking his off after glancing at the rack of discarded shoes by the door and the state of everyone else's feet.

"Jesus." Phoebe gazed up at the dragon. "He's magnificent!" Her kid sister's obvious approval was oddly gratifying. It wasn't as if the dragon was her date.

"Ione picked him up in a bar," Rhea offered helpfully, ducking out of Ione's way as she made a menacing grab for her.

Kur's stance stiffened at the appearance of two new people, muscles rippling beneath the scales, the ridged tail uncurling and moving slowly back and forth. He sniffed the air, nostrils flaring, and emitted a sort of warning puff of steam as Rafe entered the living room.

Ione moved closer to the dragon. "It's okay. Rafe's a friend."

Rafe kept a respectful distance, sizing the dragon up. "Impressive. I thought Rhea had to be embellishing a bit, but that is definitely a dragon."

"Do you think you can help—put him back?"

"I take it his transformation came about as a result of your unique chemistry." Rafe gave the tiniest sexy wink in Phoebe's direction. "You Carlisles should come with a warning label."

Rhea helpfully offered one. "Dangerous when wet."

Both Ione and Phoebe let out the same mortified groan.

Theia balanced her twin's irreverence with her usual pragmatism. "We think the pentagram tattoo on his chest is a magical ward intended to keep the dragon suppressed. Now that he's out, the magic is working against him, making him sick. His blood isn't clotting and he has a fever." She paused and shrugged. "At least, I think he has a fever."

Rafe rolled his shoulders as though warming up for

something, but Ione suspected he was actually triggering his own tattoo to activate his wings, though they were still invisible, somehow contained within his shirt.

The dragon growled in warning, emitting twin plumes of steam through its nostrils that glowed as if fueled by something molten within the beast.

Rafe went down on one knee and bowed his head. “I’ve come to help you, my friend. Peace.”

The growl came again and the dragon rose slightly on its limbs.

Ione stepped toward them. “Rafe, I don’t think this is a good idea.”

“It might be best to get everyone else out.”

“Rafe—”

“If we’re going to bring Gideon back before this magic kills the dragon and Gideon with it, we need to do it fast, and we don’t need an audience.”

Phoebe sighed behind her. “He’s right, Di. We’re all just gawking. We’ll wait outside.”

Ione pressed her mouth together in a thin line and turned to follow as the twins and Phoebe headed out to the driveway.

“Not you, Ione,” Rafe clarified. “I need you in here. You walk out of this thing’s line of sight and I’m pretty sure he’s going to go for my throat.”

“Sorry. Right.” Ione came back to where he knelt. “The dragon’s name is Kur, if that helps. Rhea got the name by reading his tattoo.”

Rafe nodded, unbuttoning his shirt. “Kur.” He trilled the “r.” As he dropped the shirtsleeves from his arms, the wings took shape like colors formed of smoke before coalescing into the brilliant solid plumage of the quetzal.

Kur’s head lowered but not in submission, his back rippling with tension.

Rafe kept perfectly still. "Ione, I need you to touch the tattoo."

Ione stepped between them, veins flooding with adrenaline. She met Kur's eyes, the glowing gold now almost a molten orange within the vivid green scales, and held the beast's gaze as she lowered herself into a crouch and put her hand against the dragon's abdomen.

"Take the knife off my belt," Rafe said from behind her.

Ione turned her head. "Do what?"

"Keep your hand on Kur but reach back and take the knife out of the sheath on my belt. I've unsnapped it but I don't dare put my hand on it myself."

"Do you know what you're doing?"

Rafe flicked his eyes up briefly to meet hers. "I'm winging it."

"God, everyone in this family is a smartass." She reached carefully for the sheath and closed her hand around the handle and felt the growl in Kur's throat beneath her other hand. Ione turned back to face him, holding the dragon's gaze once more, fumbling the knife out by feel. "Got it," she said as she pulled the knife free, though Rafe obviously knew she had it. "Now what?"

"You're going to have to give it your blood."

"What?"

"The Lilith blood is what brought the dragon out. It's the only thing that's going to put him back in." Rafe spoke calmly. "Move your hand from the tattoo and make a shallow cut on your palm—preferably on the thumb pad, because a cut in the center of your palm like you see people doing in the movies and TV is going to burn like hell when your hand sweats, and you won't be able to use the hand for days. I speak from personal experience."

Ione scrunched up her face to steel herself and drew her hand away from Kur to make the cut.

“That’s plenty.” Rafe stopped her before she went too deep.

“This is why you’re not in the coven anymore.” She said it lightheartedly to steady her nerves, but really, blood magic was the sort of thing the Covent frowned upon.

“Now you have to cut the dragon.”

Ione spun to face him. “I am *not* going to stab him.”

“I said ‘cut’ not ‘stab.’ We just need a similar shallow cut in the center of the sigil, and you have to do it fast so you don’t give the dragon time to react. Then you press your palm to the cut so your blood will activate it.”

“And what are you going to do?”

“I’m going to talk him down so he doesn’t take off both our heads.”

Fantastic. So this is how I die. Ione took a deep breath, the knife trembling in her hand, and looked into the dragon’s eyes. “I’m sorry.” She sliced the blade against the center of the tattoo, and the dragon reared up in surprise, a bellow of fury and a blast of steam belching out of it.

“Give it your blood. Quick.”

“I’m trying!” Ione reached for the dragon, but it had risen onto all fours, and she had to stand, stretching toward it on tiptoe. Tripping and falling against the creature most likely saved her life. With her hand outstretched, the bleeding palm landed just outside the tattoo, but close enough that the blood running from the dragon’s cut dripped onto hers. She dropped the knife and clung to the dragon’s bumpy protrusions with her free hand.

Rafe was chanting behind her. “By the power of Mictlantecuhtli and Mictecacihuatl, I bind you, Kur. By the Lord and Lady of the Underworld, I return you to the place where you are bound to Dev Gideon.”

Kur was roaring and steaming, and Ione’s feet were off the ground. She wrapped her legs around the dragon’s foreleg, sliding her palm up to cover the tattoo and holding her hand in place with all her might.

"Return this body to Dev Gideon," Rafe insisted. "You don't belong within this plane."

"Kur." She hoped the dragon could hear her trembling voice. "You need to go back. I won't let anyone hurt you. I promise."

The dragon stilled, snorting and huffing like a spooked horse, and Ione instinctively stroked the scales and bumps she gripped to try to calm it.

"Let the dragon rest, Gideon." Rafe shrugged the quetzal wings back into place as if to demonstrate.

With a shudder, Kur's wings retracted and, as the dragon seemed to fold into itself, Ione tumbled to the ground on top of him. But it was no longer the dragon. It was Dev, crumpled naked on her carpet, his arm ensconced in a pile of bloody towels.

Chapter 9

Ione sat back on her heels. Dev's back was scored with blood, as if the dragon's claws had somehow raked his skin. And there were older marks. Dozens of scars, suggesting he'd been through this transformation more than once, along with an unusual gnarl of flesh, like the scar tissue from a burn but with an oddly specific shape, just above his glutes. She tore her gaze away. It was entirely inappropriate to be noticing how incredible those glutes were right now.

"Dev?" His body had begun to tremble. Rafe came up beside her with a cream-colored throw from the couch and laid it over him. And there went the last thing in her living room that wasn't covered in blood. "I don't think he's conscious. Do you think he's in shock?"

"His body is probably experiencing some major adjustments, but his bleeding seems to have stopped, and his temperature feels normal." Rafe moved the towels out of the way, looking over the wound on Dev's arm. "We should probably get him to bed to sleep it off."

Ione nodded. "Maybe if we both take a side we can get him on his feet."

"Ione." Rafe smiled and placed his hand on his chest. "Quetzal." He scooped Dev into his arms and headed up the stairs as though it were effortless. Lucky Phoebe.

Ione followed him up and bit back a protest as Rafe laid Dev on top of the clean duvet. When they covered him with some extra blankets from the closet, he stirred and moaned but didn't wake.

"We can stick around if you want," Rafe offered. "Or we can get out of your hair."

"I think the less people here when he comes around, the better." It was going to be awkward enough that Ione was here, and it was her house.

Rafe nodded. "Gotcha. Just give us a call if you need anything."

"Thank you, Rafe." Ione shivered and rubbed her arms as they headed downstairs. "I think you saved his life."

Rafe smiled, pulling on his shirt. "Least I could do. You saved mine."

"Yeah, and I nearly killed *him*." Ione shook her head. "I am definitely going to be kicked out of the Covent."

Rafe squeezed her hand wordlessly. He glanced at the shattered wall as he buttoned up. "I'll come back later and board that up. First thing Monday, I'll send some of my guys over to fix the frame and replace the glass." Diamante Construction and Excavation was his family's business. His, now that his father was dead—courtesy of Carter Hamilton.

"Thanks. Just give me an estimate—"

Rafe cut her off firmly. "Family doesn't pay." He winked. "Yes, I caught that comment. You called me family." As he opened the door, Phoebe and the twins peered in, huddled outside like a brood of hens.

Rhea muscled her way past Rafe, looking disappointed. "Is the dragon gone?"

Ione grabbed her and spun her back around to face the door. "He is, and so are you."

"But—"

Phoebe tucked an arm around Rhea's shoulder. "Come on. We can all go out for breakfast somewhere. The guy doesn't need the entire Carlisle clan hovering around him. He's been through enough." She cast a glance at Ione. "Though I wouldn't mind a peek—"

"No peeks." Ione ushered them onto the doorstep and pulled the door closed behind her. "I can't thank you guys enough, though. I don't know what I would have done." She smiled at Theia, standing behind the others. "Even if I did tell you not to tell anyone else."

Theia shrugged. "You're welcome. Just stop shooting things. Plus, I made fifty dollars." Rhea opened her wallet to hand over two twenties and a ten to her twin, waggling her eyebrows at Ione with an evil grin.

Ione rolled her eyes. "Okay, get out of here. All of you."

Phoebe took Rafe's hand and headed for her Jeep, throwing a look at Ione over her shoulder before she got in. "I *will* be getting all of the details from you later."

Ione stepped inside and closed the door.

Stabbing pain in his arm and a hangover that felt like a Mack truck had run him over greeted Dev as he opened his eyes. Pale evening light made soft shadows against a bedspread he didn't recognize.

Dev sat up and gripped his head with a groan. Where the hell was he? As he turned to look around the immaculate bone-and-ivory room, the familiar pull of torn skin at his back made him wince.

Shite. Kur had gotten out. How the hell could he have gotten out? And how was he *in*? He had a vague recollection of someone chanting unfamiliar words at him while his sigil burned. Dev rubbed the mark below his breastbone, the edges raised and red, and pinched the bridge of his nose against the ache in his skull. The last thing he remembered was driving to the bar and—

"Oh, my God."

A moment later Ione Carlisle appeared in the doorway. "Dev? Thank God, you're awake."

Dev's eyes narrowed on her. *"You."* He flung the covers off and threw his legs over the side of the bed, wincing again at the fiery pain in his left arm. He tugged his elbow forward to see the bandage taped over it and peeled the tape back. His head darted up. "Did you *shoot* me?"

Ione's face flushed red. "I didn't know I was shooting *you* at the time."

And he hadn't known he was having sex with Ione Carlisle at the time. "Did you do this on purpose?" Outrage propelled him to his feet.

Ione blinked at him, taking a step back in the doorway. "Do what? Turn you into a dragon? Yeah, I do that all the time."

"You bloody well know what I mean. You lured me here, pretending to be someone else. Did you know about the demon?"

"What demon?"

"The sodding dragon!" Dev had crossed the room and grabbed her by the arm, inadvisably. There was an intense magical current running between them.

Ione recoiled and jerked her arm from his grasp. "I didn't know anything about Kur. And I didn't lure you here. I had no idea who you were when we met at the bar. The first time."

"Ha!" He couldn't help the outburst at that little three-word addition. Then the rest of her words sank in. He felt heat coming off his eyes almost as if they were Kur's. Dev took a step closer, backing Ione against the door frame, one hand braced on the wall beside her head. "How do you know it calls itself Kur if you didn't know about the demon?"

The gray-green eyes flashed defiantly as she glared up at him. "Because he told me—us." She made a semi-strangled sound of exasperation in her throat, like she was trying not to swear. "He told my sister when she read your tattoo."

"Your *sister*?" Dev's head ached as he tried to process this. There had been someone trying to reach him inside Kur's cage, someone communicating with the demon. And there had been…others. "What did you do, have a fucking party with my demon?" He made a grunt of surprise as Ione shoved him backward with both palms against his chest, that brief contact igniting the current like a ripple through his skin.

"Having a dragon tear my house apart and nearly rip my head off is not my idea of a party!" She shoved past him out of the room and Dev saw the landing behind her, the iron railing bent and torn away, and the gaping hole in the glass wall where the last of a magnificent sunset was fading over the rust-colored rocks. Ione paused on a spiral wooden staircase scored with claw marks to look back. "Your clothes are on the chair by the closet. And you're fucking welcome."

Dev turned and found his clothes laundered and folded, the belt neatly coiled on top. The belt he'd bound Kylie—*Ione*—to the bed with before he'd made her come till she was crying and then screwed her brains out. He dressed furiously, hissing at the pain of the claw marks at his back against the fabric of the T-shirt, holding on to the anger to keep the memory of those little kitteny sounds out of his head as he shoved his feet into his boots.

Pulling on his jacket, he clattered down the stairs to where Ione stood watching him from the edge of the living room, arms folded tightly around her.

Dev flung open the front door with a growl. “Send me a bill for the damage.”

Ione’s voice was perfectly calm. “You don’t have a car here.”

“I’ll get an Uber,” he snapped and then paused on the doorstep. “And I’m fucking welcome for what?”

Ione crossed to the door and grabbed the knob. “For saving your bloody life.”

The door slammed in his face.

Ione melted onto the bottom step of the spiral staircase and hung her head between her knees with her arms crossed over it. She’d expected things to be awkward, but that could not have gone worse. He thought she’d played him, deliberately hooking up with him at the bar—apparently par for the course in the long list of unethical practices he believed her capable of. She supposed she couldn’t blame him for the assumption, but the idea that he thought she’d done it to manipulate the demon inside him made her stomach churn.

Dev had turned her inside out, leaving her like a quivering bag of jelly. She hadn’t even had time to deal with how intense the sex had been. But now that the threat of danger from the dragon and the fear of Dev dying was past, all she could think about was how unexpected and amazing that connection had been. And Dev probably thought the entire thing was an act she'd put on just to get to his demon.

She raised her head, hands still clasped on top of her crown. "Who the hell has a demon? A *demon*?" Somehow the idea of a magical dragon had been easier to take. It was sort of romantic, the enchanted knight under a dragon spell, perhaps, to be released by true love's kiss. But how had he managed to become bound to a demon? And who was he to judge her and report on her minuscule drop of demon blood while he was walking around sporting a full-on demonic possession? That was definitely against Covent doctrine.

Her phone rang, the Caller ID announcing Phoebe's number. She wasn't up to being ribbed by Phoebe for another sexual indiscretion. Her little sisters had been shocked to learn she'd been dating Carter Hamilton, but at least they hadn't been able to tease her about it, given how despicable and deceptive he'd turned out to be. There was simply nothing amusing to rib her about. But annoyingly pious, stickler-for-the-rules big sister picking up a guy in a bar and accidentally releasing his secret dragon with a night of wild sex? That was Phoebe fodder she'd never hear the end of.

She let the call go to the machine, sighing as she surveyed the wreckage of her living room. She'd managed to clean up some while Dev was sleeping, but the blood and the shattered glass were going to take a professional. Maybe Rafe would have some contacts in industrial cleanup.

Phoebe's voice came over the machine as Ione got up to search the utility closet for heavy-duty rug cleaner. "Hey, it's me. I forgot to tell you what I found out yesterday at Florence."

Ione paused and turned toward the phone.

"It turns out the bag of dicks has been getting weekly visits from one person in particular. Someone calling herself Lorelei Carlisle. Seems a little too close to home, right? I ran a search and there *was* a Lorelei Carlisle living in the Phoenix area, but she passed away six weeks ago. What do you make of it? Think someone's trying to cash in on the family name? Call me later and we'll put our heads together."

"Tell her the other thing," Rhea—or maybe Theia—chimed in from the background.

"Oh, yeah. We have reservations for six at Blue Moon tonight at eight o'clock. You can bring your dragon boy as long as he doesn't shift and go on a rampage."

"We'll make sure they serve raw steaks." It was definitely Rhea. Ione sighed and went to get the cleaning supplies as the call ended.

After Rafe stopped by to board up the windows, Ione asked him to give her sisters her regrets for dinner. He didn't ask about Dev, and she didn't volunteer an explanation. Her sisters left increasingly annoying messages from the restaurant, trying to get her to change her mind, until she finally silenced the machine and the ringer in exasperation and went to bed.

Without the dragon's presence downstairs or at the foot of the bed, knowing the house was wide-open made it impossible to sleep. Magical harm might be kept out by Rafe's wards, and the alarm would be triggered if anyone tried to come in through the garage or the front or kitchen doors, but if an ordinary, determined prowler decided to go around back, he could yank out a plank and crawl in.

She fell asleep from exhaustion around dawn, waking after nine to the arrival of Rafe's construction crew. They were extremely professional, asking no questions about how the glass and frame had been shattered and making no mention of the blood stains on the carpet she'd only been able to scrub to a dull pinkish-brown. One of them even straightened and re-anchored the railing on the landing while another reinforced the cracked frames on the bedroom and bathroom doors without a word. When they were finished, a cleaning crew showed up, ostensibly to clean up the glass and plaster and any sawdust the workers had left, but they also steam cleaned her rug and buffed out the scratches on the wooden stairs, which she was sure was why Rafe had really sent them.

Family or not, she'd have to repay him somehow. Money meant little to him—in addition to the thriving business, he owned two of the most astonishingly gorgeous properties in a town full of astonishingly gorgeous property, despite his preference for staying at Phoebe's tiny 1950s ranch house—so Ione would have to come up with something other than cash. At least she could give the workers a sizable tip to express her gratitude for their efficiency and discretion.

They left her with an immaculate home that no one would have guessed had been the scene of a demonic dragon rampage the day before. It occurred to her that Diamante Construction might have a crew dedicated to such events. The Diamantes had been one of the founding families of the Mexican branch of the Covent. According to Rafe, journals belonging to Rafael Diamante Sr. had spoken—albeit in couched terms—of the legacy of the quetzal. Rafe's transformation had been anticipated, though his father had never suspected the quetzal would be his own son.

But if feathered serpent god scions were an expected part of the world in which Covent families like the Diamantes lived, other arcane creatures most likely were, as well. Within the European branch of the Covent, Ione's own ancestors had been known carriers of the recessive gene from which she'd inherited the blood of a demon. Creatures like Dev's Kur, then, might be more common than she'd thought.

Dragons, demons and divine scions had belonged only to the realm of myth and allegory for Ione just a few months ago. Now they'd become shockingly commonplace. More than ever, the events of the last forty-eight hours made her long for the comfort of the church, even as she felt less worthy of it.

The invitation to apprentice at the Covent had come a few months after the death of her parents, when her responsibilities had been slowly subsuming her individuality. She'd jumped at the chance to prove herself as something other than a substitute mother. She'd practiced her own eclectic version of the Craft in her teens, but with her formal studies, the reality of how far she'd drifted from the laws of the church had finally sunk in. Ione had been too ashamed to attend Mass and take Holy Communion, so she'd compromised by taking part in the weekly Taizé prayer service at the Chapel of the Holy Cross. But since discovering she had demon blood, Ione had stayed away.

Tonight was Taizé night and the service was in an hour. Ione had never needed it more.

After straightening her hair and dressing in a long, cream-colored silk skirt with a pair of knee-length black boots and a lightweight black sweater, she headed out. The chapel was just north of Covent Temple, four miles from her place, tucked into the rocks at the top of a winding road. She could see the temple from the chapel parking lot. Though, thanks to the glamour, she knew the white spires were passed over by the eyes of the rest of the tourists and visitors taking pictures from the gorgeous vantage point.

It was a constant reminder to her of who she really was, and she always took a moment to acknowledge it when heading in to prayer services.

Ione sat in the back row of the simple wooden pews, the atmosphere completely different from that of the temple. Soft light passed through the chapel in a straight path from the patchwork of leaded panes on the front and back walls of the A-frame building. The flames flickering within the red votive glasses lining the altar on either side added to the gilded effect of the early evening light. Even without the singing, this moment was magical for Ione in a way no temple ritual could ever achieve.

A few minutes before the service began, Ione turned at a tap on her shoulder to find a sweet-looking older woman standing behind the pew.

She gave Ione a tentative smile. "Are you Ione Carlisle?"

"Yes, that's me."

The woman handed her a folded note and the smile faded as her eyes focused on the pentacle Ione had forgotten to tuck into her sweater. "God may welcome all, and far be it from me to tell anyone they shouldn't attend the services here, but true children of God don't dabble in all this New Age pagan nonsense. It's nothing more than devil worship prettied up with crystals and chimes. You should be ashamed of yourself."

She was too shocked to respond as the woman moved away to one of the side benches and fixed her with a disapproving glare. Ione opened the note. Beneath a hand-drawn red pentagram were the words *"damnatum cum diabolo, et angelis ejus, et omnibus reprobis in ignem aeternum."* They were part of an excommunication ritual declaring a person anathema for heresy. If she remembered her Latin correctly, it translated as "condemned with the devil and his angels and all the wicked into everlasting fire." In case she hadn't understood the reference, the note writer had added the more recognizable final invocation of the ritual in English. "Ring the bell. Close the book. Quench the candle."

She didn't need to see the signature to know whom this had come from. Which meant Nemesis might still be there.

Slipping her purse strap up onto her shoulder, Ione rose, trying to make the movement casual despite the heat in her face. As she approached the deliverer of the note, the woman pursed her lips and glowered, her expression as unwelcoming as it could possibly be. She turned her head when she saw Ione wouldn't be deterred and pretended to be intently interested in something at the front of the altar.

Ione wasn't going to waste time trying to avoid further offending the woman's sensibilities. "Don't pretend you don't see me. Who gave you this note?"

The older woman turned. "I'm sorry?" She clearly was not.

Ione waved the note in her hand. "Someone gave this to you to give to me. Who was it? Are they still here?"

Seeing Ione wasn't going to let it go, the woman lifted her chin, though it wavered slightly—she obviously hadn't expected to be challenged. "A young woman who is evidently one of your ilk."

Ione ignored the slight. "What woman? What did she look like?"

"I only promised to hand you the note. I don't know her. Or you."

"But you didn't mind reading correspondence between two people you don't know and making judgments about them."

The woman reddened, glancing at the people seated near her as if they might defend her from this obviously deranged person. "I believe she was short, dark hair in a sort of pageboy cut." She leaned toward Ione as if delivering a confidence. "Said she belonged to your *coven*." She hissed the final word as though she'd been forced to say "whore" in the middle of a church service. "She left as soon as she gave me the note and I'll thank you to do the same and stop harassing me." Apparently believing she'd now turned the tables, she drew herself up straight. "And take your disgusting little satanic incantation with you."

They'd attracted the attention of everyone around them. Sound carried in the little chapel. There was no point in telling the woman the words were part of a Catholic ritual and not a pagan one. The end result was the same.

Ione tucked the note into her purse and walked to the door with as much dignity as she could, going against the grain of those still coming in. Though it was difficult not to be noticed given the chapel windows now illuminating her back with the shadow of the cross within a golden arc of light. Luckily, she'd parked at the top of the hill, so it wasn't a long walk of shame.

She sat in the car for a moment as people continued to walk up the drive to the chapel from the bottom while others who had only come for photo opportunities began to head down. She'd lost her place in the Covent and now her last refuge within the church had been taken from her. She could attend the services glamoured, but God would know who she was.

Tears prickled behind her eyes and she blinked them away, taking the note from her purse to look at it once more. Bell, book and candle. The final excommunication of the witch. If Nemesis was doing Carter's work, Ione had him to thank for all of it. Sitting in his prison cell, Carter was destroying her life piece by piece. This "Lorelei Carlisle" who was visiting him had to be Nemesis, and Ione was going to find out who she was.

As Ione pulled out of her parking space on the shoulder of the drive, the car seemed to lurch forward, accelerating even when she lifted her foot off the gas pedal. Ione stepped on the brake but the car only seemed to pick up speed, as though the accelerator was stuck. People walking on the side of the road edged farther onto the shoulder, staring at her like she was a lunatic as she barreled down the twisting drive among the walls of red rock, pumping the brake pedal and trying not to lose control of the car on the turns. Another car pulled out ahead of her at the bottom and Ione laid on the horn, swerving around it and narrowly missing another coming up. Even with her window up she could hear the expletives being hurled in her direction.

Hitting the relatively flat grade slowed the car down some, but the brakes were still useless, and with the accelerator apparently stuck in place, she was far from out of the woods. There was a stop sign coming up with potential cross traffic. Thinking quickly, she signaled right and swerved around the corner and onto the narrow shoulder of the residential road, pulled the hand brake and turned off the ignition as the car lurched to a stop and the engine sputtered down. Her heart was racing, but at least the engine wasn't anymore.

Afraid to start it up again, she sat on the side of the road for a good fifteen minutes before she finally got up the nerve. The car purred when she turned the ignition as if nothing was wrong with it. After pulling out slowly and turning around, she tried the brakes. They worked like a charm.

The car showed no sign of problems for the rest of the drive home, which meant the defect had most likely been magical and not mechanical. Another little "gift" from Nemesis, no doubt, to make sure Ione got the message. Whoever this girl with the pageboy was, Ione was having thoughts of repaying her in ways neither the church nor the Covent would approve of.

As she pulled into her driveway something moved in the dull stone-colored shadows of the falling twilight, a hooded shape lurking in the entryway. Instead of opening the garage door, she parked in front. Better not to give some creep access to the inside of the house before she could close it. She'd started carrying the Glock in her purse, and she slid it out, acting like she was searching her purse for a compact. With the gun at her side, Ione got out of the car.

As the shape moved forward out of the shadows, Ione raised the pistol. "Not another step."

The hooded figure paused, hands rising in the air. "Seriously? You're going to bloody shoot me again?"

Chapter 10

Ione lowered the gun and clicked the safety on, jade eyes leveled on him in the fading light. "Dammit, Dev. Why are you skulking in front of my house in a hoodie?"

He tried to ignore the odd tingling that seemed to animate his nerves as she came closer. "Sorry, in a what?"

"Your sweatshirt."

Dev blinked at her and glanced down at the garment. "You mean my jumper?"

Ione sighed. "You're lucky I watch PBS."

"I have no idea what you're trying to say."

"I know, and it's oddly amusing." She dropped the gun into her handbag and unlocked the door. "Are you going to tell me what you're doing here?" Ione stepped inside and turned on the light in the entryway before punching in her code on the alarm panel. "Did you forget something? Another wall you wanted to destroy perhaps?"

Dev cringed. "I—think I owe you an apology."

"Are you going to deliver it standing on my porch?"

"Well—"

"Dev, just come in."

He cleared his throat as he stepped inside, lowering his hood as Ione closed the door. Oh, *hoodie*. He'd gone for a run after finishing up interviews at the temple.

"That wasn't why I came by, actually."

Ione folded her arms. "Why did you come by? Actually."

"I have some news, and you weren't answering your telephone."

She glanced toward the blinking light in the kitchen behind her. "Yeah, I guess the machine may have gotten full. I turned the ringer off." She prompted Dev when he didn't continue. "So what is this news?"

"Oh." It was annoying how he kept losing his train of thought when he looked at her, especially as it didn't seem to be Kur's doing, after all. "There are several things, actually, and…could we perhaps sit…?" His eyes widened as he took in the immaculate living room. "How did you…?"

"I just wiggled my nose and, *poof*, everything was back to normal."

Foolishly, Dev gaped at her, almost believing it until he realized it was a reference to the American television program *Bewitched*.

The corner of her mouth lifted in a devious smile. "My sister's boyfriend owns a construction company. They're very efficient."

"Right. Rafael Diamante was here." Dev had to work to keep the heat from his face. Kur's memories had begun filtering to him as soon as he'd left Ione's house the previous afternoon. "That was one of the things I wanted to talk about."

Ione slipped off her shoes and nodded toward the couch.

"Have a seat. Would you like something to drink? I have sparkling water and tea."

Dev followed her lead in leaving his shoes by the door before following her into the living room. "A pot of tea would be lovely." As soon as he'd said it, he realized she'd probably meant iced, but Ione put the kettle on without hesitation while he sat. "The first bit of news is that I've found out who's been visiting Carter Hamilton in prison."

Ione glanced at him over the open countertop as she took two boxes of bagged tea from the cupboard. "Lorelei Carlisle." She held up the boxes. "Earl Grey or Darjeeling?"

"Earl Grey, thank you. How did you know about Lorelei Carlisle? Is she a relative?"

"Not that I'm aware of. I doubt that's even her real name. Phoebe's gone to work for a private investigator, so she was able to check out the visitor logs. How did you find out?"

Dev cleared his throat. "Well, I...bribed someone."

She tended to frown at him most of the time, but her unexpected laugh transformed her features, her jade eyes recalling the pleasure in them Dev was trying desperately to forget. The kettle whistled, saving him from having to meet those eyes until he'd gotten himself together.

He jumped up when she came around the partition carrying the laden tray. "Let me help you with that." Despite the bagged tea, she had a proper tea service, complete with creamer and sugar bowl, and had even included a plate of what looked to be lemon-cream biscuits.

Dev set the tray on the coffee table and waited for her to sit in the chair adjacent to it before he took his seat on the couch.

He might as well get this over with. "Before I say anything else, I want to thank you for how you handled Kur.

You would have been well within your rights to shoot the demon straight between the eyes and call it a day."

"That's what I was aiming for."

"Ah. Well, at any rate, you didn't finish us off, and you cared for the wound. And however you managed to cage the demon again—which I still don't quite understand—I'm indebted to you. And I suppose I owe you an explanation."

Ione poured the tea. "I probably owe you one, as well. Except I don't really have one. I picked you up that night at the bar—"

"I thought I'd picked you up." Dev gave her a half smile as he took a lump of sugar.

"You thought you'd picked *Kylie* up, but in actual fact I was the one doing the picking up."

"We'll have to agree to disagree on that point."

Ione shrugged and poured milk into her cup. "The point is, I had no idea who you were or that the Covent was sending anyone to investigate me. When I saw you the next day, I recognized you, of course. But I didn't expect you to come back to the bar."

He stirred his tea deliberately, studying her. "Why were you glamoured?" It was a spell he'd never mastered.

Ione took a sip of her tea and a bite of biscuit, delaying her answer. "I don't like to be judged. As the high priestess of the Covent, I have a reputation to uphold. But there are some nights when I need to not worry about that reputation."

"So you go out as Kylie, and Kylie can have as much fun as she wants."

She nodded, giving him a challenging look. "I suppose I sound 'a bit mental' as you'd say on your side of the pond."

"Yes."

She paused in taking another bite, obviously surprised he'd agreed with her.

"But I live with a demon, so who am I to throw stones?" Dev sipped his tea, formulating his thoughts. "And the second time?"

Ione concentrated on her cup. "I suppose I got carried away." She set the cup in its saucer and glanced up. "So what about you? How did you become bound to a demon?"

"That's rather a long story."

"I've got plenty of time."

He hadn't really come there to bare his soul to her. He was more interested in determining how she'd managed to control his demon. But he'd endangered her life and trashed her house. He supposed he owed her the truth.

"When I was eighteen, I started my apprenticeship with the Covent under an elder whose methods were rather... unconventional. After I'd spent several months with him learning the basics of the Craft, he took me into his confidence. He'd spent his later years delving into the art of conjuring." Dev focused on her eyes, watching him with their usual controlled expression, giving nothing away. "I was faced with the choice of reporting him to the Covent and ending my apprenticeship or becoming an accessory to unsanctioned magic. I was young and stupid. And intrigued. I chose poorly."

"By conjuring, you mean...?"

"Summoning spirits. The dead—and other entities." Dev finished his tea and Ione poured him another. "I suppose what particularly intrigued me was that he was successful. Until that point, I'd assumed there were no such things as demons. But Simon had one. An ancient Sumerian demon in dragon form. He kept it caged within a warded circle, studying it. His motto was that one couldn't effectively use magic for good if one couldn't harness its opposite. Unfortunately he couldn't harness it for long.

"Something happened and the wards were broken. I'm

not sure whether he thought he could control the demon and broke them himself or whether the demon somehow managed to overcome them, but I came down to the study looking for Simon and found him lying twisted in a pool of blood. I thought the demon had escaped, but it was lurking in the shadows and, when I bent to help Simon, it attacked and nearly killed me.

"When I awoke in hospital I thought that was the worst it had done. But I discovered later it had become a part of me. Luckily, I was alone when I transformed, and no one else was injured. I wasn't even sure what had happened at first, but I had a suspicion. But when it happened again, I'd rigged up a camera to record it in advance. At the time, Kur was apparently in a weakened state and my consciousness was able to reassert itself after a bit and return me to my own form. That's when I had the warding sigil to cage it permanently tattooed on my body. And it's been physically dormant ever since, though it seems to have grown stronger mentally over the years."

Dev had been focusing on the tea tray, temporarily delivered straight back into that time as he related it, almost forgetting Ione was there. But when he looked up, he was surprised to see a look of skepticism on her face. Surely she couldn't doubt the demon's power over him after encountering it herself.

She set down her untouched cup. "That's not how it happened."

"I beg your pardon?"

"Rhea saw what happened when she read your tattoo. Kur was tortured and bound to you forcibly."

Dev's mouth dropped open and he couldn't seem to make it work. What she was saying was impossible. Because he had been there. He remembered…almost nothing.

He shook his head. "No. It killed Simon and attacked me. No one tortured it."

She was studying him, trying to gauge whether he was lying.

"There's a mass of scar tissue at the base of my spine from its claws where it tore its way inside. I'll show it to you if you don't believe me."

"I've seen the scarring at the base of your spine. And it isn't claw marks."

"What are you talking about? Of course it is." He'd risen to his feet, his agitation amplified by Kur's own inside him.

Ione looked up at him calmly. "Have you ever taken a good look at the scar?"

"It's not exactly in a place I can easily see, but I can feel it and I've gotten a good enough look in a mirror to know what I'm feeling." And what he was feeling now was defensive, as if she was trying to take something from him, to change what he knew.

"Your flesh is burned. It's a brand."

"No."

"Some kind of ancient symbol I don't recognize. Maybe it's Sumerian."

"You're out of your mind." He'd had enough of this. She was *completely* mental. Dev headed for the door, grabbing his shoes on the way.

"I think your mentor died in the act of binding the demon to you. Kur was in agony, and I'm guessing you were, too."

Dev reached for the door handle but it slipped from his fingers and a mournful sound rose from his throat. He thought for a moment it was Kur—until he realized it was himself. Kur was merely observing his breakdown.

Dropping his shoes, Dev turned with his back to the door and collapsed against it, sliding down to sit with his knees raised and his head in his hands. It was true. Every word of it. He hadn't allowed Kur to share those images with him. He'd suppressed what he recalled because Simon wouldn't do that to him.

Simon had pretended to be injured. It was the demon's blood. He'd told Dev to open the cage, to collar the beast while it lay injured itself—stabbed by Simon in self-defense, he'd said. Dev had stepped in and something had seared into him from behind like the fire of the demon's claws. But the demon had been lying on the floor of the cage in front of him.

Ione was beside him. "Dev? God, I'm sorry. It's none of my business. I should have kept my mouth shut."

She placed a hand on his shoulder and he reached for her blindly. He needed her touch. He was going mad.

Ione dropped to her knees and put her arms around him and Dev found her mouth with his. He gathered her against him, drinking her in, moaning into her then drawing back, afraid he was presuming. But Ione climbed over his lap and pulled him to her by the collar and he was lost for a few blissful minutes in her kiss.

Until Ione broke the spell.

She took her mouth away and made him look at her as he tried to reach for her once more. "Dev. *Dev.* I don't think this is what you need right now."

"Don't tell me what I bloody need!" The sharp rebuke merely proved her point. He leaned his head back against the door with a thud, staring at the ceiling.

"For the record, it's taking a lot of willpower for me not to just ignore what you need and keep doing what I want." Ione slid off his lap and stood, holding a hand down to him.

Dev took it and let her pull him to his feet. "What you want?" He laughed bitterly. "You can't even stand me."

Ione folded her arms. "I'm not sure where you got that

idea. Was it while you had me on top of the washer with my arms hooked over my head or while I was facedown and tied to the headboard having four orgasms?"

Dev had opened his mouth to point out that it was Kylie he'd been engaged in those activities with, but he paused as the last bit registered. "You had four orgasms? I thought the second was just one…really long one."

She gave him a teasing wink. "I'll show you how it works later." Before he could react to that, she took his hand and headed back to the living room. "Come sit down."

Dev looked down at their hands where the live current seemed to dance between them. "Your skin, it's…"

"Electrifying?" Ione drew him to the couch. "Not bragging. You have the same effect on me. I think Kur's blood has mixed with your own and it responds to the Lilith blood in mine. As mine does to yours."

He sat beside her, bemused.

"I'm not sure what it means, but I'm not going to bother trying to figure it out right now. Suffice it to say, you're the last person I should be attracted to. You've been sent to take everything away from me. You think I enabled a necromancer and a serial killer."

"That's not exactly—"

"And yet I find you irresistible."

Dev smiled despite himself. "You did describe me as—'so hot it's almost cruel,' I believe your words were."

Ione raised an eyebrow, her cheeks tinged with pink. "You heard that, did you?"

"A few things came back to me after Kur settled, yes."

"Well, don't get a big head about it. I suspect the blood connection has us both charmed."

"If you say so."

"You said there was other news besides Carter's visitor. That you came to talk about something else."

"A couple of things, yes."

Ione took a biscuit from the tray and scooted into the corner of the sofa, legs crossed toward him beneath the silk skirt so she could look at him directly. "So?"

"I had hoped to understand how you released the demon. And how you put it back."

"I can tell you how I got him to go back, but I'm afraid I have no idea how I released him." She munched on the biscuit thoughtfully. "Rafe said it was my blood that had called Kur, and I had to cut us both to put him back—my palm to your abs over the tattoo. You don't remember that?"

"I…" He put his hand against his jumper where the tattoo was. "The demon's memories aren't as clear at the release and the return. There's… Kur fears sharp things. Perhaps that's why it's vague."

Ione nodded soberly. "Rhea said he had images of 'beatings, burning and sharp things' from the time with 'the Sorcerer.' Simon, I guess."

Sorcerer. It was an apt term. And the Sorcerer had apparently been tormenting the demon from the beginning. Dev's stomach turned at the thought. And he'd helped torture the beast without knowing it every time he'd followed Simon's orders.

"Your blood," he said idly, and ran his tongue along his bottom lip. "I bit your lip and tasted blood when I…"

Ione touched her fingers to her lips and left a fleck of lemon cream behind. Dev couldn't resist. He leaned close to her and licked it off then kissed her hungrily. "I know it isn't necessarily the wisest thing," he whispered against her lips, "but it is definitely what I need." He rose and swept her up, hiking up her skirt as she wrapped her legs around him. "Is it still what you want?"

Her jade eyes met his, full of desire. "Yes."

She gasped as he slipped his fingers into her knickers from the back and pressed them inside her, warm and wet and ready for him.

"I want to make you come so many times you can't count them." He pumped his fingers inside her and got a head start on the first one.

Ione draped her arms around his neck and leaned her head against his shoulder and the kitteny sounds began just moments after that as she rocked against his fingers. She moaned into his jumper, biting the fabric, until the pitch of her moans rose to a crescendo and her hips locked on him.

Dev slipped his fingers out, rewarded with a plaintive mewl, to tug her sweater over her head and unfasten her bra, hoisting her up so he could suck on one of the hard nipples.

He let the wet point slip from his mouth and whispered against her ear. "One."

Chapter 11

Ione stared up at him, still tingling from head to toe, as he tossed her onto the center of her bed. He'd stripped her as he'd carried her upstairs. Except for her panties—which he was sliding down her thighs.

She shivered and tried to speak without slurring. "I hope you're planning to take off that 'jumper.'"

Dev cocked his head slightly, slipping one of her legs out of the panties. "Does it bother you to be naked when I'm fully clothed?"

"Not particularly. It's just not a very appealing garment. It's hiding your rather marvelous physique."

"I'll take it off, then." He lifted the sweatshirt over his head and tossed it aside, revealing the formfitting black T-shirt underneath that made a firm shelf of his pecs. "But I rather enjoy having you on display while I'm not. It makes me imagine we're in public somewhere and I've simply denuded you for my pleasure."

Ione squirmed at how wet the suggestion made her. "Pervert."

"I did mention that, didn't I?" He tugged the panties over her other foot. "Nothing too weird. Don't worry. Just—" he trailed the panties over her skin, tickling her breasts "—enough to make it interesting." Dev prodded down her lower lip and leaned in as if to kiss her, instead, pushing the panties into her mouth as she reached up to meet him. Ione blinked up at him in surprise, totally unwilling, somehow, to spit them out on her own.

Dev smiled and pushed her legs apart, kneeling between them fully dressed, and continued his quest to make her lose count with a generous application of his tongue.

Ione had lost all sense of time when she finally collapsed beside Dev against the sheets, sweaty and sticky and thoroughly satisfied. It might have been hours later, or days. She decided she didn't really care. He *had* eventually undressed, but not until he'd played with her like a cat with a new catnip toy, teasing her mercilessly, savoring the taste of her on his tongue while she begged him to fuck her. Even after the shirt had come off, giving her the uninterrupted pleasure of his washboard abs, he'd kept his jeans on, open at the fly. Entering her while he had her on the bed on all fours, he'd raised her onto her knees, leaning her back against him so she could watch herself in the mirror as he slowly drove himself into her again and again.

He seemed to have endless patience, and endless stamina, having finally kicked off his shoes and his jeans to drag her onto his lap, weak from her last orgasm, and pump his hips up into her with impressive speed until he came inside her while holding her wrists behind her back in one broad hand.

She had never been so thoroughly enjoyed, nor had she

so thoroughly enjoyed anyone else. But she had to come back down to earth eventually, and it was while she lay curled against his hip with an arm draped across his chest, humming contentedly as she kissed his bare skin, that he revealed the other bit of news he'd neglected.

"You'll probably want to get some rest tonight."

Ione traced her finger over the tufts of curls that decorated his pecs. "What makes you say that?"

Dev placed his hand at the back of her head and leaned in to kiss her hair, breathing in as if memorizing the scent of her. Which should have clued her in that he was about to drop a bombshell, but she was too blissed out to focus on such details.

"The Covent has decided to convene the Global Conclave to make a determination about your status. They arrive tomorrow."

Ione's finger stopped circling and she raised her head, chin resting on his chest. "They…huh?" Her extremities were still feeling floaty and numb, and her brain was wrapped in a postcoital fog. "Who's coming where?"

"Members of the College of Elders. They want to interview you directly."

Ione propped herself up on her elbows, arms folded over Dev's chest. "The College of Elders? Why? I don't…wait, when did this happen?"

Dev came up onto his forearms as Ione rolled onto her side. "It's what I wanted to tell you earlier, but I'm afraid I got a little sidetracked." He smiled apologetically. "I received the notification as I was heading home from the temple. I was going to drive over here to tell you because I couldn't get you on the phone, and then I decided on a walk instead because I remembered it wasn't far and I needed some time to formulate my thoughts around it."

She sat up, drawing her knees to her chest. "But why? I

don't understand. You haven't even made your report yet." She studied his expression, which was starting to look suspiciously like guilt. "Have you?"

"No, not the official report." He sat up fully, definitely looking guilty. "But when I left here yesterday, I may have jumped the gun a little." Dev swallowed. "I reported the vandalism at the temple—I had to—and I gave them a copy of the note from Nemesis."

Though it hadn't bothered her a moment ago, Ione suddenly felt every bit of her nudity. She drew the extra blanket toward her from the end of the bed and wrapped it around herself like a bath towel.

"You gave them the note?" She hugged her arms, suddenly chilled. "You told them about my demon blood?"

"Not directly, no. But I was obligated to keep them apprised—"

"You said you'd let me tell them in my own time."

"That wasn't exactly what I said. I said it wasn't my place to do so. That it was yours. I do have an obligation to keep the Council informed of threats against a member of the Covent that take place on temple grounds."

"And you just happened to choose to do your duty after you'd decided I was a conniving slut who'd tricked you into bed."

"No. That's not—"

"And then you came over here so you could get me to explain how I'd managed to manipulate your demon before I found out about the Conclave."

"Now, wait. I don't believe 'manipulate' was the term I used—"

Ione swung her legs over the side of the bed and stood, hugging the blanket to her chest. "You need to go."

"Ione—"

"Get out of my bed."

Dev slipped off the bed on the other side and collected his clothes. It was painful to watch him cover everything he'd taken so long to uncover. But it was more painful to realize she'd let herself be blinded by her hormones once again. Dev's own standing in the Covent was more important to him than any concern for whether he might be instrumental in stripping Ione of hers. No matter how much he obviously enjoyed stripping her of other things.

"I didn't send the report out of spite. It wasn't because I was cross with you when I left here." His head disappeared for a moment as he pulled on the hoodie. "I want you to understand that I wouldn't do that."

Ione took a breath, feeling like her lungs were on fire. "I could forgive you for spite."

Ironically it was his devotion to the very principles that had always been so important to Ione—the insistence on always following the rules to the letter, regardless of the consequences to actual people—that left her feeling betrayed.

The walk back to his car in the temple parking lot seemed endless, far longer than it had taken him to get to Ione's place. He felt empty and unanchored without the touch of her skin against his, as if he'd lost one of his crucial senses. The air didn't seem right without the scent of her body in it.

He knew he was being melodramatic, but he'd never been so affected by a woman before. The truth was he'd never truly been himself with a woman before. Not the way he was with her. She'd seen his uncensored desire. And she'd also seen him at his worst. She'd seen his demon.

For that matter, it was the *way* she saw his demon that had affected him so deeply. Never mind the static electricity that seemed to zing and pop between them whenever they touched. She'd treated his demon with kindness, even tenderness. His *demon*. He'd never even afforded the creature more than mere grudging tolerance, had never given a thought to the demon as a being with feelings, just something to keep under control, like a bad temper or an addiction. And the revelation that Kur had been tormented into joining with Dev had shattered his perception of himself, the self-righteous image he'd maintained all these years as the wronged party.

In truth, Kur's memories had been there all along but Dev had refused to see them. Knowing that he'd been an unwitting party to the creature's torture filled him with conflicting feelings of revulsion and rage. He now felt, dare he say, *protective* of the demon. In that light, his memories of Ione's compassion for the creature had touched him more than he'd thought possible.

I won't let anyone hurt you. I promise, she'd whispered to calm Kur's fear.

How could Dev not fall for—? Oh, hell, no. He was not *falling* for Ione Carlisle. Because that was madness. He hardly knew her. Not to mention the fact that she felt he'd betrayed her trust—and had engaged in quite a bit of extremely intimate sex with her before he'd admitted to it. Damn, he missed being able to blame all of his worst qualities and impulses on the demon. *Right, the devil made me do it.* That had been Dev's modus operandi.

"So now what, Kur?" He spoke aloud to the demon, though it wasn't necessary. "What the devil do we do now?" A heavy sigh reverberated deep within him. He echoed it with one of his own.

As Dev neared the temple, Kur's hackles seemed to rise inside him. The murky sense of something off about the place was stronger than ever.

The moment Dev stepped onto the car park, the fetid

smell of death assaulted him. Something dark and hulking swung before the doors of the temple, and Dev gagged and covered his nose. Nemesis had apparently upped his or her game. The carcass this time appeared to be that of a several-days-rotting dog, strung up from the overhang above the entryway by a noose. Flies buzzed about it, and the desiccated thorax was wriggling with maggots.

This was beyond simple disposal. He'd have to call the local animal control. And, possibly, law enforcement, because this was getting serious. The note had been attached this time with a stick driven into the eye socket of the crushed skull. Dev was barely able to read it without losing his gorge.

This temple remains defiled. Purify it, or we will be forced to take matters into our own hands.

The smell seemed to cling to him as he took refuge in his car to ring the authorities. But with his finger poised over his mobile to enter the American emergency digits, Dev realized the temple's glamour would make ringing the authorities pointless. Anyone who came to investigate would drive in circles and eventually decide it had been a prank and give up.

With a sigh and a lurch of his stomach, Dev headed back to the temple entrance, ducking around the obscene thing, and unlocked the door. Ione had procured a bin bag from the cellar for the cat. The dog's carcass was considerably larger, but he thought it would fit in one.

Downstairs, he found the gardening supplies and fetched a couple of the bags, plus a pair of garden shears and some long gloves, and headed back up. He took pictures from every angle to document the crime before he cut the dog down. Grabbing it in his arms so it wouldn't hit the stone pavement and burst, making a worse mess, took tremendous willpower. He'd bagged the corpse and tied the plastic handles around the neck beforehand, but it didn't make hugging the horrid thing any less unpleasant. He slipped the other bag over the top and managed to stuff it all into this second layer of plastic, tying it off as tightly as he could. There was an industrial rubbish bin around the side of the property that someone must haul to the dump on a weekly basis. It would have to do.

Dev peeled off the gloves and tossed them in after. He'd have to buy the temple a new pair. He glanced down at the jumper and grimaced. It seemed Ione was going to get her wish. The dreaded jumper was going in, too. Not that she'd give a damn what he wore now. Still, it gave him a bit of grim satisfaction to see it go. He sent the pictures with a quick account to the members of the Conclave and the Leadership Council, but he could at least spare Ione having to see it.

As he drove away from the temple, the sense of uneasiness receded. Though he knew it was only the negative energy of Nemesis's actions combined with the presence of the rotting animal carcass, he was beginning to dislike the otherwise beautiful and peaceful edifice intensely.

Ione received the summons to appear before the Conclave first thing Tuesday morning. The last time a conclave had been convened in Sedona it had been to censure Rafe for his unorthodox views on the crossing of shades. That was when Carter had arrived in town as part of the regional convention. Ione herself had filed the report that had set that conclave into motion, and she'd had plenty of opportunities to regret it since—not least because it had brought Carter here.

The Global Conclave, however, was serious business.

The outcome of such a convention was generally disgrace and banishment. It was just such a conclave that had expelled Ione's distant ancestor for her demon blood. Of course, that had been in the Middle Ages, so perhaps the current Council's directives were more lenient. But somehow Ione doubted it.

She'd dressed as conservatively as she could in a much staider clerical-style jacket—no pinstripes this time—and with her hair in an unassuming ponytail.

When she arrived at the temple, they were already assembled, only three officials necessary for this level of judgment, the ceremonial chairs placed on the dais before the altar. As Ione approached, she was careful not to acknowledge Dev standing off to the side of the sacristy with so much as a glance.

She stopped in front of the dais and bowed her head to the authority of the College of Elders.

The female elder in the center addressed Ione with a thick French accent. "This Conclave, so ordained by the College of Elders of the Global Coventry, consisting of myself, Elder Clémence Dupre, and my colleagues, Elders Florien Grimaud and Théo Guerry, is now in session. Dione Margery Carlisle, is it your intent today to speak the truth before this Conclave?" For once, someone had gotten the pronunciation of her given name spot-on.

She answered without a tremor in her voice, though her knees felt like they might give out at any moment. "I pledge my troth to the Covent and swear to speak nothing but the truth, in the name of the Threefold Goddess and before all assembled."

"Then the Conclave shall hear you."

Ione raised her head in acknowledgment and waited.

Florien, to Clémence's left, spoke first. "This Conclave is troubled by the reports that have come from this Coventry.

We would be willing to allow Assayer Gideon's investigation to conclude in its natural course, but the two incidents at the temple itself over the past few days are a grave indicator that your presence here continues to be a source—if not *the* source—of this trouble for the Covent."

"Two incidents?" Ione couldn't help but speak out of turn. "I'm sorry, Elder Grimaud, but I'm aware of only one attack, on Saturday morning."

"You were not made aware of what took place here last night?"

Despite the fact that it broke protocol, Ione threw a dark glance at Dev, but he looked down at his folded hands. "I was not."

"Another dead animal was found at the door of the temple, with another note demanding your expulsion."

Clémence gave her a firm but compassionate look. "Understand, Dione, that the Covent will not accede to the demands of such a person. Any action we take as a result of these proceedings will be done in accordance with Covent doctrine and bylaws."

"I understand. Thank you."

"Nevertheless," said Théo, "it is troubling that you've withheld information about your potential conflict with the tenets of the Covent."

"My conflict, Elder Guerry?"

"The allegations that have been brought against you that you have an undesirable relative who was once expelled from our ranks."

Ione clasped her hands behind her back and met his gaze. "I assume you're referring to an incident that allegedly occurred sometime during the fifteenth century. We have no idea what evidence, if any, was presented to support those allegations. And even if it could be proved, surely there are many laws from the fifteenth century we would all be ashamed to stand by today."

Clémence frowned sternly. "That is not for you to decide. It is your responsibility to inform this body when such information is brought to your attention. Had you done so, perhaps all of this unpleasantness could have been avoided."

"All of it?" Ione bristled. "If you mean to include the actions of Carter Hamilton in that 'all,' you're mistaken. I only learned of his obsession with my supposed ancestor when he was in the act of draining the blood from my coven member, Rafael Diamante, and attempting to murder my sister."

"The events of that evening remain to be verified by Assayer Gideon's investigation. What we are here to determine is whether you willfully withheld information you believed to be detrimental to your eligibility to serve as high priestess of this coven—which I believe you have just confirmed—and what the consequences of this breach of faith with the Covent shall be."

"You mean to say the consequences of my blood lineage."

The spark in Clémence's previously dull blue eyes said Ione had gone too far. "I mean to say exactly what I did say, Mademoiselle Carlisle. As for your blood, you are quite correct in your assessment of the differences in beliefs between the Covent of the present day and the Covent of 1462. Modern witches do not believe in demons, only in the practice of dark magic through the cultivation of malevolent energy within oneself—with the exception of the practice of necromancy, of course, which involves the manipulation of purely human spirits that are not one's own."

Ione might have applauded such a statement a few months ago. But regardless of her doubts about the fact of her own demon blood—doubts that were, in truth, mostly wishful thinking—she had met a demon in the flesh. She couldn't resist a quick glance at Dev, but his neutral expression revealed nothing.

"Hypothetically speaking, what would the Covent's policy be about demon ancestry if such beings *were* real? I mean, I'm sorry to sound doubtful of what you're saying, Elder Dupre, but I can't quite understand why the Global Conclave would have assembled here in my insignificant little town simply because I neglected to report that someone had suggested I had the blood of an imaginary creature in my veins. If my ancestry has nothing to do with my eligibility to serve as high priestess, how exactly am I in breach of faith with the Covent?"

Théo answered. "No one has said your ancestry has nothing to do with your eligibility. Demon blood notwithstanding, there is a reason your ancestress was expelled from the Covent. The Covent's recordkeeping has always been quite exhaustive, and it seems we do, in fact, have an idea of the evidence presented against one Madeleine Marchant in Briançon in what was then the province of Dauphiné, France, in 1462—the woman we have determined to be a common ancestor of both your mother and your father, confirming the claims of this 'Nemesis.' Madame Marchant was found guilty of exploiting her supposed demonic ancestry by using it to instill fear in the other members of her coven and in local villagers.

"Her actions drew attention to the Covent, which in France in the fifteenth century, as I'm sure you can imagine, was a very dangerous prospect. Though the Covent would not be formally established for another seventy years, then, as now, the name was used in secret among its members, and there were those in positions of power who knew of it. The Covent was forced to disavow affiliation with Madeleine. She was later tortured and burned at the stake due to accusations among the locals that she was a witch."

Ione shuddered involuntarily. Every witch knew the history of the Burning Times, but it had never seemed so immediate and personal to her before.

Clémence inclined her head. "As you see, Mademoiselle Carlisle, the Covent does not take a favorable view of those who claim to ally themselves with demonic powers in order to intimidate other Covent members."

So they were back to that: her "intimidation" of Carter Hamilton. "Even if those members happen to be serial killers, rapists and necromancers?"

"That is quite enough, *mademoiselle*. We will adjourn for the morning and let you know if we need further testimony from you before making our decision. I suggest you keep your mobile phone to hand, as we may wish to call you at our convenience." Before Ione could demur, the older woman added, "We have the number."

Chapter 12

Per tradition, she waited with bowed head for the Conclave members to step down and proceed toward the exit. Even without looking, however, she felt Dev's approach.

"I thought you didn't have a mobile phone."

Ione glanced up, annoyed that he looked fantastic in a tailored suit. "I have one. I just don't give the number out."

"I see. It would have made it so much easier to reach you yesterday."

"And I live to make your life easier. Tell me, is that your excuse for not bothering to inform me of the attack on the temple last night? Because I do have email and I provided you with the address on Saturday."

Dev frowned. "No. I just didn't see the point in upsetting you with more harassment from this person that you couldn't do anything about."

"At least until later today, I am still the high priestess of this coven, Mr. Gideon—"

"Please don't do that. I know you find the way I've handled this unforgivable, and you'd just as soon forget any intimate connection between us, but please don't call me Mr. Gideon. It makes me feel like some crusty old wizard." Dev sighed when Ione pressed her lips together tightly. "I wasn't going behind your back in reporting the incident last night. I was thinking that you had enough on your mind without those images in your head. As with nearly every decision I've made since I've arrived, I see it was the wrong one, but I did it to spare you, not to undermine you."

Ione shifted her weight and crossed her arms to keep from giving away her discomfort. "What images?"

"I documented the scene before I cleaned it up once I realized ringing the authorities was impractical given the proximity glamour."

"Let me see."

"You don't want to—"

"Do *not* tell me what I want. This is my coven and this person was attacking me. Show me the pictures right now."

With a controlled breath, Dev removed his phone from his coat pocket, thumbing the pictures into view. Ione took the phone from him and expanded the first thumbnail. She had to fight not to shove the phone back at him in revulsion. She'd asked for this.

"As with the cat, this is clearly an animal that had lain on the side of the road for some days before Nemesis brought it here." Dev took the phone back from her before it fell out of her hand. "I only mention it to ease your mind in case you were worried that someone is sacrificing these animals as part of this campaign against you. I think it's safe to say that isn't the case here. Not that it's much comfort but this tells us 'Nemesis' is most likely not someone who would easily kill a human, either."

Ione wasn't so certain. "Every budding psychopath has to start somewhere. I ought to know. I've dated one." From the startled look on his face, she realized he might be assuming she meant him—not that what they'd been doing could be called dating. "Carter Hamilton," she clarified. "Maybe I should get Phoebe on this. Have her look further into this Lorelei Carlisle person. If she isn't Nemesis, she may be Carter's go-between, getting information to someone else who's doing his bidding."

"You said Phoebe just started apprenticing. Are you sure we shouldn't call in a professional?"

"I've learned not to underestimate my sister." Ione picked up her purse from the bench where she'd set it and took the cell phone out of the little pocket where it was tucked inside. Might as well start using the thing. "Besides, Phoebe has an advantage most investigators don't."

Dev eyed her phone with a lifted eyebrow. "And what would that be?"

Ione turned on the phone and dialed Phoebe's number. "She's an evocator." She wasn't sure Dev would know the term. It wasn't one she'd been familiar with before Carter. But the stunned look on his face told her he was well acquainted with the concept.

Phoebe's voice mail picked up before Dev had a chance to speak.

"Hi, Phoebe. It's Di. I don't know if you have this number—it's my cell—but give me a call back as soon as you get this. I need your help." She recited the number before hanging up.

Dev observed her. "Wouldn't it be easier to just text her?"

Ione gave him a withering look. "Why does everyone find it so difficult to just listen to a message? It takes thirty seconds."

Dev seemed amused. "And a text takes five."

"Maybe for you it does." Her face warmed slightly as she realized that might have come off as an unintended innuendo but Dev seemed too preoccupied with Phoebe's talent to notice.

"So your sister conjures spirits?"

"Not conjuring per se. Not usually. She communicates with the shades as a temporary host. She's been doing it since she was a kid. Apparently they just 'come' to her." Ione sighed. "And don't think I haven't tried to warn her of the dangers. We've had words over it, believe me."

"Is that why Carter Hamilton…" Dev paused, looking uncomfortable.

"Chose to seduce me?" Ione filled in. "Yes, it is. That and our demon blood. He believed it was necessary to wake the quetzal within Rafe."

"You mean the way—"

Ione gave him a warning look. "We don't have to go there." She put the phone away and slung her purse over her shoulder. "If we're done here, I have some errands to run."

Dev called after her as she turned to go, the rich tones of his voice echoing against the temple walls. "I don't suppose I could have that mobile number now. For strictly official purposes of course."

Ione paused and turned back to observe him. "Strictly official," she warned before giving him the number.

As she walked out to her car, the phone buzzed in her purse. Ione fished it out, thinking it was Phoebe getting back to her, but a text message displayed on the screen from an unrecognized number. Thought you should also have mine. Strictly officially.

Ione turned off the phone. If the Conclave couldn't reach her when they were ready to cast judgment on her, they'd just have to add her failure to obey their request to the list of her sins.

* * *

When she arrived at the house after stopping at the grocery store on the way home, Ione was surprised to find Phoebe's little blue Jeep in the driveway. Including these two recent visits, that made possibly three times Phoebe had ever even been out here since Ione had bought the place. Phoebe hopped out of the Jeep as Ione parked on the street, hitching a messy ponytail up high behind her head.

"Phoebe?" Ione rolled down the window. "What's wrong?"

"What's wrong? You leave me this weird cryptic message saying you're calling from your cell phone—and, hey, *news to me* that you even have one—and you need help, and then I call back and get a generic recording saying the person I'm trying to reach is unavailable? I thought someone had abducted you and you were trying to send me a coded message. What the hell was that about? Whose number was that?"

"Like I said, it's my cell phone number. I've had it for a while. I just don't like using it." Ione got out of the car. "Sorry. I didn't mean to alarm you. I turned off the phone because Dev persuaded me to give him the number and then immediately started texting me."

"And that's a bad thing because?"

"Because he turned me in to the College of Elders and I've just come from facing the Inquisition before a Global Conclave." Ione unlocked the front door and Phoebe followed her in.

"A *Global* Conclave?" Phoebe made herself at home on the sofa. "What do you mean he turned you in? I thought they'd sent him to investigate you. Did he find you guilty of something?"

"Of having demon blood." Ione tossed her purse down and flopped into a chair.

"Uh, isn't that the pot calling the kettle black? Isn't his dragon pal a demon?"

"Yes, but technically, he doesn't have demon blood. He just transforms into one because they share the same corporeal form."

Phoebe rolled her eyes. "Right. How stupid of me. That makes it all better. I assume you turned him in right back."

"No."

"No?"

"It's complicated, Phoebe. Anyway, that's not why I called. I was hoping I could enlist you to do a little digging on our mystery woman, Lorelei Carlisle."

Phoebe's look was suspicious. "You want me to investigate her? You didn't trust my skills as a lawyer after I'd spent three years in law school and another year in practice, and now you're going to trust me to do PI work after a few weeks?"

"That's not fair. I never said I didn't think you were a good lawyer. In fact, I recall telling you just a couple of days ago that I thought you were a *very* good lawyer. That's why I'm a little dismayed that you've given it up." Ione held up her hand as Phoebe started to object. "I'm not criticizing you. I'm just surprised. But I respect your choice. And as long as we have a PI in the family I thought I'd take advantage of it." She tried to grin but she was losing her ability to make light of things. "I also figured since there's a Lorelei Carlisle among the recent dead...your evocation skills might come in handy."

Phoebe crossed her arms and leaned back against the cushions. "Uh-huh. Now you're starting to seem more like you."

"Look, if you don't want to do it—"

"No, don't worry. I didn't say I wouldn't do it. I just

think giving you a little bit of crap is fair play after all the crap you've given me." Phoebe managed a much more effective impudent grin.

"Thanks. I think." Ione opened her purse and took out the note from Nemesis she'd received at Holy Cross. "I don't know if this will help, but here's a sample of Nemesis's normal handwriting. Maybe if you find this Lorelei woman, you can compare it with hers."

Phoebe took the note and opened it, scanning over it. "When did you get this?"

"Last night at Taizé. Where, thanks to Nemesis, I'm no longer welcome. She gave the note to someone in the congregation to give to me and claimed to belong to my coven."

"Ouch. Outed at church." Phoebe glanced up. "Did you get a look at who dropped off the note?"

"No, I never saw her, but my judgmental 'friend' said she was young and had short dark hair in a pageboy cut."

Phoebe tucked the note into her pocket. "Not much to go on, but I'll see what I can rustle up." She gave Ione a sidelong look. "So, do you want to tell me more about this Dev guy?" Her eyebrows waggled. "Maybe compare stories about turning guys into dragons with our magic pussies?"

Ione, having long since learned not to show any reaction to Phoebe's provocative speech, didn't even crack a smile. "No."

"Okeydoke." Phoebe rose. "Guess I'll get on this, then." Ione went with her to the front door and Phoebe turned back when she reached the driveway. "Oh, and I'm going to call your cell from now on so I suggest you turn it back on if you want to know what I find out."

"Nice. Brat."

Phoebe grinned as she climbed into the Jeep. "Well, as you're so fond of saying...*you* raised me."

"Which you're only willing to acknowledge when I'm pointing out a fault."

"I refer you to Article 2 in the previous sentence." Phoebe started the engine and pulled out into the road as Ione closed the door.

Though the Conclave hadn't left any messages, predictably there were more texts from Dev when she turned the phone back on, continuing periodically throughout the day. The general theme was apologizing for choosing to tell her about the Conclave when he had—though he was careful not to say anything specific about when that had been as though expecting the messages to be monitored. And each message ended with a promise that, henceforth, his use of her number would be strictly official.

Ione finally figured out how to leave the ringer on with text notifications set to silent. The little bluish illumination of light of the periodic notifications was oddly comforting as Ione fell asleep that night with the phone on the nightstand. She wasn't forgiving him, and his persistence was somewhat annoying, but she couldn't help feeling secretly pleased that he was trying anyway.

The phone woke her in the morning, and Ione fumbled for the landline only to get a dial tone when she picked it up. Slightly more awake, she answered the cell phone, her heart pounding as she braced for Clémence's soft accent.

"Di, it's me."

Ione sat up, rubbing her eyes. "Phoebe?" She yawned uncontrollably. "Did you find something?"

"I did, indeed. And Theia's found something, as well. You should come over and have brunch so we can go over it."

"I'm kind of waiting for an important call. Can't you just give me the highlights over the phone?"

"Sure, you want highlights? Dad had a second family that he hid from Mom for fifteen years. How does that grab you?"

The phone slipped out of Ione's hand and hit the floor.

Chapter 13

She had to get down on the carpet and halfway under the bed to get the phone back. How the hell did the thing manage to get so far on its own?

"Ione? Are you still there?" Phoebe's muffled voice grew clearer as Ione fished the phone out.

"I'm here." Ione sat on the edge of the bed. "What on earth are you talking about? What second family? And why are you researching our family instead of following up on Lorelei Car…lisle."

"Exactly. I drove down to the address in Glendale that Carter's visitor provided when she signed in at the prison. It turned out to be the address of one deceased octogenarian of the same name. I found her shade hanging around—she's one of those that hasn't realized she's dead and isn't bothered by it—and I managed to talk with her. She spoke of 'that nice girl who used to bring her groceries,' and I eventually got a name out of her. Laurel Carpenter."

Ione's foot jiggled against the bed frame as she tried to be patient. "So she borrowed her dead neighbor's name because it was similar. What does this have to do with our family?"

"That's where Theia comes in. The shade thought Laurel had moved home to Flagstaff to work for Animal Control, so I called Theia to ask her if she knew anyone through her veterinary connections there who could find out about her. She knew, all right. Back when Theia was researching the Lilith connection, she'd found another Peter Carlisle on the genealogy site with the same dates of birth and death as Dad, but he was connected to a different wife and kids—Peggy Carlisle and three daughters, Rosemary, Rowan…and Laurel."

"So? That could just be a coincidence."

"That's what Theia thought at first. But after we'd confirmed her Lilith hypothesis by combining our energy, she'd gone back to the genealogy database and dug around a little further. There was no question about it. Peter Carlisle, husband of Renée, was also Peter Carlisle, husband of Peggy."

Ione ran her fingers through her sleep-mussed hair. "So what are you saying? Dad was married before?"

"No, I'm saying he was married *during*. Dad was a bigamist."

Ione's fingers caught in her hair. "That's not possible. I would have known."

Phoebe made a scoffing sound. "Exactly how would you have known when the rest of us didn't?"

"I'm older. I would have seen something odd going on. You don't just have two completely different sets of wives and kids without anyone noticing. Besides, if she was actually married to him—legally or not—why wouldn't she have made a claim on his money when he died?" As soon as she said it, Ione's stomach sank. The will *had* been contested. By an anonymous party. But the claim had been dismissed by her lawyer as invalid.

"Apparently, Peggy Carlisle died fifteen years ago," Phoebe explained. "While Dad was still alive. The kids ended up in foster care. After Theia confirmed all of this, she didn't know how to tell us, so she kept it to herself. Didn't even tell Rhe. When I told her the name, she just knew. And my sources have confirmed the same. Laurel Carpenter, an employee at Flagstaff Animal Control, is the current legal name of the youngest daughter of Peter and Peggy Carlisle."

Ione couldn't believe what she was hearing. "She's our sister? Our *sister* is Nemesis?"

"Well, we don't know for sure that she's Nemesis."

"But she's been visiting Carter in prison. You're absolutely certain."

"I ran her prints and found her picture in the DMV database. It's the same woman who's calling herself Lorelei Carlisle."

"But why? Why would she be involved with Carter? Does she know she's our sister?"

"No way to find that out except talk to her. Which I'm planning to do later today."

It was too much to comprehend. Ione tried to put it out of her mind as she checked compulsively for a message from the Conclave. Still nothing...though Dev had texted her a half dozen more times. He was becoming insufferable. Ione went to delete his latest message and instead ended up clicking on Dev's phone number and automatically dialing. Before she could hang up, he answered.

"Ione." His voice was warm, and even over the phone

it seemed to buzz through her with that peculiar vibration that went right to her core. "Everything okay?"

"Yeah, I just…" She might as well not let on that it was an accident. "I just figured you weren't going to stop 'officially' texting me."

Dev chuckled against the mike—more vibrations. "Sorry. I couldn't help myself. I really want to find a way to make this right."

"There's nothing to make right, Dev. You chose duty and loyalty to the Covent over me. Which is perfectly understandable. You hardly know me. Why risk your own standing in the Covent for someone you don't even know?"

Dev was quiet for a moment. "I don't think that's fair. Fairly represented, I mean. It's perfectly fair of you to feel that way, of course. But it wasn't a matter of choosing the Covent *over* you. It was simply choosing to do what I thought was the right thing regardless of how I felt about you. And I do know you," he added before she could interrupt, his voice dropping into that warm, lower register that danced along her skin as if the current between them had traveled through the airwaves, bouncing off cell towers and satellites to alight on her flesh. "I believe I know you as no one has ever known you before. Just as I believe you know me. You can't imagine intimacy has been easy for me with Kur to worry about. I don't make a habit of fornicating with strangers in car parks."

Ione had felt her resolve melting as the sound of his voice caressed her, but she was suddenly bristling. "How charmingly put, Mr. Gideon."

"Oh, Lord. I didn't mean that the way it sounded."

"Didn't you?"

"I meant that my attraction to you is like nothing I've ever experienced." Dev made a soft groan of dismay into the phone. "Can we go back thirty seconds?"

"The thing is," said Ione, "I do make a habit of it. Not usually in parking lots, but that wasn't the first time I hooked up with someone at a bar knowing I'd never have to see them again. You were nothing out of the ordinary." The quiet that followed said more than words. "And since our values are clearly so different—"

"Oh, for God's sake, stop it."

Ione glared at the phone. "I beg your pardon?"

"Stop pretending that I'm shocked at the idea of a woman picking up a man in a bar in the twenty-first century. You seem to have this peculiar need to set yourself up as this fallen woman or something so that I can play the villain."

"I'm not doing anything of the—"

"What I was trying to say is that I'm not afraid of being judged by you for who I am—and that is a first in my experience. Just as I am *not* judging you. Or labeling you. Or anything else. What I *am* doing is asking you to give me another chance. To give *us* another chance."

Ione laughed to cover her conflicting emotions. "A chance at what? All we did was sleep together twice."

"Was that really all it was to you?"

"You know, it sounds an awful lot like you judging me from here."

Dev let out a frustrated growling sigh that Ione tried to pretend didn't make her squirm in her seat. "You're being deliberately obtuse. Can I take back my declaration from the other night that I didn't inform the Council out of spite? Let's just say it was spite. You said you could forgive spite, so…it was spite. Forgive me?"

The squirming was forgotten. "Well, since you've asked so nicely…" She ended the call and tossed the phone aside.

Chapter 14

Dev stared at the phone in his hand. Perhaps that last little gambit had been ill-conceived. Ione Carlisle was maddening.

Might as well get on with the job he'd been sent to do. He had interviews to finish with the members of the coven. Regardless of whatever action the Conclave decided to take about Ione's sins of omission, Dev was tasked with determining whether the high priestess had been at fault in allowing the incident with the necromancer to, well, *necrotize* within the coven. He couldn't allow his personal feelings for Ione to color that. Especially now that the Conclave was involved. He was walking on very thin ice. If he showed her any favoritism, the Conclave might start taking a closer look at Dev, too. And that, he couldn't afford.

The soft sound of chimes tinkling over the entryway to the temple announced the arrival of his next appointment. He glanced at his notes. Margot Kelley, the young witch he'd been about to interview when the first volley had been lobbed by Nemesis on Saturday. Dev rose from the desk in the office and went out to greet her.

"Miss Kelley." He extended his hand as they met before the altar. "Thank you for taking time out of your schedule to come by. I apologize for the unpleasantness that occurred the last time you were here."

Margot seemed to size him up with curiosity. "You didn't put that thing out there." She paused. "Did you?"

Dev blanched. "Certainly not. I just meant…it was unfortunate, and it happened under my watch. So for that, I apologize." He seemed to be doing a lot of that today, come to think of it. "Would you like to sit down in the office or would you prefer to talk here?"

"Here's fine." Margot took a seat in the front row.

"Let me get you some water." Dev retreated to the back and returned with a bottle for each of them, along with his notes, then sat beside her at a respectful distance, turning his body diagonally to face her.

But before he could pose his first question, Margot launched into her own testimony. "Like I told you before, we all stand behind Ione. She had absolutely nothing to do with Carter Hamilton's actions—and, frankly, I would think *you* people ought to be apologizing to *her* for letting him weasel his way in here."

Dev frowned and paused in opening the cap on his water. "You people?"

"All of you Covent bigwigs. Didn't he come up in the ranks in the Phoenix branch? Who let him get so much power without any oversight? He was a member of the Regional Conclave. Ione trusted him because you folks told her to trust him. You should be ashamed of yourselves."

Dev took a gulp of water to hide his smile. She was a good person to have on one's side.

"I'll certainly take that into consideration. What I wanted to determine, however, was whether, to your knowledge, Miss—Ms. Carlisle was ever a party to any of Carter Hamilton's unauthorized rituals."

Margot's eyebrows drew together in irritation. "Didn't I just say you all sent him here and she trusted him because of his standing with the Covent? Where do you get, 'Oh, and while she was practicing the Great Rite with a necromancer between sabbats, she sacrificed a few goats on the altar, and the occasional baby' out of that?"

Dev choked on his water and nearly did a spit-take. "No one is suggesting that level of impropriety—"

"Well, what *are* you suggesting?"

"Not suggesting anything at all. I just want to confirm, for my report, that you personally never witnessed the high priestess engaging in any unauthorized magic with Carter Hamilton."

"Well, you can write a big, fat *no* to that on your little report."

"Very well." Dev set the water bottle aside and picked up his tablet to look over his notes. "Do you recall the exact date Carter Hamilton arrived in Sedona?"

"Why would I recall that?" He'd gotten her dander up and it seemed there was no getting it down. "He showed up with the Conclave, so whenever they say they came here, that's the exact date."

Dev nodded and made a note. "That's fine. These are general questions to establish a timeline, so please just answer to the best of your ability. I'm not grading you on this." He tried to give her an affable smile but Margot wasn't having it. "So you never saw Carter Hamilton before the Conclave convened."

Margot sighed. "No, I never saw him before that."

Dev made another note, aware that every time he did

so, Margot seemed to get more irritated. "And did Ms. Carlisle appear to be acquainted with him at that time?"

"You mean had *she* met him before? *No.* How many times do I have to tell you that?" Margot opened her water and drank it forcefully.

"So she told you that they'd never met."

"No, it was clear to me that they'd never met."

"Were you aware of their subsequent relationship?"

Margot opened her mouth, clearly ready to tell him off, and then paused. "Well…no, actually. That came as quite a surprise. I wouldn't have thought she'd fall for someone like him. He was a little too perfect, you know? Kind of… glossy." Margot made a slight shudder of distaste.

Dev wasn't quite sure what "glossy" signified but it was obvious that Carter Hamilton had left an unsavory impression with the lot of them, based on the interviews so far. He couldn't help but be somewhat pleased at the thought that Ione's ex-boyfriend hadn't been well liked. But Margot was still waiting for him to continue.

Dev cleared his throat. "So you would characterize Ms. Carlisle as being good at being discreet about such things."

"I guess so. I mean, if she was carrying on with him, none of us knew it. She's very private."

"Then you wouldn't necessarily have known if she actually hadn't met him before his arrival with the Conclave or whether she was just being discreet."

"I…what are you, a lawyer? Because you kind of talk like him, you know."

Dev smiled. "No, just English. And I'm merely trying to be thorough. I'm not trying to entrap you."

Margot eyed him with arms folded. "Mmm-hmm."

"Just one more question and then we're through. To your knowledge, prior to the incident at Rafael Diamante Senior's house on eleven August, had the high priestess engaged in any magical practice for the purpose of personal gain?" Of course, he knew the answer to that. Ione had used a glamour to pick him up in a bar. But he wasn't about to put that in his report.

"Absolutely not. Ione has always been very clear on that with the coven. She's a stickler for the rules. Which is why all of this is so absurd. And, frankly, insulting. You couldn't do better than Ione Carlisle." Margot jabbed a finger against the screen of his tablet. "You put *that* in your little notepad."

Dev tried not to let his response to that statement show on his face. Because he quite agreed with it. "Thank you, Ms. Kelley." He switched off the tablet and rose, offering his hand once more. "You've been a great help."

She eyed his outstretched hand dismissively as she rose and straightened her billowy skirt. Dev let the hand fall.

Margot picked up her water to take with her. "How many other interviews do you have to do before you make up your mind about Ione? I mean, how much longer are you going to be here before we find out if we get to keep our high priestess?"

"I have six more members to interview. But if they're anything like the rest of you, which I'm sure will be the case, I won't have anything negative to report back to the Council." He smiled, though of course his report wasn't going to matter much if the Conclave voted against Ione. And that was his fault, too.

He walked Margot to the door and found his next appointment waiting in the atrium. The older woman exchanged a warm greeting with Margot before the younger went on her way.

It wasn't until later, after the interview finished and he was closing up the temple for the day, that he noticed the marks on his rental car. Someone had written something in red letters across the metallic-silver paint job. Dev crouched to examine it. *The impure shall be cast out, and all those who consort with the impure.* The words appeared to have been written in nail lacquer and it wasn't quite dry. And Margot's nails had been adorned in a similar shade.

Ione fretted when Phoebe didn't get back to her that evening. Mulling over the revelation of their father's infidelity and his secret life, she'd never wanted a drink more. Maybe it was time for Kylie to give Officer Paul a call. She could kill two birds with one stone. She tried not to think about the fact that with her double life as Kylie she was following in her father's footsteps.

The cop expressed surprise and enthusiasm when "Kylie" phoned him.

"Absolutely, I remember you. Can you meet me at Bitters in an hour? There's some people I'd love for you to meet."

His group had reserved a private section of the club, and he waved Ione over when she arrived. The tall, dirty blond was built like a bouncer—or a cop, she supposed—barrel-chested with a thick middle that on anyone else might have looked like paunch, but she had a feeling it was just more muscle. Not someone she wanted to have to tangle with if things got ugly. She'd earned a green belt in krav maga, but he'd likely had his own fair share of martial arts training.

"Glad you could make it." He gave her a side squeeze around her middle that confirmed her suspicions about his build. And pretty much gave her the creeps. "Guys, this is Kylie."

The group of half a dozen men and a couple of extremely young-looking women greeted her without bothering to introduce themselves, though several of the men gave her appraising looks that made her feel like she was naked.

"Have a seat." Paul indicated the spot he'd vacated on the U-shaped cushions surrounding the large table in the booth, and Ione slid in reluctantly, immediately hemmed in by him as he sat beside her. "We were just talking about the big Halloween party a couple of the guys are throwing." He waved over a waitress. "What can I get you?"

Her need for a drink had evaporated. The creep factor at this little gathering was sending wholly unpleasant tingles up her spine. Someone at this table was definitely practicing dark magic.

"Just a Coke. I can't stay long, and I'm riding."

"Nah, you gotta stay. We're just getting started." He leaned past her to add a "rum and" in front of her Coke order. Looked like the sobriety elixir was going to come in handy tonight. "So this little shindig is going to be *the* place to be Friday night. You have to come."

"Do I have to wear a costume?"

One of the guys, who looked like another cop, laughed as he set down his drink. "You can wear whatever you want to, sweetheart. As long as it doesn't stay on long."

"Hey, come on, now." Paul laughed good-naturedly. "We don't want to scare her off."

The rum and Coke arrived, and Ione picked it up. "I don't scare easily." She took a sizable sip.

One of the girls eyed her across the table as if sizing up a rival. "Maybe you should." She snuggled under the arm of the cop, who grinned at her as if they were sharing a private joke.

"Don't mind them," said Paul. "They're just trying to keep the fun to themselves. But everybody gets to have fun at the party. We might even have some magic tricks. You like magic?"

Ione shrugged. "I've never seen much that impressed me."

"This will impress you," the other cop assured her.

"Bonnie, here, can go into a trance and channel the spirit of a dead warlock."

"What's the use of that?"

"He's a *warlock*," said Bonnie, as if that answered it.

Her friend elaborated. "The warlock has power over the spirits of the dead who haven't moved on. He can conjure up any sort of spirit you like…and he can put it into anyone at the party he chooses." It was as good as an admission of the nonconsensual magical sex trade as she was likely to get.

Ione suppressed a shudder of disgust. "You mean like my friend Barbie told me about? The ride-alongs?"

Paul cut in before the girl could answer. "That's kind of privileged information that Barbie shouldn't really have been giving out." He smiled as if making light of the idea. "But you should come to the party and see."

"So what's in it for me?" She smiled at Paul. "Besides a little fun, I mean."

"How would you like to make a thousand dollars?" The cop next to Bonnie wasn't playing around.

Ione downed the rest of her drink. "For a thousand dollars, I'll do the dead guy myself."

She managed to extricate herself from Paul's clutches after a couple of drinks on the pretext of having work in the morning. "Being a receptionist is the most boring job ever," she complained as she picked up her helmet off the floor behind her feet. "I am so over being friendly to jerks for shit pay. If I'm going to be friendly to some rando, I'd like to get paid for my real skills." She winked at Paul and made her escape, the address of the party saved on her phone.

After she'd ridden home and shaken off the glamour, Ione's skin was still crawling, as though the unpleasant vibes that had emanated from someone at that table had followed her home like necromantic feelers being sent out in her direction. She needed to beef up the wards around the house, but she also needed to start using some real protection. A handgun wasn't going to cut it against necromancy. And if Carter meant to come at her through this Nemesis, whether it turned out to be her own half sister or not, Ione needed to be ready for him.

She gathered the supplies for the first protection spell she'd ever learned: the Amulet of Isis. Her altar room, originally designed as an under-the-stairs storage closet, allowed just enough room to stand before the altar fashioned from an old vanity she'd picked up at a flea market. The mirror was still intact and could be tilted forward and back on a hinge. She'd scraped off the old paint and left it "distressed" to complement the crackled appearance of the aging glass.

From her apothecary cabinet she gathered the ingredients: dried lavender and laurel, pine and ash, and oils of agrimony and eucalyptus—along with a lump of dragon's blood. The name of the red, powdery resin couldn't help but bring Dev to mind, but Ione pushed the thought away. She burned the herbs and resins in the broad shell bowl that served as her cauldron, placing a drop of essential oil on the tips of each index finger as she recited the incantation.

"Isis, Giver of Life, lend me your protection from those who would seek to do me harm. I draw your shield around me like the cloak of night over which you preside." As she spoke the words, Ione concentrated on the droplets of oil and willed them to rise. It was her signature, the trick she'd thought only that, but she felt the power in her blood now as the droplets hovered and circled in the air over the bowl. "East, west, north, south, from every direction, the goddess's protection." The droplets moved through the air above the altar in a figure eight with the motions of her finger.

As the still-burning ashes in the bowl took on a red glow, she released the droplets over them, sending the pungent fragrance hissing and puffing into the air. When the ashes had cooled, she wrapped the remnants in a small rectangle of red cloth cut from a silk scarf she rarely wore and tied it off with another strip to hang down like arms while the knotted ends of the original piece formed the "legs" of the amulet—the Isis Knot.

Ione repeated the ritual three more times to create amulets for Phoebe and the twins before going up to bed. She briefly the entertained the idea of driving Phoebe's amulet over to her tonight. Nemesis hadn't left Phoebe or Rafe any more unpleasant surprises since the first one, but there was no telling what Carter might still have up his sleeve. She glanced at the clock on her nightstand. After eleven. Phoebe was probably all tucked into bed for the night and wouldn't appreciate the late-night intrusion into whatever she was doing in it. And they'd had enough awkward conversations lately.

Chapter 15

Odd dreams assailed her throughout a night of fitful sleep. She couldn't remember them in the morning, but the sun had barely risen when her phone started ringing.

Theia's frantic voice carried upstairs from the answering machine for the landline as Ione scrambled for the phone in the semidarkness.

"Theia? What's the matter?"

"It's Rhe. I mean, this is Theia. But it's Rhe. Well, it's me, too—"

"Theia! Calm down. Tell me what happened."

"I had a vision, or a bunch of visions, really. Of terrible things happening to you and Phoebe and Rhe. All night long. Every time I closed my eyes." Theia paused for breath. "Nothing happened to you? You're okay?"

"I'm fine. What happened to Rhea?"

"I called to check on her and she said she woke up in the middle of the night with her left arm feeling like it was on fire. She thought she'd broken out in a rash, but when she turned on the light, it was like someone had tattooed her in her sleep but without ink. Perfectly smooth, flat, red lines, like freshly healing flesh, showing the words 'The impure shall be cast out, and all those who consort with the impure.' And then she watched as it spelled out 'abomination' below it, a little bit at a time, exactly the way the design would have appeared with a tattoo machine."

A shiver rose up Ione's spine. "She *saw* the word being tattooed into her arm?" Before Theia could answer, Ione's cell phone rang. "Hang on, that's Phoebe."

"You have another phone?"

Ione didn't bother to give her the obvious answer. "I'll put her on speaker." It took her a moment, but she managed to figure it out. "Phoebes, I've got Theia on the landline. Are you okay?"

"Yeah, just a little spooked. I had this shade flinging things around my house like a poltergeist all night. It didn't try to step in, but it was hopping mad or crazy or something. I've never experienced a presence that could affect the material world like that without the help of a host. And of course it had to be the one night Rafe sleeps at his place. Otherwise, he'd have been able to see who it was and try to talk some sense into the damn thing."

"Well you aren't the only one who had a visitor last night." Theia repeated what she'd told Ione about the visions and the attack on Rhea.

Phoebe whistled. "I think maybe somebody wasn't happy about the fact that we found Little Miss Laurel. Do you think Rhea's up to driving back up here this morning, Thei?"

"She's already on her way up to stay with me, but I'll call her and tell her to head to your place. I can be down there in an hour."

* * *

Ione was the first to arrive at Phoebe's place. Not even Rafe had arrived yet. She and Phoebe were closest in age, but Ione never felt quite as comfortable around Phoebe by herself as she did around the twins.

Phoebe must have felt the same, because she busied herself in the kitchen making scones. "So what about you?" she asked as she rolled out the dough. "Did anything creepy happen at your place?"

Ione stroked the cat as he made himself at home in her lap. "I had some weird dreams, but nothing more than that. I think the protective amulet I made for myself yesterday may have had something to do with it." She opened her purse and took out the ones she'd brought with her. "I made some for you three. Wish I'd done these a day sooner and brought them over yesterday."

Phoebe looked up, her expression surprised. "You made me an amulet?"

"Why wouldn't I?"

"I don't know. I just...thank you, Ione. That's really nice of you."

Theia's arrival, followed by Rafe's a few minutes later, saved Ione from any more awkwardness. By the time Phoebe's scones had come out of the oven and tea was steeping, Rhea had arrived, as well.

"It looks worse than it feels," Rhea insisted as she held out the arm for Ione and Phoebe's inspection after Theia had looked her over. The marks had scabbed over, but the words were still perfectly clear.

"This has to be Carter's doing." Theia followed Phoebe to the kitchen as the timer went off. "What did you find out about Laurel?"

Phoebe brought out the tea and let Theia bring the scones. "Rafe and I went to see her while she was at work, pretending to be looking for our lost dog. I gave her a fake name and she didn't let on that she recognized me. But there was something really odd about her."

"Odd how?" Ione set the cat aside, to his vocal objection, and Rafe answered.

"She smelled like death. I don't mean physically," he clarified when Ione blanched. "Not something that anyone else could smell. But it's a scent I've come to recognize since the quetzal's awakening. I've often smelled it when the dead were near, preceding the appearance of a shade or spirit."

Phoebe nodded. "I've smelled that too before a step-in. It's like…something oddly sweet. An almost cloying, flowery perfume."

Rafe nodded. "And there were no shades around. But somehow death was clinging to her. It seems she's somehow touched by it in a way that doesn't make sense for a living person."

"Necromancy," said Rhea and Theia together.

Ione shuddered, wondering whether she had ever carried the scent. "Did you question her about Carter?"

"I couldn't just come out and ask her if she was visiting him without giving myself away." Phoebe snagged a bite from Rafe's scone. "But Rafe and I tried to steer the conversation around to the murders and Carter's notoriety. She was wearing a pentacle, so I used that as my opening to turn the conversation toward paganism and the goings-on in Sedona over the past few months. Unfortunately, I think I tipped my hand and she clammed up."

Ione sighed. "Which means you're probably right about this attack on the three of you last night. Maybe Carter found out you'd talked to her and he found some way to magically strike back." And if he had, Ione was through sitting around and waiting for him to attempt something worse. It was time she had words with Carter Hamilton.

While the others continued to speculate about Laurel, Ione followed Phoebe into the kitchen to help with cleanup after breakfast. "Phoebes, I need a favor," she said quietly as she loaded the dishwasher.

Phoebe gave her a wry look. "I was wondering why you were being so helpful."

"I need to get in to see Carter."

Phoebe nearly dropped the plate she was rinsing. "Are you out of your mind?"

"I'm through being manipulated by him. I'm going to get some damn answers."

"And exactly how do you intend to accomplish that? You need to apply for prison visitation two months in advance."

Ione took the plate from her and set it in the rack. "His legal counsel doesn't."

Phoebe leaned back against the sink. "You want me to try to get you in as part of my team somehow?"

"Not exactly." Ione glanced over the breakfast bar to make sure no one was listening. "I want to get in *as* you. I want to borrow your ID."

Phoebe let out a short laugh of surprise. "I hate to break it to you but you don't really look that much like me. Switching identities is more of a twin thing. I'm pretty sure the prison personnel would be onto you in a second."

Ione lowered her voice even further. "Not if I used a glamour."

Phoebe blinked at her. "You're going to glamour yourself…as me."

"Only with your permission. A specific glamour is a little more difficult than the one I usually use. I'll need something of yours to wear. And some DNA."

Phoebe nearly choked. *"DNA?"*

"Just a small lock of hair would do it."

"You're serious."

"Deadly."

Phoebe glanced at the others, still absorbed in their own conversation. "And I suppose if I say no, you'll just pull some of my hair out and steal a blouse."

Ione crossed her arms and leaned against the counter with a smile. "You know me so well."

With a shirt from Phoebe, a clipping of her hair and Phoebe's driver's license in her bag, Ione drove back to the house to change—literally. It was unsettling to look into the mirror and see Phoebe's heart-shaped face and blue-gray eyes instead of her own thinner oval and muddy green, with Phoebe's signature bangs framing her forehead. Ione brushed the dark hair back into Phoebe's usual ponytail, pulling it up high so that it swung a bit when she turned her head.

It was a little annoying that Phoebe looked better than she did in her biking leathers. Taking the bike for the trip to the Arizona State Prison Complex in Florence made her feel more in control. She wasn't just Ione Carlisle, high priestess, going to confront the necromancer who'd deceived her and her coven, she was Badass Ione Carlisle—even if she looked more like Badass Phoebe Carlisle—ready to deliver a verbal smackdown to the piece of crap who'd threatened her sisters.

There was a brief delay when Ione arrived at the prison since she'd come without scheduling it. But after making a fuss about being concerned for her client's welfare and threatening to file a complaint about being denied lawful access—something she wasn't even sure was valid—

she was ushered into the noncontact visitation kiosk. She couldn't help but be relieved about the noncontact part.

Carter somehow managed to look cool and collected as he entered the room on the other side of the glass, as if he were wearing one of his four-thousand-dollar suits instead of an orange jumper. He eyed Ione with something like mild amusement as he sat, making her wait a moment before picking up the telephone receiver on his side.

"That's an interesting look for you. To what do I owe the pleasure of this visit, Ms. Carlisle?" He was just as smooth and sure of himself as ever. "I can't imagine you've done anything helpful like move up my sentencing hearing or arrange for a better plea deal." His blue eyes twinkled almost merrily in his still unnaturally tanned face. Maybe Little Miss Nemesis had been smuggling in bronzer.

"I want to know why you're messing with my sisters. If you have a problem with me, you deal with me."

Carter's pale eyebrows flicked upward with shrewd interest. "Ione, my dear. Your skills never cease to impress me. The leather should have clued me in. You rode your bike down."

"My method of transportation is irrelevant."

"Not to me. Not when it means you're playing that little game you like to play where you throw off the confines of your prim—dare I say, prissy—persona to play dress-up. Is it titillating for you to pretend to be your sister, as well? Is this something you've done a lot?" Carter's smile was vicious. "Do you sneak into Rafael's bed and f—"

"You shut your mouth." Ione moved her hand forward on the counter in front of her as if to form a silencing hex. "Or I may just shut it for you."

Carter gave her an exaggerated shiver. "Ooh. Come to play rough, have you? Why were you never this much fun in bed?" He gave her a rude up-and-down glance. "Do you play Phoebe for that glorified metaphysical auditor… *Dev*, is it? Does naughty Phoebe like a bit of slap and tickle?"

"Enough!" Ione clenched her fist to keep from accidentally throwing a hex in his direction that would do more than silence his tongue. Not that she was really versed in such things.

Carter laughed softly into the phone. "You're quite out of your league, you know. This isn't the kiddie pool you've waded into. There are sharks in these waters, my dear."

"I didn't come here to play who can throw more shade."

"Why did you come here, sweetie? Just missed me?"

"I want to know what business you have with Laurel Carpenter."

Carter touched his finger to the end of his nose. "Ah. Direct hit. I see I've struck a nerve. Am I not allowed to have whatever visitors I choose?"

"I don't care who visits you, Carter. I just care why. Why Laurel Carpenter? How did you get in contact with her?"

"Laurel is a sweet girl with a tender heart. She visits me because she's kind and she hates to see any sort of injustice done."

Ione knew she was letting him manipulate the conversation, but she couldn't ignore it. "What injustice have you suffered? You murdered four people in cold blood. That we know of."

"Did I? Or did you and your sisters conspire with Rafael Diamante to frame me—using necromancy against me to force my confession? Which makes more sense—that a respected attorney such as myself would randomly kill four people I had no connection with for no apparent gain? Or that a spoiled rich boy who paid for magically enhanced sex lost control and strangled a hooker, tried to cover it up by offing his own apprentice, and then killed another hooker he'd knocked up? After he'd gone that far, it's not much of a leap to imagine he'd had enough of his politician father and poisoned the old man to get his inheritance sooner."

"That's a lovely story. Too bad it's a complete fabrication and you've already confessed and pleaded guilty to all four crimes in a court of law."

"That's your story."

"And it was your story, too, and everyone's already heard it. Stop playing games and tell me what you want with Laurel."

Carter sighed and looked as if he might hang up the phone but seemed to think better of it. "Do you know she has Phoebe's eyes? I hadn't noticed it before but now that I look at them, lovely Laurel has that same periwinkle blue that turns almost violet when she's passionate about something. Deeper skin tone, which makes it much more striking, but really the resemblance is rather uncanny." Carter smiled at Ione's scowl. "You know, don't you? You've worked it out that Laurel is your sister. That your father sowed his seeds in more than one fertile field to make sure he was able to pass on what he carried."

"You're suggesting Laurel inherited the recessive trait."

"I'm not suggesting it, I'm stating it. All three of your father's illegitimate children possess it." There was no way to know if anything Carter said was true. Ione filed the information away for later.

"And you think you can get your hands on Laurel's blood and use it to regain your power."

Carter laughed. "I don't need your silly little strain of demon blood to regain my power."

Ione's breath caught in her throat as Carter's hand turned in a gesture similar to the one she'd threatened him with. He didn't have any natural power. It was one of the reasons he'd been so covetous of Rafe's. Once they'd bound him from Covent spell-casting, they'd rendered him harmless. Or ought to have. He couldn't possibly have the power to cast a hex with will and thought the way Ione might. Her amulet would protect her if he tried, but it was bad news if he was able to do it at all.

Carter paused and narrowed his eyes at her before lowering his hand and sitting back to observe her with calculating interest. "Laurel is helping me in a much more practical way. In fact, she's already helped me immensely."

Ione hated that she'd walked into his trap, allowing him to lead the conversation, but she had to know. "How has she helped? What do you mean?"

"You've seen how she's helped. Have you been enjoying my little presents?"

She wasn't going to let him get a rise out of her. "Exactly what is this vendetta against me about, anyway? All I did was believe your lies. It was Rafe you couldn't win against. I've done nothing to you."

Carter's blue eyes darkened through the glass. "Ah, but that's not quite true, is it, sweetheart? You've been meddling in my affairs. Throwing glamours all over town. It wasn't enough for you to let them slander me and put me behind bars. You're trying to ruin more innocent men because of their connections to me."

"Innocent men? They're running a prostitution ring right under the noses of the Sedona Police Department!"

"Nothing wrong with a little free enterprise."

Ione's fist curled around the phone. "Well, I'm going to make sure they aren't operating their little enterprise with anyone who can't consent. I'm coming after the source of your power. However you're doing it, I'm going to stop you."

"Do you sincerely believe you're any kind of a match for me?" The corner of Carter's mouth lifted in a sneer. "You may be good in the magical makeup department, but when it comes to real, potent magic, your silly little glamours aren't going to cut it."

"What power do you have?" The words were scoffing, but she was starting to think he wasn't bluffing.

Carter smiled and leaned closer to the glass. "How was your sleep last night? Or should I say, how was Phoebe's sleep? And those clever twins… I imagine they didn't get much of it."

Ione pounded her fist on the counter, earning a frown from the guard. "How, dammit? How are you doing it?"

"How did I do it before? With the power granted me by the guardians of Mictlan. With the bones of the dead."

"No." Ione gripped the receiver. "You couldn't possibly—"

But Carter had hung up the phone. He gave her a sweeping bow and blew her a kiss before turning to be escorted back to his cell.

What the hell had she accomplished? Nothing at all. Carter had gotten the best of her. He'd controlled every moment of that conversation, giving her only the information he wanted her to have, making sure she left there more agitated and worried than when she'd arrived.

Ione waited impatiently to be buzzed back out to collect her things. She'd promised to call Phoebe as soon as she'd finished to let her know she was okay, and she'd had to leave the cell phone in a locker. Funny how the device she'd scorned now felt like a necessity.

As soon as she had the phone in her hand, her notifications flashed, showing more text messages from Dev. God, did the man never give up? She ignored his messages and texted Phoebe as she walked out the door—and collided with a man coming in.

Ione opened her mouth to apologize and stared up into the face of Dev Gideon.

Chapter 16

Ione's borrowed features were flushed as she gaped up at him. "Oh…aren't you…? You're the Covent…what was it? Assayer?"

The fact that she seemed intent on maintaining her charade made him irritable. "Before you embarrass yourself, let me just state that I'm perfectly aware that it's you, Ione. Your leather alone would have given it away. Besides, Phoebe told me you were here."

Ione's blush turned a shade pinker. "Of course she did. What are you doing here?"

"I might ask you the same."

"I thought Phoebe told you."

"Yes, I know what *you* told Phoebe, that you intended to find out what Lorelei Carlisle's—or rather, Laurel Carpenter's—connection is with Carter Hamilton."

"And?"

"And…" Dev paused. If he told her he knew she'd

threatened Carter with magic, he'd have to explain how. And explaining that he'd used Kur's magic to conceal himself from detection and eavesdrop on her conversation just now—magical practice definitely not sanctioned by the Covent—would deprive him of the moral high ground. Not that he really had it in the first place, but neither was he ready to relinquish the illusion that he did.

Ione was eyeing him shrewdly through those blue-gray eyes.

"And I couldn't help but wonder if there wasn't more to it than that."

"What more would there be to it? What are you insinuating?"

"I'm not insinuating anything, but it *is* part of my mandate to determine your involvement in Carter Hamilton's oath-breaking." He regretted the words as soon as he'd uttered them. He'd have done better to simply say he was jealous. Lord, *was* he jealous?

There was no mistaking the expression on Phoebe's features. The outrage was purely Ione's.

Shoving her phone inside her jacket and zipping it with a jerk, she brushed past him without a word. The helmet was already on her head when he caught up to her. She ignored him and got on the bike.

Dev watched her go with a sigh. It was just as well. He had no idea what he was going to say to make up for shoving that large of a foot into his mouth.

He contemplated using Kur's magic once more to slip inside and beat the information out of Carter Hamilton, but that would get him nowhere. He'd be playing right into the neutered necromancer's hands. He also had the nagging suspicion that the necromancer might not be as impotent as the Covent believed. Hamilton's boasts about having his power restored notwithstanding, there had been a moment as Dev had paced behind Ione while she sat before the glass barrier when Hamilton had seemed to look right at him. If he'd been able to detect the magic Dev was expending to keep himself hidden, he clearly had some kind of magic of his own.

Heading out of the prison complex in his rental, Dev caught up with the black-and-red Nighthawk after just a few blocks. He stayed a few car lengths behind Ione all the way back to Sedona, worried she'd be distracted by her anger—at both him and Hamilton—but she drove with careful precision.

He wasn't sure if she'd caught on that he was following until they'd turned onto Highway 179 from the interstate just before dark. The traffic was light and Dev's rental car was a dead giveaway in the burnished glow of the vanishing sun against the magnificent rocks.

Ione pulled onto the shoulder and got off the bike. When Dev followed suit, she yanked off her helmet, shaking off the glamour as she shook out her hair—no longer Phoebe's dark brown but the ombré russet fading to chestnut that mimicked the setting sun.

Dev turned off his engine and stepped out of his car. "Ione—"

"Don't you talk," she ordered as she stalked toward him. "You've forfeited your right to make excuses or give me any more of your lame apologies. I'm going to talk and you're going to listen."

She stopped in front of him, legs apart and boots planted firmly in the dirt, and glared up at him in a way that made him sure she was actually expecting him to say something, after all, though he had no idea what. Her cheeks were bitten by the wind and there was fire in the green of her eyes. He wanted to kiss her. He was equally certain she'd deck him if he tried.

"Okay," he offered finally. It seemed to be what she'd been waiting for.

"You don't get to come marching in here—into *my* town—from your fancy London Coventry to judge my actions. I don't care why the Covent sent you and I don't care what the Covent thinks of me. The Global Conclave can go to hell as far as I'm concerned. I did what I had to do to keep my family safe and I'd do it again. I will use whatever magic I have at my disposal to keep Carter Hamilton and his cronies from enslaving and trafficking any more shades and to keep him from harming my sisters or my coven."

She stepped closer and Dev had to resist taking a step back. "So you listen to me carefully, Mr. Gideon. I had *nothing* to do with what Carter did. I abhor everything about what he did and I am mad as hell that he did it in my temple. And if you can't see that, if you can't understand that, or if you so much as stumble into my path as I defend myself and mine from his attacks, you can expect me to treat you with the same contempt as I would him. So if that's what you intend, why don't you go write up your little report, tell the damn Conclave that I want nothing more to do with their rules, and get the hell out of my town."

Dev waited, following the furious rise and fall of her breath. "Are you…should I speak now?"

Ione flicked her dark brows upward as if daring him to try.

He cleared his throat. "You're absolutely right. I've made a complete cock-up of everything since the moment I arrived. I keep trying to do the right thing, to follow the rulebook and stick to the straight and narrow, as it were, because this job is very important to me. It's my first assignment as an assayer, and I came here fully expecting to be exposed as a fraud who had no business taking on such an important role—and exposed for what I carry inside me. So I've tried to set aside my personal feelings for you, to do my job and to be rational. And in the process, I've treated you shabbily, and I'm sorry."

Ione's green eyes blinked at him with confusion, as though he'd been speaking in a foreign language. "I… What?"

"Sorry, was that another lame apology? I promise to keep trying until I get one right."

"Are you mocking me?"

"Absolutely not. I had plenty of time to think on the drive back and I realized that continuing to treat you as some kind of a suspect was grossly unfair. You've proved to me beyond a shadow of a doubt that you couldn't possibly have been Carter Hamilton's accomplice. Even if everything you'd done and everything you'd said since my investigation began hadn't already assured me, the way you handled Hamilton today has made it perfectly obvious."

Ione stared at him for a moment, the fire of indignation rekindling in her eyes, and Dev couldn't figure out what he'd said. "How do you know how I *handled* Hamilton today?"

Dev blinked and this time he did take a step back, carefully, out of range of a possible swing of her fist. "I…oh, bollocks."

"Were you *spying* on me?" Ione followed his step, keeping the barest of space between them. "Did you actually use *unauthorized magic* to eavesdrop on my private conversation?" He couldn't help fixating on her nails as they dug into the strap of her helmet. "You're absolutely unbelievable. Did you really think you'd catch me conspiring with my necromancer lover to spring him out of prison so we could go on a murderous magical spree?"

"No, no." Dev held up his palms in a gesture of surrender. "That came out all wrong."

"So you *didn't* use magic to sneak into the prison with me and listen to every word I said to Carter Hamilton, without my knowledge, to see if I was secretly in collusion with him."

"Well, I—"

"You complete *wanker*. I can't believe I actually thought you were a decent person for a moment, that I actually entertained yet another fake apology from you." She shoved the helmet back on as she turned to stalk to the bike.

"Ione, wait."

"Drop dead." The visor snapped down over her words.

Thick dust bloomed up around him as her wheels spun in the dirt while she whipped the bike around. Dev had to jump out of the way, rubbing dust out of his eyes, as she barely missed him on her way back onto the highway. He felt Kur moving restlessly inside him, pacing and growling in rebuke of his stupidity. The demon didn't care for having been the tool Dev had used to pull the stunt that had angered Ione.

Dev considered slinking off like a coward, but he could tell Kur was having none of it. With a sigh, he got back in the car and drove to Ione's place. She'd already driven the bike inside the garage and parked it before he pulled into the drive, but she came outside at the sound of his car and stood in front of her door, arms folded like one of the bouncers at that pub she liked.

"What do you think you're doing?" Ione's tone was sharp and biting as Dev got out of his car.

"Preparing to present the next lame apology, it would seem."

"Well, I don't want it. So get back in your car and go away."

Dev folded his arms, echoing her stance. "Wouldn't

you rather just get good and mad at me and let it all out? Take a swing at me or something? Wouldn't that be more satisfying than sitting in your house by yourself stewing about what an arse I am?"

Ione's body language and expression didn't change. "Do you think this is endearing in some way? Do you think you're being cute?"

"Not in the least. I was prepared to take my lumps and go home, as you suggested, but Kur, it seems, would have it otherwise."

A tiny ripple of reaction flickered across her face. "*Kur* would. You're trying to tell me that you're standing in front of my house behaving like a sad little stalker because your demon made you do it?"

"Well, in a word, yes." Dev unfolded his arms with a sigh and put his hands in his suit pockets. "Kur has a way of making me miserable until he gets what he wants—indigestion, gas—I won't bore you with the details. Suffice it to say, I give the demon what he wants when it's at all convenient, and particularly when it coincides with my own needs and aims. And it seems he's taken a liking to you."

"A *liking*."

"Yes. I've never known him to be partial to anyone else but he's left me with little doubt that he's grown quite fond of you." Dev allowed himself a brief smile. "As have I, as a matter of fact. And, as it happens, it was Kur's innate magic I exploited in order to effect my stupid stunt at the prison, and he's rather displeased that I've dragged him into the doghouse with me. So to speak. If I'm on the outs with you, so is he, and he doesn't care for it."

Ione was tapping her foot with irritation, but at least she wasn't glaring her own brand of dragonfire at him for the moment. "So you're appealing to my fondness for the dragon. That's how you expect to somehow get back into my good graces, by trying to make me feel guilty for upsetting Kur even though you're the one who did it?"

Dev opened his mouth to say something but forgot what it was as her words sank in. "You have a fondness for him?"

"Well it's hardly the damn dragon's fault he's stuck with you, is it? I doubt it's a picnic. Truth be told, I think I like him a great deal more than I like you."

Something akin to a smug purr sounded inside his head. "So you do like me, then."

"Oh, for God's sake." Ione turned to go into the house.

"I followed you into the prison because I was jealous."

She paused but didn't turn around.

"I called Phoebe looking for you because your phone was off and I was worried, and she told me you'd gone to see Carter. Instead of hearing 'she's gone to demand the truth from Carter about this Nemesis business,' I heard 'she's gone to see her ex-boyfriend.' I told myself I was driving up there because it was my duty as an assayer and because I was concerned for your safety. But it was because I was suddenly afraid you still had feelings for him. Which, of course, would be none of my business in any event. But it felt like my business."

Ione turned slowly to face him. "Why? Why would it be your business?"

"Because I feel a connection to you that seems preposterous given how little we know of each other and how recently we met. And yet it's there." Dev took a step closer. "There's a sort of...well, it sounds absurd, but it's not just the electrifying connection when we touch. Even when we're meters apart, there's a..."

"Vibration."

Dev felt it in the ground right now as if it was flowing down through her and into the earth to get to him. He couldn't help but smile. "You feel it, too."

"What I feel right now is a strong desire to slug you. Frankly, I find you infuriating."

"I can work with that." He took another step toward her. "Perhaps you'd feel less inclined to slug me—or at least to tell me you wanted to slug me—with your knickers in your mouth."

Ione's eyes widened and she shifted her weight. "I'm pretty sure I'd still find you infuriating."

"But you'd still let me do it."

"I…don't know." The color in her cheeks said she did.

"Shall we find out?"

Ione moistened her bottom lip and regarded him for a moment before she turned and went inside—leaving the door open.

Chapter 17

She heard the click of the latch behind her while she unzipped her jacket. The vibration of Dev's demon-enhanced blood crackled in the air as he closed the space between them and his hands came around to her front to finish unzipping the jacket for her. He wrapped his arms around her and brought his hands up under her shirt to stroke her skin.

"Still want to slug me?" he murmured against her ear.

"Your mouth's still moving, isn't it?"

Dev chuckled, his breath tickling her neck. "I can move it somewhere else if you prefer." He turned her to face him, his hands sliding around to her back, and Ione closed her eyes as his lips brushed hers. As the kiss deepened, the vibration went all the way from her head to her toes—becoming particularly noticeable at the midpoint.

Dev released her, moving his hands to the waistband of her leather pants, and slipped out the top button. Ione shivered at the touch of his fingers making their way through the buttons inside the fly.

With two fingers inside her panties, he teased them downward. “Still find me infuriating?”

Ione bit her lip as she looked him in the eye. “Completely.” His fingers slid down and curved inward, seeking entry. Ione groaned softly as the top joint of his middle finger found its way.

“How about now?”

Ione made an incoherent noise that was neither affirmation nor denial as he stroked the finger inside her, his other rubbing the hood of her clit.

“Sorry, I didn’t catch that.”

All she could manage was a high-pitched whimper. He could make her come standing right here in her foyer with just two fingers barely inside her, and it wouldn’t take long.

Dev smiled and kissed her again while she rocked her hips into his hand but he pulled away much too soon. “I don’t think you need your knickers in your mouth, after all.” He wriggled his hand deeper into her pants to penetrate her with both fingers, pumping them slowly. “Tell me again that I’m infuriating.”

“You’re—” The word morphed into a long, drawn-out moan.

“That’s what I thought.” He drew his fingers out against her whimper of protest and ran the slick tips of them along her upper lip before sliding them into her mouth. Ione sucked and moaned around them as his other hand took their place below. Dev mimicked the motions of the fingers between her legs with the fingers in her mouth. “Like that?”

Ione made a moaning sound of assent, rocking her hips faster.

“So do I,” said Dev and took both sets of fingers away from her without warning to drop onto his haunches and wriggle the leather pants down her thighs. “Quite a bit.”

He closed his mouth over her swollen clit and stroked his tongue beneath it, pressing his fingers inside her at the same moment, and Ione had to grab the hair at the side of his head to stay on her feet.

He was dogged in his determination, and Ione's knees nearly buckled as the vibration she could no longer differentiate from his mouth and fingers and her own quivering response broke into a shuddering climax. He lapped at her with his tongue as her body rocked with it, and Ione's moaning turned into a breathless wail.

Dev looked up at her while she trembled with aftershocks. "Still want to slug me?"

Ione tried to answer and he had to stand and catch her as she stumbled into him. "I don't care," she finally managed to gasp.

Dev laughed and tilted her head up to kiss her with the salty musk of her own desire. "Poor thing. I think you may need to lie down. Best get these off you." He proceeded to tug off her pants, and Ione gripped his shoulders to keep from toppling over. Without further conversation, he scooped her into his arms, carried her steadily up the spiral stairs and tumbled with her onto the bed.

With Dev reclining beside her, Ione wriggled out of her jacket and pulled off the black sports turtleneck she'd worn for warmth while riding on the freeway. The removal of the snug compression fabric freed her breasts and Dev eyed her with appreciation, hands cupped behind his head.

She smiled wryly as she moved to unlace her heavy boots. "See something you like?"

Dev smiled back. "You look cold." Ione laughed, but Dev picked up her leather jacket and held it out for her.

She paused at the bootlace with eyebrows raised. "You want me to wear my jacket?"

"And the boots. And those red lace knickers."

"Oh, *now* you want me to wear my 'knickers' as you so adorably call them."

"That's right. Why, what do you call them?"

Ione shrugged, letting him slip the jacket over her arms. "Panties."

"And yet you think *knickers* adorable." Dev shook his head. "Stand up."

Ione bristled slightly, leaning back on her elbows. "Are you giving me orders?"

"Only in bed, darling. Come on. Up."

Ione considered. She'd indulged his kink so far…and enjoyed every minute of it. She slid off the mattress and stood in front of him. Dev turned her around to face the bed, cupping her breasts and holding her body close, the firm heat beneath his suit pants pressed against the curve of her back.

She shivered as he toyed with her nipples. "You planning to keep wearing that suit?"

"Heavens, no. It's terribly uncomfortable." He unzipped and she felt the head of his cock nudging the cleft of her ass through her panties. "Just the trousers." Dev gave her a gentle push toward the bed. "Hands on the bedspread."

She heard him undressing behind her while she followed his orders, the tie sliding out of his collar with a snap that made her jump.

Dev stepped up behind her. "Spread your legs farther." He gave her a nudge with his boot to direct her then put a hand on her back and lowered her onto the bed so that her bare breasts rubbed against the rough fabric. Then he was drawing her hands behind her back and wrapping the necktie around her wrists. Ione's breathing quickened when he slipped his hand along the inside of her thighs and cupped the damp heat between them.

After he'd finished removing his jacket and shirt and

laid them neatly on the bed beside her, he stood back to observe her. Ione's heart raced with anticipation, the uncertainty of wondering what he'd do next making her hotter than she'd ever been.

"This won't do," he said after a moment. "Stand up."

When Ione obeyed, she only had a moment to realize he'd been putting on a condom before he sat on the bed and whisked her onto his lap, nudging aside her panties, and buried himself in her.

Ione gasped and Dev's hands paused lightly at her hips.

"All right?" he murmured at her ear.

"God, yes." The words were breathed out on a moan.

Dev turned her head to kiss her, but the angle was awkward. "Do you want me to untie your wrists?"

Ione only hesitated a moment. "No." His cock responded with a sharp twitch inside her, and a soft groan accompanied it. As Dev's hips began to move rhythmically beneath her, she tried to wriggle back against him, but Dev gathered her hair in his hand and held her still, pushing her forward so that her weight tugged against his grip.

In the mirror over the bureau across from her, his eyes met hers. "Don't move." He braced his boot heels against the frame of the bed and thrust upward rapidly with his powerful hips, watching her in the mirror as her breasts bounced inside the leather jacket, pushed forward by her bound arms.

As Ione began to moan, he tugged sharply on her hair. "No moving and no sound. I want only the quivering inside you and the flush in your cheeks to tell me when you come."

With her own boots braced firmly on the ground to hold herself still, Ione struggled to keep silent. The vibrations coiled inside her like a spring being wound tighter and tighter while Dev watched her in the mirror, drawing her down to meet his repeated thrusts. She bit her lip, seeing the flush rise in her cheeks as the spring uncoiled with a bang, the tightness in her muscles from trying not to move or cry out making the orgasm more intense than any she'd ever had.

"My God, you're beautiful," Dev groaned. Ione fixed her gaze on him in the mirror as every muscle in his body tensed when his cock jolted inside her with his release, the groan ending on a joyous roar.

She let out her breath with a cry, no longer able to hold it in, and Dev drew her back against his chest and rolled with her onto the bed as she whimpered and moaned, kissing her neck and her throat until they'd both stopped shuddering.

"I wish I could keep you like this for days," he murmured at her ear as he cupped her breasts.

It occurred to her that, given her experience with Carter, perhaps she ought to have been more cautious. Dev might have been a psychopath, and she'd let him tie her up twice. Yet somehow that was part of what made it so hot. Surrendering completely despite that tiny kernel of doubt. Even as she pondered it, he was loosing the silk tie from her wrists.

He nuzzled her ear as he pulled the tie away. "I love you in this jacket."

Her heart stopped for an instant until the full sentence registered.

"Especially with nothing under it," he continued. "Always wear this jacket."

Ione laughed shakily, trying to ignore what she'd thought she'd heard. "I think that might be a bit awkward when I'm at the grocery store."

"Oh, God. Now I'm picturing you at the market in this outfit. And riding there on your motorbike. Oh, you're killing me." He rolled himself away from her and finished undressing at last, heading into the adjacent bathroom to relieve himself.

Ione rolled onto her side and watched him return, the deep brown skin rippling with nothing but muscle.

"Seriously. You're still killing me." He put his hands on his hips. "Do you have to keep being that insanely sexy? Stop it this instant."

Ione laughed and then squealed in surprise as he dove onto the bed and smothered her with kisses before scooting down to unlace her boots and toss them aside with her socks.

"Come on then, off with that jacket before I hurt myself." Dev helped her remove it, pausing to kiss her navel, before tugging off the red lace panties. He sat back and shook his head. "Nope. Dammit. Still killing me. Under the covers." He hustled her between the sheets and wrapped himself around her as he joined her. "Although I have to admit," he murmured sleepily, "there's no way I'd rather die. If I don't wake up, have me buried with those knickers."

Ione giggled softly to herself, picturing him wearing them, which was likely not what he had in mind. She snuggled closer, realizing she'd never felt so relaxed—or so safe—with anyone.

The musical tones that woke her sometime later made no sense to her sleepy brain.

Dev reached across her and grabbed his phone off the nightstand. "Dev Gideon." He listened for a moment. "Why, yes, as a matter of fact. She's right here."

Ione rolled over to face him, coming swiftly and horribly awake. "The Conclave?" she mouthed.

Dev nodded grimly and handed her the phone.

She sat up and took the phone, answering as calmly and professionally as she could. “This is Ione Carlisle.”

“Mademoiselle Carlisle, this is Clémence Dupre. We’ve been trying to reach you on your mobile number.”

“I’m sorry. My battery must have died. I’m not used to carrying it. I was just here with Mr. Gideon—”

“The Conclave has taken a vote. We wish to see you at the temple at ten.”

“At ten. Yes, certainly. I’ll see you th—” But Clémence had already hung up. Ione handed the phone back to Dev, propped on his arm beside her. “The Conclave is convening at ten.” She glanced around, still disoriented. With the curtains drawn, she couldn’t be sure whether they’d meant ten at night or ten in the morning. “What time is it?”

Dev clicked the button on the side of the phone and the screen lit up. “It’s ten after nine—” he glanced up “—a.m.”

“Oh, God.”

“Come on. We’ll shower together. It’ll be quicker.” He threw off the covers, revealing a rather optimistic morning hard-on. Dev grinned at Ione’s obvious glance and took her hand to pull her from the bed and drag her with him to the bathroom. “Entirely a function of biology, I assure you. Pay no attention to it.”

Ione shrugged as he turned on the water. “It’s not as if I can do anything about it now.”

“Indeed.” Dev took her hand and led her into the shower. “Let’s just get you bright-eyed and bushy-tailed, shall we? We’ll worry about my anatomy later.”

He winked, but she was too preoccupied to smile. She felt like she was on her way to the gallows.

“Ione.” Dev took her face in his hands and looked her in the eye. “Don’t worry. I’m sure they’ve come to the right decision.”

She didn’t doubt it. But the right decision for whom?

She was beginning to have serious doubts whether what was right for the Covent was right for her.

Dev managed to look as if he'd been up for hours, his hair towel-drying quickly and his suit relatively unrumpled. At least it might not be obvious that they'd slept together. Except for the fact that he'd been with her at nine o'clock in the morning and she'd only just showered. They took his rental and, as Dev drove, Ione tried to come up with some scenario about having met him for breakfast just before Clémence's call.

The Conclave had arrived before them—perhaps had been here at the temple when Clémence had called—and Ione walked up the aisle feeling their eyes upon her with judgment. Well, she'd know what that judgment was soon enough.

"Elder Dupre." Ione bowed to each of them. "Elders Grimaud and Guerry."

"Mademoiselle Carlisle." Clémence nodded. "Let us get right to the point. First of all, let me reiterate that we are not here to make a determination of your level of responsibility in the incident with Carter Hamilton. That remains for Monsieur Gideon to decide." She glanced past Ione to where Dev stood off to the side. "We trust that he will weigh the evidence *impartially* and fairly. What we are here to determine is whether your failure to be forthright with this body regarding your ancestry constitutes a breach of faith with this institution."

Ione nodded. "Yes, Elder Dupre."

Clémence glanced at her two companions and one of them leaned in to whisper something to her before she continued. "We have come to a split decision of sorts. Because this is a Global Conclave, technically, we need only two to be in agreement. But, given the circumstances, I feel we must have a full consensus to make a binding ruling. The member who cast the dissenting vote didn't feel that we could separate the oath-breaking from the possible necromancy. We have therefore agreed to withhold our final determination until such time as Monsieur Gideon's report is complete."

Ione felt like she'd missed a paragraph. "Forgive me, Elder Dupre, but I'm not sure I'm following you. Am I to understand that you're now charging me not with a breach of faith and negligence, but with oath-breaking—and *necromancy*?"

"It was agreed that if Monsieur Gideon determines that you were complicit with the necromancer Carter Hamilton in any way, the guilt of necromancy must be considered yours as well as his. And if you are guilty of necromancy, well…you will most certainly be guilty of oath-breaking."

"You mean to label me a warlock."

"I must repeat that no determination has been made."

"But two of you came to a consensus. May I inquire as to which way the vote was leaning?"

Clémence sighed. "I'm afraid, *mademoiselle*, that would serve no use. Because we have new information to consider, there is no guarantee that our final findings will 'lean,' as you put it, in the same direction."

"I see." Ione knew bullshit when she heard it. "And by new information, you mean Mr. Gideon's report? Or is there something else?"

Florien leaned in to confer with Clémence before he turned to address Ione himself. "We are given to understand that you have made some progress in identifying the person calling herself Nemesis. Is that not so?"

Ione couldn't help whipping about to stare at Dev in disbelief. Was she really this stupid? Had he gone behind her back and reported on her again? Dev's face was unreadable.

Florien cleared his throat. "Mademoiselle Carlisle."

Ione turned back to the dais. "Not precisely, no. My sister Phoebe has done some checking and managed to track down Carter Hamilton's frequent visitor in prison. It seems likely this person may be acting on Carter's behalf to exact revenge, but so far we have no proof to substantiate our suspicions."

Clémence folded her hands on the table and leaned forward. "*Mademoiselle*, we are quite aware that this 'person' of which you speak is also a sister of yours. We are also aware that you visited the prison yesterday to confer with the necromancer. That is the new information, *mademoiselle*. That we believe, given this unexpected complication, it is possible you yourself are involved in this vandalism."

Ione couldn't comprehend what she was hearing. "Are you…? You're accusing me of…of what? Of *faking* these attacks from Nemesis?"

"No one is accusing you of anything, my dear. Not yet. As I said, we will await Monsieur Gideon's report before making our final determination. That is our decision for today."

"But you can't just—"

"Good day, *mademoiselle*." Clemence's voice was firm. The three stood as one and made their way down the steps without glancing in Ione's direction before marching down the aisle and out the door.

Ione couldn't stop staring after them with a parted mouth.

Dev approached her carefully. "Ione, I swear to you—"

"You swear?" Ione whirled on him. "What is it you're about to swear this time? That it's your duty to report every move I make to the Conclave and this isn't personal? Because I have had it up to here with you screwing me blind and then—then—*screwing me blind*!"

Dev raised a finger in the air. "No, no. Just a minute—"

"If you say 'no, no' to me one more goddamn time, I will flatten you. I know krav maga."

Dev swallowed, his eyes widening. "Sorry. Please, just give me a moment to respond before you resort to violence."

Ione folded her arms.

Dev placed his hand over his heart. "Upon my honor, I did *not* make any reports to the Conclave or the Council or anyone else. Not about your activities or your sisters' activities or my own. Except for the interviews I've been conducting with your coven members, I've had no communication with anyone in the Covent since the Conclave last convened. The only thing I ever reported was the incident with the cat's corpse. And the dog's. I didn't even tell them about…" Dev paused, looking guilty.

Ione advanced on him. "Goddammit, Dev."

"No, n—" Dev swallowed the second no before it was fully formed, his cheeks burnished with color.

"What have you not told me? What are you keeping from me?"

"It's not that I was keeping it from you. I'd just forgotten to mention it. I have this tendency to forget my own name when I'm standing in front of you. Did you know you smell like—?" Dev shut his mouth as if realizing he'd said something he hadn't meant to.

Ione's hands went to her hips. "What do I smell like, Dev?"

"You'll think I'm completely mental. Never mind. I was just trying to say you have this effect on me—"

"What do I smell like?"

This time Dev crossed his arms defensively across his

chest. "All right, then. You smell like toasted marshmallows."

"I… What?"

"I told you it was mental. Forget it."

Ione stared him down, trying to determine if he was messing with her. "Did you just make that up to get me to forget that you're keeping something from me? Because I haven't forgotten."

"I most certainly did not. It's not my fault you smell delicious. I expect it's some essence of vanilla extract. Perhaps it's in one of your toiletries."

"Then *you* would smell like toasted marshmallows, because you just used everything I used."

"O—kay then, I'll give myself a smell later."

"Dev. What did you forget to tell me?"

Dev sighed and drew himself up. "After I interviewed your friend Margot Kelley, Nemesis struck again. Or at least I assume it was Nemesis. Someone had graffitied my rental. It looked like women's nail lacquer. Specifically, it looked like Margot Kelley's nail lacquer."

"What?" She shook her head as if to clear water from her ears because she couldn't have heard him correctly. "Now you think Margot is Nemesis?"

"No, no, I—" Dev reddened, apparently realizing he couldn't stop saying "no, no."

"I'm not saying that at all. It's just an observation. I don't know whether there's any significance to it or whether it's simply a peculiar coincidence."

"Well, what did it say? Maybe she was just playing a little joke or something." Though it didn't seem like Margot to damage someone else's property for a joke.

"'The impure shall be cast out, and all those who consort with the impure.'"

"Oh. Mother of God."

Chapter 18

It seemed Dev hadn't been the only one who'd failed to disclose that something significant had taken place.

He studied Ione as she chewed at her bottom lip, trying not to fixate on the arousing nature of the unconscious gesture. "Does that have some significance beyond Nemesis's previous threats?"

Ione pulled the elastic band out of her hair and twisted the still-damp sheaf of hair in her hands. "Nemesis—or Carter—launched a four-prong attack the night before last. That's why I went to the prison to confront him. My sisters and I were each attacked in our sleep, though I had an amulet that seems to have rendered the attack on me little more than bad dreams. Theia had horrifying visions, Phoebe was plagued with a poltergeist and Rhea's arm was tattooed—with those same words."

Dev gaped at her. *"Tattooed?"*

"She woke up to find the words being written into her

flesh as if with a tattoo machine but without ink. The marks are still raw on her arm."

"My God."

"Carter alluded to it during my visit. I suppose you were there when he asked how my sisters were sleeping."

Dev nodded. "I did wonder what you meant when you asked how he'd done it."

Ione shuddered. "And he said he was using the dead."

"But if he's practicing necromancy again from inside the prison…that means he's gotten his hands on a corpse somehow. Or bones at the very least."

"Or he has access to someone who has." Ione met his eyes. "Someone like Laurel Carpenter."

"I know Phoebe and Rafe already tried to feel her out—Phoebe mentioned it to me when I called looking for you yesterday—but I think it may be time for you and I to have a word with Ms. Carpenter ourselves."

"Oh, God." Ione's hand flew to her mouth.

"What? What's the matter?"

"I forgot to call Phoebe. I never charged up my phone. She's got to be worried sick."

Dev gave her a sheepish smile. "I suppose I did rather manage to distract you." He took his phone from his pocket. "Here. You can use mine."

While Ione called her sister, Dev wandered through the temple to give her privacy, studying the uniquely pagan stories depicted in the images in the stained glass. There was one in particular, however, that seemed to be straight out of the Bible—the story of Eve being tempted in the Garden of Eden. Dev studied it, the ruby red of the apple in Eve's hand standing out among the vivid greens of the grass and trees and the brilliant azure of the sky. There was also the poison-green serpent, coiling out of the branches of the tree—the color reminded him of Kur's scales.

As he studied the image, however, a deviation from the standard narrative of the biblical story became obvious. Images of Eve generally showed a nude young woman, either looking innocent and pure in her nudity in the moments before taking the forbidden fruit, or covering her breasts and genitals in shame after having eaten of it. But the woman in this depiction was no innocent, nor did she seem ashamed of her nakedness, judging by the satisfied and secretive smile. And the snake was coiling about her limbs and trunk as it slithered from the tree. This wasn't Eve. It was Lilith.

Peculiar that the Covent would castigate one of its members for bearing the blood of this same lady in her veins and yet celebrate Lilith as one of the icons of the goddess decorating its own temple.

Ione approached him to return his phone. "Well, I'll never hear the end of *that*."

"Oh?"

"She said she wasn't bothered that I hadn't called because as soon as she told you where I was, she figured I'd be too busy 'making the beast with two backs,' as she put it, to remember common decency."

With his hands in his pockets, Dev rocked back on his heels with a grin. "Well…she's not wrong. The lap of these pants still smells like—"

"That's quite enough of that." Ione glared at him, but she couldn't hide the flush of pleasure in her cheeks and the brightness in her eyes at the reminder.

"I was just going to say 'toasted marshmallow.'" Dev grinned but made a little skip backward as she moved toward him as if to slug him. That mention of krav maga had him both wary and aroused.

Ione chose instead to head past him toward the door.

Dev tried to keep up mentally as well as physically as he trotted after her. Was she cross with him again?

He touched her arm as she reached the atrium. "You're not leaving?"

Ione glanced at him. "Aren't you?"

"Well I..." Dev fumbled, at a loss for words, which he seemed to be more often than not around Ione. At least when she was clothed.

"You said you wanted to talk to Laurel, didn't you? So let's do it."

Ione smiled to herself as Dev opened the wrong car door for her after unlocking his rental in the parking lot. She couldn't help but be amused by his awkwardness around her. There was something extremely satisfying about being the cause of it. And it made his confident, take-charge attitude in the bedroom all the hotter.

She glanced over at him as he maneuvered the car onto the freeway. "Are you sure you wouldn't rather I drive? It has to be a bit disorienting to drive on the opposite side from what you're used to. I don't think I could do it if I were in England."

Dev didn't take his eyes off the road as he spoke. "I've become accustomed to it. Besides, I thought you needed to review Phoebe's notes." Phoebe had sent all the information she had on Laurel to Dev's phone when Ione told her she and Dev were planning to take the drive.

"There isn't that much to review. Just a few notes about Phoebe's impressions of Laurel's responses to her leading questions." Ione didn't add that she found reading on a little screen nauseating. "The important thing is that she's given us Laurel's place of work and her schedule, along with her home address. She's scheduled to work today, and she should be at work when we arrive, so it should be easy enough to catch her there. The drive takes less than an hour."

"Have you mapped it?"

"Mapped?"

"Phoebe gave you the address of the place, didn't she?"

"Of course. I figured we'd get directions at the gas station when we get into town."

"All you have to do is plug the address into the mapping application and it will give you the route." Dev glanced at her briefly. "Do you want me to do it?"

Ione sighed and started poking around on the screen. "I'll figure it out."

It took her most of the drive to do it, but Ione wasn't about to let on. She pretended to be engrossed in reading until at last she'd gotten the app to show her the text version of the directions from the highway.

"You'll want Exit 341," she said as if she'd had it all along.

When they arrived at Flagstaff Animal Control, Ione decided to be direct and ask for Laurel at the front desk.

"Don't you think we ought to be a little more discreet?" Dev murmured as one of the employees led them through the pound.

"I'm tired of being discreet. I intend to get answers."

When they were ushered into a separate area beyond the rows of cages, Ione was taken aback by the sight of the waifish young thing in a drab, baggy uniform hosing out an unpleasant-smelling room.

"Laurel." Their guide raised his voice over the barking echoing from the interior and the spray of the hose. "These people are here to see you."

The waifish girl shut off the water and turned her head—and went so pale that Ione made a swift move toward her, afraid she would faint. Laurel dropped the hose and scrambled back, causing her to slip on the slick concrete. Though Ione grabbed for her, Dev was faster.

"Ms. Carpenter!" He steadied her with his hands on both arms. "Are you all right?" Dev was in his most proper British mode. Laurel gaped at him wordlessly, shrinking under his grip, and Dev let go and stepped back. "Forgive me. You looked quite ill for a moment."

Laurel swallowed and attempted a smile. "Can…can I help you with something?"

Ione folded her arms. "Yes, you can. You can tell me why you've been terrorizing my family."

The color came back into Laurel's face with a vengeance. "I beg your pardon?"

"Oh, I'm sorry. Perhaps you didn't know what your victims looked like. I'm Ione Carlisle. The one with the impure blood you're so fired up about."

Laurel looked helplessly to the door. Ione was blocking her only route of escape.

"Ms. Carpenter." Dev threw Ione a look that said he disapproved of her methods. "My colleague and I represent the Sedona Coventry. Perhaps you're familiar with it. I believe you may be acquainted with a former member of our society, Mr. Carter Hamilton."

Laurel stiffened. "I'm afraid I don't know what either of you are talking about. I've never heard of this 'Coventry' and I don't know any Carter Hamilton."

"Funny," said Ione. "This picture of you visiting him in prison says you do." She held up Dev's phone displaying the security camera photo from the prison that Phoebe had managed to obtain. "Are you going to pretend that isn't you? That you aren't 'Lorelei Carlisle,' the name you've appropriated to hide your identity?"

Laurel looked to Dev as if to gauge whether he might

be the more reasonable of the two, before glancing to the door once more and apparently deciding there was figuratively and literally no way out. "All right. That's me. So? Since when is it a crime to visit the less fortunate and offer them comfort and companionship?"

"Is that what you offer him?" Ione couldn't help the sarcastic tone. "In that case, I'd say you're the one who's less fortunate. Carter is using you."

Laurel had lost the deer-in-headlights look, her blue eyes—with a grayish tinge like Phoebe's, just as Carter had said—bright with anger. "I may not be a high priestess in some ancient secret society, but I'm not stupid."

Ione folded her arms. "So you do know who I am."

"I know you're the fraud who framed Carter for those murders and used witchcraft and possession to force him to give a fake confession." She cast a disparaging look at Dev. "And I'm well aware of who your demon familiar here is."

"What did you call him?" Ione felt a sudden rush of protective anger.

Dev put a hand on her arm. "Ione, let it go."

"Your familiar spirit." Laurel practically spat the words. "No wonder the Covent is falling apart if you're the sort of people they promote to positions of authority. A demon mongrel and an unclean carrier of the blood of the Whore of Babylon."

Ione was speechless with rage for a moment before she centered herself and took a few deep breaths. Laurel was smarter than she looked, and she'd gone for both of their weaknesses. Carter had taught her well.

"Why don't you tell me what you expect to gain by playing your little tricks on me? What's in it for you in playing Carter Hamilton's pawn?"

"I'm not anyone's *pawn*. I'm his friend. After what you did to him, he had no one. You've turned everyone against him, poisoning the minds of every member of your precious *Covent* with your contaminated blood and your lies. There's a reason your ancestress was expelled from the Covent—the same reason your earliest ancestress was thrown out of Eden. You're a mistake. And I'm going to do what I can to help rectify it."

Ione gaped at her, unable to comprehend how this demented, deluded girl could be her own sister. She wondered if the other two—Rosemary and Rowan—were as messed up as this one was. It also made her wonder what their mother must have been like. With a pang of guilt, she recalled what Theia had said about them growing up in foster care. Their father had still been alive at the time—and he hadn't bothered to claim them. She couldn't imagine what that must have been like.

Laurel was still glaring at her defiantly, daring Ione to challenge her. It dawned on her then that Laurel had said "*your* ancestress" not "ours." Was it possible she didn't know they shared the same father? Or did she believe the "contamination" had come only from their mother's side? If what Carter had said was true, Laurel's mother must have had the recessive gene. But that didn't necessarily mean Laurel was aware of it. Carter would have used any information he had about Laurel to suit his own aims, which surely wouldn't include sharing what he knew with his little protégé if it served him not to.

"If you don't mind, I have work to do." Laurel picked up the hose and looked like she might aim it at Ione. "I want you to leave, and if you or any of your sisters or coven members harass me again, I'm going to file charges."

"Thank you for your time, Ms. Carpenter." Dev took Ione's arm to lead her out, but Ione shrugged him off.

"I want an answer to my question. What do you get out of helping Carter? Besides your wonderful, warm feeling of helping the less fortunate, of course. I can't believe you're committing these acts of terrorism just because you feel sorry for him."

Laurel twisted the nozzle on the hose and water began to trickle out of it at her feet. "I don't know what you're talking about. I haven't terrorized anyone."

"You're going to stand there and tell me you're not Nemesis?"

Laurel's uncannily Phoebe-like eyes were unreadable. "A minute ago you claimed I was Lorelei Carlisle. Now I'm Nemesis?"

Ione let out her breath in an exhausted sigh. "You've made no secret of your feelings for my 'unclean' blood. You came to my Taizé service at the Chapel of the Holy Cross and gave a woman in the congregation a note that was signed 'Nemesis.' She described you to a T. And I'd be willing to bet with all the tourists constantly taking pictures in the chapel that someone will have evidence that you were there. All I'd have to do is run a quick image search for Holy Cross photos posted online in the past week. You said you were willing to do anything to help Carter, and someone is helping him with this campaign against my 'impurity.' It's absurd to deny it."

Laurel's disconcertingly familiar eyes never blinked. "You have no proof that I've done anything but pass along a note to give to you. That's not illegal. It wasn't even a threat. So, yes, I admit that was me. But I'm not helping Carter in order to get anything. I'm helping him because he's a dear, sweet man who's been treated horribly by you and your precious sisters, and I believe in him. It's also my duty to help him." She lifted her chin proudly. "I happen to be his apprentice."

Dev must have sensed the explosion of disbelief and rage about to erupt from Ione, as he took her firmly by the hand and turned her about, leaving the little room and Laurel Carpenter before it could happen. "This is one of those battles you must walk away from," he murmured when she stiffened and tried to turn back.

She pulled her hand out of his as they entered the interior. "But she's as much as admitted she's Nemesis. We have her. We need to call the police and press charges against her for her threats."

"Carter Hamilton is a dangerous, conniving necromancer, and he's put this girl under his protection. We have to walk away. For now. We'll figure something out."

"He's in prison," Ione snapped. "What difference does his protection mean? If he had any real magic, he'd have done far worse than his stupid tricks. He'd influence someone, and he'd be out on the street. The only possible explanation for the magical attacks is that he's trained her—and she has the advantage of my family's blood."

"Be that as it may," said Dev patiently, "if we continue to accuse her, or if we even keep trying to contact her after she's invoked the claim of apprenticeship with a member of the Covent, there will be consequences. And you're in enough trouble as it is."

They'd stepped through the front doors into the parking lot and Ione stopped and turned to stare at him in shock. "A member of the Covent?"

Dev rubbed the back of his neck. "Hamilton remains a Covent elder for the present. There are official procedures to formally revoke his standing and permanently expel him."

Tears of anger sprang to Ione's eyes. "He's a murderer!"

Dev took her in his arms and drew her against him, despite the fists clenched at her sides. She resisted until the anger turned into despair and she collapsed against his chest.

"I know he is. I know, love." Dev placed a kiss on her brow and kept his lips against her skin for a long moment. "And he's not going to get away with it. The wheels of justice turn slowly, and the wheels of Covent bureaucracy make those wheels seem straight out of an installment of *The Fast and the Furious*." Dev's voice grew hard. "But he *will* pay for what he's done. And if the Covent doesn't see that it happens sooner rather than later, I may see to it myself."

Chapter 19

The drive back to Sedona was silent. Ione was obviously full of conflicting emotions, and there was nothing Dev could say to help. Silence seemed the most respectful option.

He took comfort in the little pulses of their vibration that traveled between them like the rhythm of a heartbeat or a wave against the shore. He wasn't quite ready to examine what it meant that they shared such a visceral connection. But he knew he wanted to pummel anyone who dared to hurt her. Well, maybe not Laurel Carpenter. She was being used and lied to by Carter Hamilton, just as Ione had been used and lied to by the filthy necromancer.

Though Laurel referring to Dev as Ione's demon familiar had punched him in the gut. Hamilton had definitely seen him in the prison. The magic he'd invoked with the demon's cooperation had the effect of throwing a "glamour" of invisibility, and the expenditure of magical energy had given him away. Which meant Hamilton definitely had access to power he shouldn't be able to wield. Hamilton claimed to be in possession of another soul, and Dev was reluctantly inclined to believe him. But as brainwashed as Laurel appeared to be, Dev found it hard to believe she would commit murder for Hamilton.

She had access to the animal carcasses—and a willingness to desecrate them on Hamilton's behalf. That much was clear. But murder…? It would be quite a leap for a young, idealistic woman who clearly believed her mentor innocent of the crimes of which he'd been convicted. Could Hamilton have committed a murder in prison? It seemed too far-fetched to imagine he could get away with such a thing with no one raising a hue and cry, even if he did have allies among the guards. And, besides, how could he possibly accomplish the ritual with the bones? No, more likely someone else on the outside was doing his dirtier work. And Laurel, perhaps, had been employed as their go-between. But whether she would go along with murder even if she herself wasn't willing to commit it, well… that remained to be seen.

Dev glanced at Ione as he turned onto the rugged stretch of highway within the cloister of Sedona's spectacular stones. "There's something I've been meaning to ask you." When she didn't respond, he continued. "When Hamilton said you'd been meddling in his affairs by throwing glamours…" Dev let the words hang in the air.

Ione turned her head away from the window at last. "That's not exactly a question."

He drummed his fingers along the steering wheel. "Is there anything you want to tell me about that?"

Ione let out a sigh heavy with resignation. "The reason I've been going out in a glamour wasn't to pick up hot British guys." She gave him a wan smile. "I've been looking for the men who were part of Carter's ride-along business."

"Ride-along?"

"It wasn't brought up in the case against him because there was no way to prove it, but Carter was using necromancy to allow men to purchase sexual experiences with prostitutes possessed by the shades he enslaved. Or, worse, to have his shades step into unwitting victims so these men could take revenge on women who'd wronged them."

Dev jerked the wheel and nearly ran off the road. "Christ. That's…probably one of the most repugnant practices I've ever heard of. And I've heard some of the worst."

Ione's profile was grim. "He did it to Phoebe to take salacious pictures of her, and threatened her with releasing them. The good news is that I found some of the bastards the night before last. A couple of Carter's cop friends, it turns out. I got the address of a little party they're planning for tonight. They claim to have access to the spirit of a warlock and a girl who can channel him."

"Tonight? On Samhain?" Dev shook his head in disgust. "Taking advantage of shades when the veil between the living and the dead is at its thinnest."

Ione nodded. "And I intend to call in an anonymous tip to the police and get them shut down."

"Sounds like a splendid idea." And he had a few ideas of his own. Dev slowed as they neared the turnoff to Ione's street. "So what do you want to do now? Shall I take you home?"

Ione considered. "I should tell Phoebe what I've learned."

"So…to Phoebe's, then?"

After a moment she shook her head. "No. No, let's just go home."

He wondered at the meaning of that "let's." He couldn't be sure if it was just an American figure of speech or whether she actually meant to include him. It was best not to assume. He pulled into her driveway and kept the engine running.

Ione's eyes crinkled with that peculiar amusement he seemed to elicit in her. It did funny things to his internal organs. And some external ones.

"Aren't you coming in?"

"Certainly, if you wish me to. I didn't want to presume."

"Yes, I *wish* you to." Her smirking little smile and her emphasis on the word "wish" had that quality that made him certain she was mocking his Britishness.

She got out of the car as he turned off the engine, and Dev followed her in, not sure what to expect. They'd gone from intensely intimate to uncomfortably polite—and not so polite—so many times he couldn't keep track. But Ione set the mood, taking him by the hand and leading him to the sofa.

She sat beside him, drawing her legs up onto the cushion, and curled herself against him. "I just want to be close," she said as he wrapped his arms around her. He had no objection to the proposed activity.

Despite the best of intentions on both their parts, it didn't last long. The vibration between them was simply too strong to ignore.

Ione played with the lines of Dev's tattoo as they lounged in bed later, tracing the pentagram along the firm terrain of his upper abs. "So this keeps Kur in his cage."

Dev tucked his arms behind his head, causing the muscles to contract into a tighter six-pack. "I couldn't manage him otherwise. I couldn't take a chance that he'd emerge and harm someone."

She glanced up, studying the wary brown of his eyes.

"Oh, I'm not judging. Just musing. Is he aware of what goes on…with you? Do you share a conscious connection?"

The corner of Dev's mouth turned up. "If you're asking whether he's aware when I'm getting busy with a lady, that's a question I rather doubt you want the answer to."

"Really." Ione raised an amused eyebrow. "Do you 'get busy with the ladies' often?"

The turned-up corner gave an amused twitch. "I sense that you're mocking me."

"You have a unique way of wording things." She crossed her arms on his chest with a smile. "I won't deny enjoying your peculiarities."

"My peculiarities."

"You're very proper sometimes. And then you're not."

"Oh? When I have been improper?"

Ione shrugged, still thinking about Kur. "You drank out of my toilet, for one."

Dev sat up, looking outraged, unseating Ione from where she'd propped her chin. "I did *no* such…" His voice trailed off and his face went crimson as the shared memory with the dragon apparently surfaced. "Oh, bugger me."

"And there's that very proper-sounding impropriety." Ione grinned. "Don't worry. Your secret's safe with me."

Dev's look of embarrassment changed to one of pensiveness. "It does seem to be."

"Sorry?"

"You've had a couple of opportunities now—both having occurred while you were quite cross with me—to denounce me to the Covent for not disclosing what I carry within me."

Ione shrugged, drawing up her knees and wrapping her arms around them. "It's not your fault you're bound to a demon."

"Nor is it yours that you have demon blood in your veins. And it's my fault the Covent knows about that. It's my fault the Conclave is even here. And yet you haven't said a word against me."

"And I don't intend to."

"I can't tell you how much I appreciate that. It's consideration I don't even deserve. You've been incredibly kind—to both me and Kur."

"I'm not trying to be kind." Ione shrugged. "Just…fair." The way Dev was looking at her was making her extremely self-conscious. She swung her legs over the side of the bed and went to the door to take her robe from the hook, wrapping the taupe satin around her.

"If you're trying to be fair, showing me that bum and then covering it up simply isn't." Dev grinned. "But in all seriousness, I've been thinking about what Ms. Carpenter said."

Ione tied the robe. "About what?"

"When she called me your familiar. Or said it of Kur, anyway."

Ione felt the disheartening venomousness of the encounter creeping back over her. "I'm sorry, Dev. That was horrible. I'm sure it was Carter talking."

"Well, yes. Obviously something she got straight from the necromancer's mouth. But the thing is… I'm not sure she's wrong."

Ione squinted at him. "Come again?"

"That marvelous vibration we both feel when we're in close proximity with each other. The connection we have that brought Kur out—and enabled you to put him back in before the warding destroyed him and me with him. It's in the blood. Kur, if my old mentor Simon was correct, is as ancient as they come, a demon from pre-biblical times. As is the origin of Lilith."

"So you think I'm somehow…"

"Genetically programmed to care for Kur—as he's genetically programmed to obey you."

"To *obey* me?"

"Perhaps 'serve' might be a better word. Quite frankly, I'm not sure what else could explain why he didn't kill you."

Ione rubbed her arms, unsettled by the idea that something in her blood controlled her responses—and Dev's. "You think the magnetism between us is only about Kur then?"

Dev blanched. "No, no. Not at all." He jumped up from the bed to come around to her side. "I didn't mean to imply that at all." Dev took her hand from her sleeve where she was nervously stroking the fabric and kissed it. "That frisson of electric energy when my lips touch your skin…that may be the part of my blood that is Kur's recognizing the part of your blood that is Lilith's. But my response to that energy, my body's response to you…" Dev glanced downward with a slight smile. "That is mine."

Ione's cheeks warmed pleasantly. "But if it's simply some biological predestination—like a pheromone…"

Dev shook his head. "Not a predestination. A predisposition. It doesn't shape my desire. It merely draws me to you."

"That and the fact that I smell like a sweet, gooey treat."

Dev grinned. "A *warm* sweet, gooey treat."

With a little smile she couldn't suppress, Ione drew her hand away, not wanting to get further distracted from the topic. "But about this 'familiar' business. You really think Kur is mine?"

"It seems the only plausible explanation for his immediate devotion to you. Whatever else Kur is, he is, in essence, a wild animal, not a tame beast. And he certainly has no love for humans—witches in particular. I've carried his seething rage inside me for nearly two decades, and his responses to people are unambiguous. He sees them as enemies. I've had to practice daily meditation just to be able to go about my business without sudden pulses of violent fury making me respond to slights in most unsociable ways."

Dev sat on the bed and gazed up at her, and in that instant he seemed as vulnerable as a child. "But I feel none of that when I'm with you. I feel—*Kur* feels—safe."

Part of her wanted to climb into his lap and tell him she felt the same. That the impulses she had to run away, to do reckless things like don glamours and have sex with strangers in parking lots, were quieted when she was with him. That she'd never felt so safe letting go and relinquishing control, calm in the knowledge that he wouldn't let anything happen to her.

But the part of her that wanted to bolt was still whispering in her ear, reminding her that she'd been betrayed before. Like Carter, Dev had learned where she was most vulnerable. And, like Carter, he could use it against her.

Ione smiled. "Well, I certainly feel safe knowing he can't get out without my help." Casually she picked up her landline since the cell phone was still charging. "I should probably check in with Phoebe and see if she can find out what Laurel's up to when she's not at work or visiting Carter in prison."

Dev blinked at her, looking somewhat dazed by the sudden change of subject. "You're going to have Laurel followed?"

"The sooner we figure out how she's helping Carter access his magic, the sooner we can stop her."

"We have to tread carefully there. Technically she has protected status as Carter's apprentice."

Though she knew it wasn't his fault, the words felt like another betrayal.

Ione tried to keep her voice light. "I'm not planning to use magic against her." She dialed Phoebe's number. "Not yet, anyway. Just gathering evidence."

Phoebe answered before Dev could say any more, and Ione stepped into the bathroom and launched into an account of her trip to Flagstaff, hoping Dev would take the hint.

It didn't stop her from feeling like shit when he did. By the time she came out, Dev was gone.

Chapter 20

The temperature had fallen as Dev drove back to his hotel, and he lit a fire when he arrived. Sitting on the floor in front of the fireplace, holding his hands out to it, he felt like he couldn't get warm. He should never have brought up his feelings—and certainly not in the context of the demon's. Why had he even broached the subject of familiars with her? It was like a security door had banged shut between them.

Inside him, Kur was restless and irritable once more. It was clear the demon already felt more loyalty for Ione than he did for Dev. Not that the symbiotic relationship he shared with the demon could be called loyalty in any but the loosest sense. Once he'd managed to cage the demon, he'd kept it on a tight leash, only indulging the demon when he needed to borrow its power.

Kur's disapproval of him notwithstanding, Dev was troubled by Ione's insistence on pursuing the investigation into Laurel Carpenter's activities. He'd known instinctively that if he'd stayed to argue with her about it after she'd finished speaking to her sister, the thickness of the metaphorical steel door between them would only have increased.

He couldn't blame her for being angry about the situation with the Covent. It was preposterous that Carter Hamilton should be given even the slightest consideration. He ought to have been expelled the instant he'd confessed to his crimes. But the fact remained that if Carter Hamilton wanted to he could file a complaint against Ione for interfering with his apprentice. Dev hoped she'd only been blowing smoke when she'd alluded to using magic against the girl.

Seeing Hamilton in action had solidified Dev's gut feeling with regard to the investigation. When it was completed, he was certain he'd find Ione innocent of any wrongdoing in taking action against the necromancer. She would have been fully within her rights to put a stop to his reign of terror by any means possible. But he couldn't very well sit back and watch her use magic against Laurel out of a thirst for revenge.

Of course…there was nothing to stop Dev pursuing further surveillance of the girl as part of his own investigation. And, technically, nothing stopping *him* using magic to do it, since he wasn't under investigation. If he could get the answers Ione wanted before she got into trouble trying to get them herself, it would hasten the Conclave's decision. And the conclusion of his report, he hoped, would lead them to the right one. He could also take care of those despicable sods and their ride-alongs with a bit of help from Kur. He'd sneaked a peek at Ione's mobile while she was in the bathroom on her house phone and snagged the address for the party.

But first he needed to find the source of Hamilton's necromantic power. Staring into the flames had given him an idea of how to go about it.

"All right, demon. You want to help your mistress? Let's see you put your money where your mouth is."

Rather than risk setting the hotel room on fire, Dev headed to the temple to conduct his experiment just after dark. He'd told Ione that the sigil kept Kur contained, but he hadn't told her he could let the demon out himself. It was how he'd accessed the demon's magic for the cloaking spell. Releasing Kur on a metaphysical choke chain allowed him to reel the demon back in without the detrimental consequences of Kur's accidental release through Ione's blood.

After stripping down before the temple altar, Dev set the stage for the ritual that would provisionally unlock the warding magic of the tattoo. The power of fire required fire—sympathetic magic. Reciting the invocations of the four cardinal directions, Dev began with the east and moved counterclockwise to end at south, the quarter aligned with the element of fire.

Dev lifted the candle from the altar and held it above his head. "Welcome Shapash and Arinitti, Ishum and Ra, rulers of the fires of the sun. Welcome Hephaestus, god of the furnace and the forge, Vulcan, god of flame and master of the eternal fires within the belly of the earth. Welcome Hestia and Vesta, goddesses of the hearth fires and the home. Welcome Agni, purifier and bringer of lightning, devourer of sacrifice, and he who commends the spirits of the dead to the netherworld. Lend me your power that I may pass safely through it."

He tilted the candle and let the wax drip down onto his abdomen, the first spatter of hot liquid making him flinch as it struck the topmost point of the star. With careful precision, he traced the symbol with drippings of wax, down to the left and up to the right, and across and down, and once more returning to the topmost point before slowly moving about the whole of the circle surrounding it.

"With the element of fire, I call you, Kur." He felt the ground shudder beneath his feet as though the dragon's weight had shifted within him. "With fire I call your fire." Heat rushed upward through his veins and collected at his heart until it felt like it might stop beating before the heat began flowing downward, centered once more on the tattoo.

Dev held the candle aloft. "Your power is my power. My limbs are your limbs. Your breath my breath. We move forward as one, the body of the man and the power of the dragon." Dev set the candle back on the altar as dragon-fire moved through him like a tide ebbing and flowing, heat radiating from his skin.

"So," he said conversationally, "let's find this corpse that's causing our Ione so much trouble." He gathered his clothes from the bench, prepared to dress and head out to use the dragonfire as a sort of divining rod, when the dragon's sense turned him swiftly toward the door that led to the basement. *Here?* It couldn't possibly be here. Kur must be picking up on something else. But with his height-ened senses, he could smell the faint reek of decomposition, the same scent he'd noticed the night he'd found the dog's corpse hanging over the entrance to the temple. Probably just a mouse in a trap, but he ought to check it out.

Dev set down the clothes and grabbed one of the candles kept safely burning in the wall sconces with a perpetuity spell and headed for the stairs. As soon as he opened the door, it was clear this was no decomposing rodent. The smell he was breathing in with the dragon's sense was mixed with the moldering odor of damp soil. *Grave dirt.* Someone or something had been unearthed.

The scent grew stronger and overwhelming as he descended, appealing to the demon and repelling the man. He paused at the bottom, lifting the candle to illuminate the shadowy corners of the basement. There were the gardening supplies he'd used that night: shears and bin bags… and a long-handled shovel he hadn't seen before.

Dev approached the shelf where the shovel stood propped and crouched to examine it. Dirt was crusted around the base of the blade. Someone had used it and put it back without cleaning it off. Concentrating the dragonfire into his palm, he held out his hand and the flesh began to glow. Heat radiated into the metal of the shovel, enhancing the scent of the components of the dirt. The demon reared inside him as if it were tossing its head and stomping its feet like a warhorse on the battlefield, ready for action. It was definitely grave dirt.

A creak on the stairs made him whirl around, but a breeze rushed in from above and the candle went out, leaving him temporarily blind. As Dev straightened, something struck him in the back of the head and he stumbled onto one knee. In the darkness, it seemed as though the shovel itself had sprung from its place to crack his skull.

"What the blazes?" He put his hand to his head and felt something warm and sticky. The blood sent Kur into a rage and Dev found himself on his feet, lunging at whoever was messing with him in the dark, his human mind too rattled to control the demon's impulses.

Someone was there. Dev—or Kur—could smell her. Kur lashed out with the heat of his fire as Dev grabbed for her, and his assailant let out a sharp cry of surprise as his hand closed around her arm.

"Kur," he managed to growl in warning, trying to temper the demon's rage. He was burning her. But before he could calm the demon, the woman stepped in close to him and something stinging and sharp pierced his abdomen at the center of the tattoo. Dev let go of her arm and she scrambled back, taking with her whatever she'd stabbed him with. His eyes were becoming accustomed to the darkness. She backed away from him, her eyes wide, and a syringe dropped from her hand.

"Miss Kelley?" Those were the words he meant to say but his voice had gone low and gravelly, and the utterance wasn't human. "What did you do?" But that had come out as a demon snarl. Beneath him, his limbs were stretching and breaking, remodeling themselves into forelegs and hind legs, and his center of gravity was changing—as well as his vantage point. The basement suddenly seemed much smaller. Dev snarled and darted his head around—in a manner a human head oughtn't to be able to turn—to see the skin on his back boiling and rippling, sparkling with the emerging scales of the dragon.

Though she'd pushed him away, Ione had secretly hoped Dev would come back and allay her fears, swaying her once more with the charm he exuded when he wasn't playing the role of the straitlaced-but-awkward assayer. Or at least call, wanting to hear her voice before bed.

She groaned at the thought. What was the matter with her? It wasn't as if they were in a relationship. She prided herself on being independent and self-sufficient, yet here she was mooning over a guy like a teenager, just because he happened to be able to curl her toes with the sound of his voice.

Annoyed with herself, she decided to turn in early after a Samhain blessing at her altar. With everything that was going on, the coven's usual ritual had been canceled. She'd asked them all to practice solo this evening to raise energy individually for the good of the coven.

Before heading to bed, Ione called in her anonymous tip. Rather than getting into the magical component, she told them the attendees at the party were trafficking underage girls. Which probably wasn't untrue.

As she climbed into bed to read a bit before going to sleep, her skin suddenly prickled with apprehension and her heart began to race. Ione sat up, her chest feeling tight, like she couldn't catch her breath. What the hell was this? She'd never had a panic attack, but this sure felt like every description of one she'd ever heard. Maybe it was another attack from Carter through his precious apprentice.

Her amulet, set aside while she was changing for bed, lay on the nightstand. Ione slipped it over her head and tucked it into her pajamas, but the rush of adrenaline in her veins didn't slow. There was something urgent and familiar about this feeling.

Ione lay back against the pillow and closed her eyes, trying to still the sense of alarm, and nearly jumped out of her skin when her phone shrilled beside her.

She didn't recognize the number.

"Ione, thank Goddess you picked up. I didn't know who to call." The rushed voice seemed familiar, but she couldn't place it.

"Sorry, who is this?"

"It's Margot. Margot Kelley. There's something going on at the temple."

"At the temple? What do you mean? What's happening?" Visions of the Conclave dousing the perpetual flames and shuttering the doors flashed through her mind. Or a Halloween attack by some ultra-right religious group who'd managed to see through the glamour.

"I saw something—or someone—Gods, I don't know

what I saw. Something's inside the temple and I'm really freaked out."

"Where are you now?" Ione rose and started pulling on clothes one-handed. "Are you still at the temple?"

"No, I'm in my car. I had to get out of there."

As she zipped up her pants, the clock on her bedside table flipped to ten thirty.

Ione paused. "Margot, what were you doing there this late at night? Did you decide to do a Samhain ritual, after all?"

There was silence for a moment on the other end and then a horn honked and Margot swore softly. "Sorry. I have to go."

"Wait. *Margot*." But the line had gone dead.

Ione finished buttoning her waistband and shoved her feet into a pair of boots, not bothering to change the frayed and faded red T-shirt she'd worn to bed as she threw on her leather jacket. Twisting her hair into a knot at the nape of her neck, she hurried down to the garage and shoved her helmet on, not even thinking twice about taking the bike.

The parking lot of the temple held a single car—Dev's rental. As she passed it on the way inside, she noticed the remnants of the nail-polish graffiti Dev had told her about. Margot had been here when that had happened, and now this. What was going on?

Inside, the place seemed deserted, the usual muted glow of the magical candlelight throwing soft shadows against the stained glass, though an altar candle had been lit by someone, and incense was still burning. Dev's clothes were folded on one of the benches nearest the dais.

"Dev?" Her voice echoed through the empty sanctuary. "Are you here?"

The initial response was more silence. And then the

silence was pierced by an inhuman bellow from beneath her feet that sent chills up her spine. Crashing sounds followed from the basement. Crashing sounds that were ominously familiar.

Ione went to the open door and peered down the stairs into the darkness. "Kur?"

The bellow came again, ear-piercing and accompanied by a jet of flame. She just managed to get out of the way before the dragon barreled up the stairs and burst into the sacristy, tearing the door from its hinges, and crashed into the altar. If dragons could be drunk, this one seemed to be.

"Kur, it's me." Ione held out the back of her hand as though presenting it to a strange dog to be sniffed.

The dragon whipped its head slowly back and forth, its eyes unfocused as though it couldn't see her, but its nostrils flared, and it made a snorting sound as if it were scenting the wind. It turned toward Ione, its movements jerky and lumbering, and she saw something orange and fuzzy bobbing at its shoulder—the end of a tranquilizer dart.

She stepped closer, holding out her hands in a pacifying gesture. "It's okay. You're safe with me. Let me get that out of you."

With glazed eyes, the dragon exhaled with heavy, warm gusts but made no move to resist her—until she closed her hand around the tranquilizer dart to pull it out. And then it bolted, madly, letting out a roar of what could only be furious indignation, and leaped through the double doors into the atrium, scattering benches and candlesticks in its wake.

"Son of a—" Ione took off after the dragon as it broke off one of the outer doors and bounded into the parking lot. How was it able to move so quickly when it was obviously half-unconscious? She hoped to God the tranquilizer was still working its way through the dragon's system and would slow the creature down soon.

She shouted after the dragon as it scrabbled onto the top of the rental car, buckling the metal. It skittered and turned briefly, and then Ione's mouth dropped open in disbelief as the dragon leaped into the air and spread its massive webbed wings and flew away.

Stupidly, she watched it for several seconds as it wove and careened through the air—a caged bird suddenly free and unused to its wings—before she thought to hop on her bike and try to keep up with it.

Like a small plane with an engine problem, the dragon soared overhead, diving and climbing several times in succession while Ione sped among the hills through clouds of red dust. Kur was heading toward the rugged saddle points of Cathedral Rock. With the full moon overhead, she could see the dragon's silhouette as it neared the formation and appeared to alight on one of the lower spires. Ione rode in as far as she could get and parked her bike at the Back O' Beyond trailhead.

The full moon provided reasonably decent visibility at first, but deeper into the trail, sight was becoming impossible. Ione considered calling Phoebe to bring help. As she took her phone from her pocket, it dawned on her that it had a flashlight built into it.

Steering clear of night fauna as much as possible, she made her way as swiftly as she could to the spot where she'd last seen Kur's silhouette. But more than half an hour had passed by the time she reached the signature saddle of the rock formation. She climbed in deeper, despairing of finding him, and then stumbled onto the dark, hulking shape of a motionless dragon camouflaged by the rocks except for its glowing gusts of breath.

"*Kur*. Thank God." Ione scrambled up the hill to where the dragon lay curled at the base of the spire. The dragon watched her out of one baleful eye, like a great beached whale wondering what the puny human beside it was about to do next. What the hell *was* she going to do next? It hadn't been her doing that had brought the dragon forth. Could the same method she'd tried before put it back?

But she didn't have a blade. Ione searched the ground for a sharp enough rock, but picking up a piece of sandstone told her instantly that even if she managed to scrape away at her own flesh to make a deep enough cut, it would never pierce the thick scales of the dragon. She was going to need Phoebe and Rafe, after all. But the button on the phone yielded only the fruitless click of a drained battery.

"Crap."

Kur made a mournful sound like a dog moaning in its sleep and lowered his head to the ground. Ione was out of options. She sank to the ground next to the dragon. The desert night was chilly, but Kur's body emitted a comforting heat.

Now that she had time to sit and think, Ione tried to piece together what had happened. Dev had gone to the temple—perhaps called there by Margot?—and had performed some kind of ritual. He'd undressed, so he'd probably been alone at that point. He didn't seem like the type to be comfortable with casual nudity. In fact, he seemed pretty fond of keeping his clothes on even while engaged in not-so-casual sexual activity. She suspected it wasn't entirely down to his particular proclivities. The brand he'd thought of as a mass of scar tissue at his back was something he was always careful to keep out of view. But thinking of Dev in the buff wasn't getting her anywhere—at least not anywhere she needed to be at the moment.

Had he let Kur out himself? But that didn't make sense. He'd spent years keeping Kur in check. Not only was the dragon dangerous, but Dev had been determined to keep his condition hidden from the Covent. It wouldn't serve any purpose to risk his career and the reputation of the Covent—not to mention people's lives.

It seemed more likely that someone else—whoever had tranquilized him—had brought the dragon out for their own purposes. And the only person Ione was sure had been there was Margot. But it didn't make sense—the magical ambush or the graffiti on Dev's car. Carter had to be behind the ambush, and he was obviously behind Nemesis. Why would Margot be working with them? There was just no way Ione could have been that wrong about her.

Leaning back against the surprisingly silky texture of the dragon's scales—they were slick, like a snake's—she stared up at the milk of stars. It was easy to forget the spectacular blessings of living in this remarkable place. Ione crossed her arms over her chest and let her mind wander with the constellations.

The next time she blinked, the stars were in a different position. She'd dozed off, and there was no telling for how long. Kur was snoring behind her, producing gentle jets of steam, and either the dragon had tucked his wing around her or she'd nuzzled under it while she'd slept. The faint noise of cars on the distant highway announcing the early work shift said it wasn't long before dawn. What was she going to do when the morning hikers arrived?

She wished she knew what trick Dev had used to make himself unseen when he'd followed her into the prison. It couldn't have been a simple glamour because his physical presence would still have set off the metal detectors with his belt buckle and keys. She'd never glamoured anything to be *un*seen, anyway. Changing the perception of one's appearance was one thing, making a person—or a dragon—not appear at all was an entirely different matter.

The dragon stirred at the deep sigh she let out. Perhaps

the tranquilizer was wearing off. Ione wasn't sure if that was a good thing or a bad thing. But one way or another, she was going to have to get the creature moving, because the headlights of an intrepid early morning hiker were pulling into the parking lot at the trailhead. She probably had a few minutes. They weren't likely to hit the trail before the sky began to lighten, and it would take them at least as long as it had taken her to hike out to the spot. Somehow in those few minutes she had to get Dev back.

"Kur."

The dragon raised its head, instantly alert.

Ione rose onto her knees to bring herself to the height of the dragon's upraised head. "I don't know how much you understand, but I need you to return to your cage. I know it's not fair, but I promise you I'll do what I can to make things easier for you and Dev to coexist."

Eyes like glittery caramelized sugar candies narrowed at her and Kur made a soft growl in his throat.

"Dev said you were bound to me, that you had to obey me. Is that true?"

With a steamy sigh, the dragon lowered its head to its paws in a gesture of subservience. She took it as an indication that it both understood and agreed.

"I'd rather you didn't have to obey me. I'd rather you do what I ask because you want to. But I have to work with what I've got." This prompted a tilt of the dragon's head that was reminiscent of a dog, apparently tapping the limits of its understanding of human speech. Ione tried to keep it simple. "Do you know how to return to your cage?"

Kur's eyes blinked slowly at her, like a purposeful signal for "yes."

"Can you do it on your own?"

The dragon snuffled, nudging its snout into her hand.

"You need my help." Ione considered. "Do you need my blood? I don't have a blade."

Once more the dragon nudged her hand, more insistent this time as if she wasn't understanding. The indistinct gray of the rocks behind him had taken on a pale pinkish glow.

"I don't know what to do." Ione had only uttered the words for her own benefit, not expecting the dragon to understand. It moved its head swiftly, its mouth opening, and Ione let out a slight cry of alarm as it caught the heel of her hand between its teeth. But sharp as they were, the teeth hadn't pierced her skin. The dragon held her firmly but gently in its grasp. As its golden eyes met hers, it nipped her ever so slightly.

Ione flinched. "You're going to draw blood?"

The amber gaze continued to hold hers, unblinking. The dragon made no move to tighten or loosen its jaws.

Ione shook her head. "I don't know what you..." She paused, idly stroking the smooth scales of the dragon's side, and studied the expectant expression. "You need me to give the order. Or at least permission."

The dragon blinked once, slowly.

Ione took a deep breath and nodded. "You may do what you need to. I give you permission to draw my blood. Do what you must to return to your cage."

The prick of a needle-sharp canine pierced her flesh before she'd finished speaking, and Ione couldn't suppress a gasp of pain. Kur's eyes had gone sharp and—if she had to put a word to it—hungry. Ione wondered briefly if she'd made a mistake. But the dragon had released her hand. As she stared at the well of blood pooling up out of the puncture wound, Kur began to lap at it with a long, prickly tongue. The sensation was something between ticklish and stinging, and Ione gritted her teeth to keep from jerking her hand away.

As Kur lapped at the wound, his motions seemed to make the blood flow faster, and the dragon's eyes had grown alarmingly predatory. It let out a deep growl and lifted its head, and Ione was certain she'd misjudged the situation. It was about to attack.

"Kur." She tried to keep her voice calm.

But the dragon was looking over her head. It raised its snout in the air and opened its mouth—Ione's blood visible on its teeth—and looked for all the world like a cat that had smelled something that had overwhelmed its senses.

Boots crunched on the gravel just yards below them.

Ione turned swiftly. In the predawn light, she could see the bobbing movement of bright-colored clothing through the brush as the hiker approached. She tried to think of an explanation or some way to distract the hiker from coming any closer, but it was too late. The lone hiker, a young hipster with a beard, emerged a yard away, stepping into the clearing.

He stopped and stared at Ione, his mouth dropping open, and then a blush crept up his face. "Oh. Sorry, I… I didn't know anyone was out here."

It wasn't exactly the response she'd been expecting. Ione turned to find Dev crouched on all fours—in all his naked, delectable glory.

Chapter 21

Ione took off her jacket with as much nonchalance as she could manufacture and draped it over Dev's shoulders. Not that it covered…anything, really.

She glanced back at the hiker. "I'm so sorry we alarmed you. My brother has a head injury—he's just back from Afghanistan. Sometimes his PTSD gets triggered and he's not sure where he is. I've been looking for him all night."

"Oh. Wow, that's rough." The hiker accepted the story immediately, probably relieved to have a reasonable explanation, and Dev's wild hair and the out-of-it look in his eyes didn't make it too hard to swallow. "You need some help?" He was already taking off his pack and offering Ione his water.

"I think I've got him calmed down, but thanks." Ione took the water and crouched in front of Dev. "You're okay, hon. You just need to hydrate and we'll get you home." From the way Dev eagerly drank from the bottle, it seemed that much wasn't untrue.

"If that's your ride down at the trailhead, you're probably going to need a little more than that jacket." The hiker fished a pair of swim trunks out of his pack and handed them to Dev, who took them with a wariness that backed up her story. "They're not much, but I won't be needing these today. It's gotten pretty chilly."

"You're a sweetheart. Thank you so much." Ione pulled out her wallet as Dev pushed the jacket back at her to put on the shorts. "Let me reimburse you for those."

"Nah, it's cool. My dad's a vet. Just giving back, you know?"

Ione smiled. "You're a godsend. Thank you." She took Dev's hand and prompted him onto the path. "Let's get you home, babe."

The hiker gave Dev an awkward salute and complicated it with a "Peace, dude."

Dev, still silent, returned the salute…in the British style, with his palm facing out. The hiker's eyes narrowed, but he shrugged and let them go on their way.

Keeping quiet until they were out of earshot, Ione glanced at Dev trudging silently beside her on the path in his bare feet. "You okay?"

Dev gave a slight shiver as if her words had startled him. "I'm… How'd I get out here?"

Ione slowed. "You don't remember?"

"Not…as such, no."

"You flew."

Dev came to a stop and stared at her. "I what?"

"The dragon."

His brow wrinkled and Dev pressed his thumb and forefinger against the knot between his eyes. "No. Wait, I… You're saying I transformed? How?"

"I was hoping you'd be able to tell me." Ione started walking toward the parking lot once more and Dev followed. "It wasn't me, if that's what you're wondering. I got a call from Margot Kelley saying something was going on at the temple. And when I got there, you were…well, Kur."

Dev continued to look puzzled and somewhat shell-shocked, saying nothing more until they reached the lot.

He stopped on the asphalt. "You brought your motorbike."

Ione nodded. "Hop on." She unhooked the extra helmet from under the rear seat and tossed it at him, and Dev barely caught it.

He stared at her in disbelief. "Like this?" He glanced down at his bare chest and feet.

Ione's eyes only made it to the chest. Good God, he was absurdly ripped. He kept his clothes on so much she hadn't really had time to appreciate it.

"It's either that or you can walk back by yourself." Ione didn't wait for him to reply, mounting the bike and starting the engine. "I'll drive slow."

Dev looked skeptical, but he climbed on behind her and wrapped his arms around her waist. She could definitely get used to that.

"Watch your feet," she admonished and peeled out onto the road.

Dev's memories of Kur's consciousness began to come back to him in blurry watercolor bits as they arrived at the temple. They drifted to him in reverse, the most recent delivered by the taste of blood on his tongue. The image of Kur lapping blood from Ione's hand stopped him in his tracks as he swung off the bike.

Ione's jade eyes regarded him from the seat of the Nighthawk as she removed her helmet. "Are you all right?"

"I just recalled…" Dev shivered and rubbed his arms. "Kur…bit you."

She shrugged, dismounting. "I told him to. It seemed he needed blood to get back in the cage." Ione put an arm around him and prodded him toward the doors. "Come on. You're turning blue."

One of the outer doors was off its hinges and Dev scanned the upended benches and scattered candlesticks as they entered. A burned-down candle still graced the altar. "Was that me? I mean Kur? Did we do this?"

Ione started righting the furnishings. "He spooked when I tried to take out the tranquilizer dart somebody shot him with."

"Tranquilizer dart…"

"You don't remember anything? Any idea who shot you? I can't believe Margot would have been involved in this."

Dev shook his head. Memories that were formed in Kur's amygdala, embedded by strong, primal emotion, were the hardest to access. But calming ones came more easily.

He sat on one of the benches after helping Ione tip it into place. "You stayed with Kur."

Ione's eyebrows arched and she tucked her hands into the pockets of her jacket. "Of course I did. You didn't expect me to leave you out there on your own trapped in the body of a dragon?"

"It wasn't me, you understand. I'm not the dragon."

"I hate to break it to you, but for all intents and purposes, it is you. You may not be able to control him or be responsible for what he does, but you feel what he feels and I'm sure he feels what you do. If something happened to Kur out there, it would have happened to you. Besides, you told me he was my familiar. That means I have a responsibility to him."

"You keep calling the demon 'him.' It's a creature."

"For God's sake, Dev. You're going to have to come to terms with him. I know you didn't ask for this, but you share the same physical matter. Somehow. He's part of you. He's not a thing, dammit." Her face was animated with frustration and passion.

Dev could feel the demon's affection for her even as he tried to suppress the connection. "You care for it. For him." He shook his head, unable to express his mixed emotions. Was he actually jealous of Kur? He almost laughed out loud but decided against it in favor of not looking completely mad. Or simple.

Ione glared. "You say that like it's a bad thing."

"No, n—" Dev cleared his throat. "It's not a bad thing. It's just…unexpected. I've been at odds with the—with *him* for so long, and I—" He paused, a distinct memory rising out of the post-transformation fog. "The basement!"

Ione looked baffled. "The what?"

"Before Kur took over. I remember what I was doing here. I'd done a ritual to tap into Kur's fire—his breath, really. I meant to use it to sniff out the source of the necromancer's new power. And it led me to the basement." He rose and headed toward the gaping basement doorway, but Ione grabbed him by the arm.

"Not that I'm not enjoying ogling you, but maybe you should get dressed first." She picked up his clothes off the floor before the altar.

Dev raised an eyebrow. "You've been ogling me?"

Ione smiled, a slight pink creeping into her cheeks. "You don't give me the opportunity often enough."

Dev couldn't help smirking as he pulled his trousers on over the swim trunks. "I'll have to see what I can do to remedy that." He put on the shirt but didn't bother with his shoes, buttoning as he headed downstairs, anxious to see if what he thought he'd discovered in the basement was really there.

As he stopped at the bottom, Ione arrived beside him and pulled the switch dangling from the bulb overhead to turn on the light. That would have made his last trip easier.

The smell that Kur's borrowed senses had uncovered was there, just under the ordinary, dusty, musty smells of the basement. He recognized it now with his human senses: the smell of death.

Ione glanced at him. "What is it?"

"Over there." Dev moved toward the corner he'd been investigating before the demon had overtaken him. The shovel still lay on the floor and Dev paused to pick it up. "This shovel—someone hit me with it." He wasn't prepared to concede that the shovel had struck him on its own. "It's been used recently, you see?" He held out the blade of the shovel and showed Ione the remnants of soil.

After examining the shovel, she handed it back. "Probably the gardener."

Dev shook his head. "No. Don't you smell it?" Her wrinkled brow said she didn't. "I suppose I'm still accessing a bit of Kur's senses. But there's a scent of decay, organic matter—and not plant."

"I'm not sure what you're getting at. You think Nemesis used the shovel when she strung up the dog?"

"No, but I suspect the dog was meant to quite literally throw us off the scent. To mask what someone was really doing that night." He lifted his head and sniffed the air. "There's something else here." Against the wall, tucked into a space between two sets of shelves, a military footlocker was notable for its lack of dust. On closer inspection, faint lines were visible on the concrete floor before the trunk where it had been dragged forward and pushed back into place. Someone had tried to sweep over them, but the strokes of the broom itself had created a hash-mark effect.

As Dev moved toward the trunk, Ione made a soft sound of dismay behind him. "God, no. It can't be."

Dev glanced at her. "Can't be what?"

She just shook her head, her complexion looking a bit gray in the harsh light of the overhead bulb. He pulled up on the lid of the trunk, but it was locked with a padlock.

"Are there keys to this thing?" He glanced over his shoulder to find Ione holding out a pair of heavy-duty hedge clippers. Though they weren't quite made for the task, by applying enough pressure, he was able to snap the shackle of the lock in two.

After setting the clippers aside, Dev crouched to work out the broken pieces of the lock and pressed up on the front lip of the lid. The smell was the first thing to hit him, though it was relatively mild as such odors went. Ione made a horrified sound and stepped back as he propped the lid against the wall. Something leathery was folded inside the trunk, like an old maintenance worker's uniform stiff with dirt. Except that Dev knew very well it wasn't a uniform. It was a desiccated corpse.

"This is it," he said excitedly, while at the same time Ione gasped, "It's him."

Chapter 22

Dev straightened and turned, eyes wide. "My God. It's someone you know?"

"I didn't know him well. It's Matthew Palacio. Rafe's apprentice." Ione shuddered, unable to look away from the horror in the trunk.

"The young man Carter Hamilton killed." Dev looked the body over carefully before closing the trunk and coming to wrap her in his arms. "I'm so sorry. I didn't realize it would be someone you knew. I just knew there was a corpse down here somewhere. Kur picked up the scent."

Ione thought back to the night Matthew's body had been discovered here the first time. Carter had offered to handle it for her—to spare her. Goddammit, she was a fool. One of his friends on the police force, maybe Officer Paul himself, had probably "handled" it.

"But there was an inquest. A burial." Ione raised her head. "How could he have kept the body? How did no one notice it down here?"

"It's only recently been unearthed. But it looks as though the body wasn't embalmed. The dry desert dirt has effectively mummified it." Dev held her tight as she shivered. "I think Nemesis's activities were meant to disguise what was really going on here. Hamilton had someone dig up this corpse to give him access to the bones and power over the soul. That's how he's been able to practice magic, despite the binding spell the Covent performed on him. Necromancy is particularly potent magic, especially so when the body of one's victim is kept from its place of rest."

Ione shuddered. "I hate that you know that."

"Sorry. It's not something I have personal experience in, you understand. But I've studied unorthodox practices extensively—partly with Simon and partly as a requirement for my current position. The good news is that we've got him now. We can report to the Conclave that Hamilton is practicing necromancy again and inciting others to help him with it, including his apprentice. There won't be any more impediments to the proceedings to expel him."

Dev loosened his grip around her and let one palm slide down Ione's arm to take her hand. "Come on. We just need to make a plan to return the body and break Hamilton's connection before he has a chance to do anything more with it, but we don't need to stay down here with the poor soul to do it."

Ione let him lead her up the stairs. "But how do we know returning the body to its grave will accomplish that? He has to have a remnant of it with him in the prison—some artifact of bone. We need to get it from him and burn it in order to release Matthew's shade. That's what Rafe did with the others."

Dev shook his head. "That's not the method Hamilton is using this time."

"How do you know?"

"There were no missing appendages." Dev stepped aside as they reached the top. "From the looks of this corpse, he's using a method more like voodoo. Sympathetic magic, wherein the corpse's exhumation—and likely the disrepectful burial itself—is merely a symbolic means of exercising control over the soul. He may have something else, an object of importance to the victim, perhaps a lock of hair, something he's used to form a kind of poppet to stand in for the corpse. In essence, he's created a zombie without bothering with reanimation." Dev shuddered. "For which I think we should both be grateful. Elsewhere in the Caribbean, there's a concept called a 'jumbee,' the spirit of one who's become an instrument of evil in death because of evil done in life. Hamilton's intent may have been to make young Matthew into such a being."

"I can't imagine what evil Matthew Palacio could have committed."

"Perhaps that was to be achieved through the ritual burial and the exhumation of the body. Defiling the corpse to defile the soul. Either way, without the body, he has no power."

Ione glanced back down the stairs. "Maybe that's why you were attacked. You were getting too close and Carter wanted to stop you finding Matthew's body. But we still don't know how he did it. How the person who attacked you was able to bring Kur out."

Dev paused with his hand on the doorknob. "The hypodermic. Hang on a moment." He jogged back down the steps and returned after a moment with an empty syringe. "The last thing I recall after being hit with the shovel was this. Whatever was in it, that's how she did it." He placed his hand on his shirt over the tattoo. "She injected it directly into the mark."

"How *who* did it?" Ione dreaded the answer she knew was coming.

"Margot Kelley."

"You're sure?"

"Positive. I saw her just before my consciousness was subsumed by the demon's. It should be easy enough to prove. I grabbed her arm while Kur's fire was burning through me, and it left a burn."

Ione zipped up her jacket. "All right, then. Get your shoes on. Let's go."

"Go?" Dev picked up a shoe and pulled a sock from inside it to tug it on. "Where are we going?"

"To talk to Margot."

The address was easily obtained from the computer in the temple office that held the contact list for all the local Covent members. Ione had never used the list for anything personal before, but practicing magic to harm another member of the Covent invalidated Margot's right to privacy.

The apartment complex in the Village, just two miles south of Ione's place, was a ten-minute drive away. It was a little early for a visit, but Margot's grandmother was all smiles to see "friends of Maggie's" as she opened the door. Margot's face wasn't quite so happy when her grandmother led them through the apartment to where she stood looking out at the view from the balcony patio.

"Maggie, company to see you."

Margot turned and started visibly, blood draining from her face.

Margot's grandmother didn't seem to notice. "You kids want some iced tea?"

Ione started to decline, but Dev had better manners. "We'd love some. Thank you, Mrs. Kelley."

Margot put her back to the rail, arms outstretched and clutching it behind her, her eyes fearfully on Dev. The burn on her left upper arm peeked out from under her sleeve. "I-Ione. What are you doing here? What's wrong?"

"What do you think is wrong?" Ione curled her fingers around the edge of her helmet to keep her temper in check. "Would you like to explain what you did to Dev last night?"

"I… I didn't…" Margot stopped and her face crumpled. "He said we were helping Rafe."

"Helping Rafe?" Ione was taken aback. "Who said? Carter?"

"Carter?" Margot blanched. "God, no. What would I be doing talking to that sicko?"

Ione folded her arms, the helmet tucked at her side. "That was going to be my next question."

"I swear to you, Ione. I have nothing to do with Carter Hamilton. I've never even spoken with him, even before he was—before we knew what he was doing."

"But you're helping Nemesis."

Margot looked genuinely confused. "Nemesis? The person that left that dead cat in front of the temple? I'm not. I swear. You have to believe me."

"You keep swearing," Dev put in. His voice made her jump visibly. "But you haven't explained whose orders you were acting under when you assaulted me last night."

Tears sprang to Margot's brown eyes. "It wasn't anybody's orders. I didn't mean to hurt you. But he said you were possessed by a demon and I had to protect the high priestess. And you *were*." Margot managed to draw herself up despite her obvious fear. "You *are*. You're some kind of…*thing*. You may have Ione fooled, but I know what I saw. I didn't imagine it."

Ione put a hand on Margot's forearm and Margot

flinched. "You didn't imagine it. You're right." From the expression on her face, it was clear that Margot hadn't expected Ione to agree. "Dev—Mr. Gideon—is magically bound to a demon. But he won't harm me. And it wasn't his doing."

"You know?" Margot looked aghast. "You're okay with this?"

"There's a lot more to it than you understand but, yes, I am okay with it." Ione glanced over at Dev with a smile she couldn't help. "I'm working with him to keep it under control. And he was. Until you shot him up with whatever was in that syringe."

Before Margot could respond, her grandmother returned with a tray of iced tea and a plate of tea cakes and set them on the patio table.

"Thanks, Grams." Margot's smile seemed close to natural as she took a glass.

"You just holler if you need anything else." Grandma Kelley seemed to have finally sensed that something was off, but when Margot said nothing else, she went back inside, throwing a glance between Dev and Ione as if to gauge whether they were a threat to her granddaughter.

Margot gulped down half a glass of tea without looking Ione or Dev in the eye.

Ione took a sip of her own. "Margot, whoever you've gotten mixed up with, they're not being straight with you. Carter Hamilton is practicing necromancy from prison, and he has people on the outside helping him, like this Nemesis. And, frankly, if I hadn't already figured out who she was—at this point, I'd be certain it was you. Now tell me who put you up to this."

Margot set down her glass, her expression grim. "I've been studying spirit communication. I know it's not exactly sanctioned by the Covent, but a lot of us were on Rafe's side when he defied them over the crossing doctrine." She glanced nervously at Dev, obviously still uncertain about him, before looking back at Ione. "I suppose you'll have to report me to the Council. But I haven't performed any rituals we haven't done in Circle."

Ione didn't comment on reporting her. "And whom did you contact?"

"Rafe's apprentice, Matthew Palacio."

Ione let her breath out in a sigh. Whatever else Margot had done, she'd hoped Margot wouldn't be implicated in the grave robbery.

"It's more like he contacted me, though." Margot took a cookie, nibbling on it absently. "I was actually trying to reach my mom. I just wanted to talk to her, you know? To be honest, I'm not even sure she's passed. She left me with Grams when I was little and we never heard from her again, so we've just assumed. But when I did the conjuring spell, Matthew seemed to be hovering in the shadows. It's hard to explain. I didn't see him. But I could sense him." Margot swallowed. "I didn't have any direct communication with him at first, just the sense that he was there. But then I found myself in the parking lot at the temple after talking to Mr. Gideon—writing on his car with my nail polish. Words I wasn't even aware I'd thought."

Dev spoke softly. "'The impure shall be cast out, and all those who consort with the impure.'"

Margot nodded, her eyes red from unshed tears. "I saw myself doing it. I was aware. But…it wasn't really me. That was when Matthew sort of spoke to me in my head and I realized his shade had stepped into me. He said Rafe had sent him to find someone like me who was a…" She paused, trying to find the right word.

"Evocator," Ione supplied.

"Yeah, that was it. An evocator. Like your sister Phoebe, huh? I never even knew—"

"Margot." Ione held her gaze as the younger woman seemed to realize she was rambling. "Why wouldn't Rafe have sent him through Phoebe? Or just communicated directly with you himself?"

"I…" Margot looked defeated. "I guess I was so excited to find out I could do it that I didn't even think about it. Matthew told me Mr. Gideon—" Margot swallowed and looked at Dev. "He told me you were being controlled by an evil spirit and they needed my help to expose you. He told me how to do the spell to bring out the spirit and where to find the special ingredient."

"Special ingredient?" Ione shot a quick glance at Dev. "What was the special ingredient?"

Margot looked nervous again. "Blood. I would never do blood magic. I know how dangerous it is—the slippery slope and all. But he said the blood was the only thing that would reveal the demon and that it was Phoebe's. That she'd let Rafe draw the blood to help protect you. They knew you wouldn't like it if you knew what they were doing so they left it for me at the temple. I picked up the vial of blood and cast the spell and made the serum per his instructions. Then I waited for Matthew to guide me. Last night he came to me and said it was time, that I had to get to the temple basement and that when…Dev…came downstairs, Matthew would make sure he was dazed so I could inject him with the serum. And that he'd know the spot when he saw Dev."

"The pentagram sigil." Dev put his hand to his solar plexus. "It's how I keep the demon from escaping."

Ione sighed and sat at the table. "And *you* let him out, Margot."

"I'm sorry." Margot's tears were finally falling. "I

thought I was helping you, Ione. I shot the demon with a tranquilizer gun, but it wouldn't go down. It was supposed to be knocked out when you came and found it in the basement. Matthew said you'd kill it, and Dev wouldn't be a danger to you anymore." She wiped her eyes, looking at Dev. "I didn't think it would kill you, just the demon. You have to believe me. I thought I was helping Ione and that it was for your own good."

Ione took a sip of tea and cleared her throat. "And whose good was digging up Matthew's corpse supposed to be for?"

Margot turned her head slowly. "Digging up…? What? What are you talking about?"

"You weren't involved in the exhumation of Matthew Palacio's remains?" Dev was as formal as ever. Ione supposed it probably helped in a situation like this.

Margot gaped at him. "His remains? His *body*? Somebody dug up his body? From the grave?"

Ione couldn't help but feel relieved at Margot's apparently genuine surprise. "We found it locked in a trunk in the basement. The same trunk he was originally found in, I imagine." It had been gone since the crime scene had been cleaned up. Ione had just assumed the police had thrown it out. Who would want to use a trunk a dead body had been found in? But someone had obviously been keeping it for Carter, planning his comeback.

"I don't know anything about that, I promise you. God, how awful." Margot paused. "Do you think that's why Matthew came to me? He'd been disturbed?"

"I think," said Dev firmly, "that Carter Hamilton has been controlling Matthew's shade through the possession of his mortal remains in order to manipulate you into helping him get rid of me."

Margot went pale. "I've been—I've been helping

Carter? But why does he want to get rid of you if it isn't about the demon?"

"To get back at me," said Ione.

"But how would…?" Margot glanced at Dev, the color returning to her cheeks as she studied his expression. "Oh." She gave Ione a slightly chagrined smile. "Well, then I guess…you did see that walking away."

Dev looked confused. "See what walking away?"

Ione tried to hide her smile. "Private joke." She glanced at Margot. "And you bet I did." She thanked Margot and rose to leave before Dev could dwell on it long enough to make the connection. "We're going to try to make sure that he can't, but please give one of us a call if Matthew tries to contact you again."

They had their confirmation. Carter was controlling Matthew's shade. Now they just needed to lay Matthew's body to rest to release his shade from Carter's clutches.

Back at the temple, they brought the trunk upstairs to take it out to Dev's car.

Ione sank onto one of the benches after they'd set it down before the altar, already emotionally exhausted. "What about the Conclave? Don't we need to show them evidence of Carter's necromancy? How are we going to hold him accountable without the body as proof?"

Dev leaned back against the front rim of the dais and nodded. "We'll take some pictures to document it. It would be ideal if they saw the body undisturbed for themselves, but, proof or no proof, there's a strong likelihood that the Covent won't allow us to do what needs to be done, magically or otherwise, to free the boy's soul. Sometimes tradition trumps common sense with the leadership."

"You don't say."

"Hopefully, if we take care of this ourselves first, our testimony will suffice, particularly when Margot adds hers." He shrugged, his smile crooked. "And as they say, it's easier to ask for forgiveness than it is to get permission. But in the event that they choose to disregard our testimonies, we will still have stripped Carter Hamilton of his ill-gotten power if we do this right."

Ione sighed. "I just want this to be over. I want *him* to be over. God help me, but sometimes I wish I could just kill him. Drive his body to some dark hole in the ground and be done with him."

"We'll do the next best thing," Dev promised. "We'll castrate him. Figuratively speaking."

With plenty of time to kill before dusk, they grabbed lunch at a brewery in the Tlaquepaque tourist trap. While Ione munched on her veggie pizza, the television over the bar caught her attention. Whatever game had been on had been interrupted by a special news bulletin. She couldn't hear the audio over the noise in the restaurant, but the words on the screen under the Breaking News banner were crystal clear: Underage Sex Scandal Rocks Sedona Police Department. Images of Officer Paul and his buddy appeared in the corners of the screen, identifying them as alleged ringleaders.

Dev had followed her gaze and he gave a low whistle. "Holy shit. You got them." He reached across the table to squeeze her hand. "I was actually hoping to take care of that for you last night with a little help from Kur before Margot derailed my plans." His smile was dark. "But your way is probably better."

They drove Matthew's body to the cemetery outside the nearby town of Cottonwood after dark. Ione had attended his funeral, and she recognized the plot by the tall cottonwood tree that stretched two wide branches over it like the arms of a guardian. It had given her comfort to think Matthew had one. And yet Carter had managed to use him all over again.

Dev was able to build the same sort of glamour he'd used to make himself invisible at the prison—the type of misdirection of energy that kept the casual observer from detecting Covent Temple—to allow them to dig up the grave without being bothered in case anyone happened by. He and Ione dug together at first, and then took turns once the hole got too deep for two. Aided by the fact that the ground had been recently disturbed, they were able to reach the empty coffin by late evening.

Ione had this horrible idea that it wouldn't be empty, that Matthew's soulless eyes would be staring up at her when they opened the lid, not desiccated and desecrated, not half-mummified and folded up to fit in a footlocker, but fresh and putrescent. But, of course, it was empty. It could have been no one else in that trunk. She suspected there was something about the body being placed at the murder site that was part of the necromantic ritual. From what they knew, Carter had lured Matthew downstairs on some pretext and strangled him, getting rid of him after using him to kill Carter's first victim, Barbara Fisher.

Mercifully, Dev lifted Matthew's dried-up corpse from the trunk himself and placed it in the coffin. After lighting candles at either end of the grave, they began the ritual to dissolve the unnatural magic keeping Matthew's shade bound to Carter. On top of the body, they crisscrossed boughs of cypress and juniper followed by a layer of stones as if to ensure the corpse wouldn't rise as one of the undead.

Dev spoke the words to sever the bond, ending with, "May your rest be henceforth undisturbed, your soul now your own to wander where you will. So mote it be."

"So mote it be," Ione agreed.

They worked in silence after that, replacing the dirt on top of Matthew's coffin and finishing it with the rectangles of sod they'd pried up before they'd begun to dig.

Belatedly, Ione realized she ought to have let Rafe know they'd discovered his apprentice's unearthed body. He might have wanted to be there to lay him to rest. Maybe it would be better, though, if he never knew. No sense in digging up all that pain just like Carter's accomplices had dug up all this dirt. It was done now. Carter was cut off and Matthew was free. Ione felt a sense of lightness and freedom herself. She'd also never been so tired in her life.

Dev echoed her thoughts. "I suppose we should both get some sleep."

"Maybe a shower first." Ione regarded him with a half smile. "You have dirt on your nose."

"Yeah? You've got a bit of nose on your dirt." Dev grinned and flicked the tip of her nose with his knuckle. "Just there. Maybe I could help you get clean."

"I suppose it might be more efficient if we showered together."

Dev nodded gravely. "I understand it's quite important to conserve water in the desert."

"Yes, indeed. Very important."

Exhaustion took over, however, as soon as they'd stripped down at the house and climbed into the shower. Ione nearly fell asleep on her feet and ended up just standing in the circle of Dev's arms for several minutes, reveling in the touch and smell of his skin while the warm water cascaded over them until it began to cool.

"You awake?" he murmured against her hair.

Ione nodded reluctantly. "I am as long as I keep standing."

"I think we're running out of hot water. Seems we're doing a poor job of water conservation, after all." Dev let go of her and shut off the faucet while Ione stepped out and grabbed a towel. "I wish I weren't so bloody tired," he said as he watched her.

Ione glanced up, mildly amused by the hopeful partial erection that seemed to say otherwise. "Not all of you looks tired."

Dev smiled ruefully. "It seems Kur isn't the only part of me with a mind of its own. But I'm afraid I'd fall asleep if I attempted to indulge it. And then God knows what mischief it might get up to without me."

Ione squeezed the water out of her hair and tossed him a towel. "I can't promise I'll keep watch on *this* one all night, but if it's still here in the morning, I'll see what I can do."

Dev laughed as he rubbed the towel across his chest. "Will you, now? That thought may just keep me up. In more ways than one."

In the end, they were both too tired for anything but sleep.

Dev's kisses on the back of her neck woke her in the morning. It was a wake-up call she could get used to. Ione made appreciative noises as she wriggled back against him, noting as Dev spooned around her that he was once again more awake than she was.

She smiled to herself. "Nice to see you, too."

Dev stroked his hand up and down her thigh, sliding the other arm beneath her and around to the front to cup her breast. "But you can't see me." His voice was warm and sensuous. "Because I have you from behind."

A shiver went through her and Dev obviously felt it, pressing her closer into him and kissing her shoulder. "And what are you planning on doing with me?"

Dev's grip tightened around her and the hand at her hip slid down between her thighs. Ione let out a breathy gasp as one finger prodded her open. He stroked the fingertip in tight circles just inside her until she was moaning and rocking her hips.

"I thought I'd just keep you in this position," he murmured against her skin, sending ripples down her spine. "While I *have* you—repeatedly—from behind."

Ione managed to make her vocal cords work. "I have no objection to that plan."

He was already opening a condom—apparently he'd been awake longer than she realized—and Ione made a sound that was close to crooning as Dev pressed between her legs and entered her.

"God, yes." His voice was gruff as he thrust deeper. "Let me hear you."

Ione happily obliged, abandoning all restraint as Dev rocked their bodies together, his quickening, vigorous motions pushing her toward more and more vocalization until she was arching back in his arms and nearly wailing with the force of her orgasm. As her cries tapered off into happy moans and whimpers, Dev dug his fingers into her hips and held her still while he sped up his pace, making noises of his own, grunts and growls of pleasure, until he spilled into her with a shout.

He turned her head toward him as his body relaxed into her, about to kiss her, when his phone went off on the table behind him. Dev groaned and separated himself from her, rolling over to grope for the device.

Ione rolled onto her hip, head propped on one hand, watching as he greeted the caller. His expression went from a pleasant smile to a furrowed, worried brow.

"No, of course it's fine that you called me. She's right here."

The Conclave again? Why couldn't they leave her alone? They'd promised to wait for Dev's report.

She took the phone when Dev held it out to her, rolling onto her back. "This is Ione."

"Ione, it's Rafe."

Ione sat up swiftly, instantly aware that something was wrong. "What's happened? Is Phoebe okay?"

Rafe's answer was several seconds too long in coming. "I don't know."

"What do you mean, you don't know?"

Rafe sounded weary. "She took a fall. She was out following a lead on Laurel, and when she didn't come home for several hours and wasn't answering her phone, I went out looking for her. Some hikers found her—"

"Oh, God. No. Please don't say—"

"She's not hurt. Physically. Just a few scrapes and bruises. But they're saying..." Rafe's voice trailed off for a moment on an odd hitch, and Ione realized he was fighting tears. That scared her more than anything. "They're saying she should have regained consciousness hours ago. They don't know why she hasn't. They're saying Phoebe's...in a coma."

Chapter 23

A moment before, Ione had believed everything was right with the world. Now she was struggling to get dressed while trying to understand Rafe's words about her kid sister being "unresponsive to stimuli."

As she tried to button her shirt one-handed and got the buttons misaligned, Dev took the phone out of her hand and pressed the speaker button.

"There's no medical explanation," Rafe was saying. "But she was out there to meet Laurel, and I don't trust that girl any farther than I could throw her. This is necromancy. I feel it. This is Hamilton's doing."

Ione struggled with the buttons. "I don't understand. I gave her an amulet. You had protective spells surrounding her. How could this happen?"

"I don't know." Rafe's voice was thick with anger and sorrow. "I don't understand how he can even have power."

"I'll get Ione over there as quickly as I can," Dev said

when Ione could manage nothing more than a string of obscenities directed at her own hands. “We’ll figure this out.”

Rafe gave them the room number at Verde Valley Medical Center. “Ione knows where it is.” His voice caught again. “Thank you, Dev.”

As Dev hung up the phone, Ione stopped fighting with her pants and burst into tears.

Dev was beside her in an instant, enveloping her in his arms. “It’s going to be all right, sweetheart. I promise. Don’t worry, love.” Terms of endearment tumbled from his lips without hesitation as he held her tight, words he hadn’t said to her before, and in the midst of her grief and worry, Ione realized that Dev loved her. But she had to put the fear and wonder of that realization on hold for now. If Phoebe was lost, nothing would matter.

When Ione couldn’t stop crying long enough to finish dressing, Dev did it for her, buttoning her pants—he would have laughed at that word, she thought idly; “pants” to him meant underpants—and rebuttoning her shirt that she’d gotten wrong twice. Dev wiped at her eyes with a tissue, handing it to her while he gathered up her hair behind her head. She’d slept on it wet, without adding any product to weigh it down, and it was wild with tight, frizzy curls. No one ever saw her like this. Crying or otherwise.

Dev glanced around, holding her hair in his fist. “Where are your hair ties, love?”

She pointed to the dish on her dresser, dabbing her eyes as she began to get herself under control, and Dev retrieved one to tie back her hair. “I must look a mess. I usually straighten it—”

“You look beautiful. I can’t fathom how you don’t know that.” Dev kissed her damp cheek.

* * *

He was respectfully silent as he drove her to the hospital, reaching over at stoplights to take her hand and give it a squeeze of encouragement. Ione felt numb, like the world was crumbling away beneath her feet and there was nothing she could do about it. She remembered this feeling from the drive home from California after getting the call that her parents were dead. But Phoebe wasn't dead. *Please, God. Don't let Phoebe be dead.*

When they entered Phoebe's room, Rafe sat by the bed, draped over Phoebe's body as if he might be asleep. Her sister looked like a stranger, stitches and bandages obscuring her features and a feeding tube taped to her nose like she was a lifeless object.

"Oh, Phoebes."

Rafe lifted his head at Ione's voice. "Ione. Thank you for coming so quickly. The girls are on their way."

Ione hugged him as he stood halfway to meet her. "I'm so sorry I missed your calls." She'd plugged the phone into the charger in Dev's car on the way and discovered Rafe's voice mails as he'd become increasingly worried at Phoebe's absence the night before. "I can't seem to get used to charging a cell phone."

Dev hovered a few feet behind her, studying Phoebe with a frown. "Where did they find her? Do they know what happened?"

Rafe rose to offer the seat to Ione. "Near Devil's Bridge. She'd fallen from a ridge on the hiking trail, but it wasn't much of a height. There's no sign of a head injury except for the shallow lacerations." For a horrible moment, Ione had pictured Phoebe falling from the precarious rock bridge itself.

She took Phoebe's hand from the blanket as she sat,

flinching at the cool, unresponsive touch. "What was she doing at Devil's Bridge?"

"Following Laurel. She called me from her car to say she'd tailed Laurel to Sedona from Florence after getting a tip that the girl was there visiting Hamilton again. I think Laurel must have known Phoebe was on her tail and led her out there to get her alone. I don't know what she did, whether she pushed Phoebe or something else—but I know there was necromancy involved." Rafe's voice shook. "I've seen Phoebe's shade."

Ione's skin went cold. "Her shade? But she's not..." She couldn't even say the word out loud.

"That's why I'm certain this is magical foul play." Rafe's hands were clenched at his sides and he seemed to notice his agitation, uncurling his fists to tuck his hands into his pockets. "Someone is using necromancy to try to control Phoebe's shade while she's unconscious, to draw it out of her."

"Draw it out of her." Ione swallowed, tasting bile in her throat. "To kill her, you mean."

"Soul murder," said Dev. His eyes were apologetic as Ione looked up at him. "If one separates the spirit of a living person from the body, the shade created cannot cross over because the body cannot die."

Ione clutched Phoebe's hand as if she could keep her shade inside her by sheer will. "Something else you learned from Simon?" Somehow she managed to sound casual, though inside her head she was screaming.

Dev regarded her. "No, not from Simon. From my studies. Simon never used magic against anyone. At least not anyone human."

"Simon?" Rafe glanced between the two of them.

"Dev's mentor," said Ione. "The man who bound him to Kur. Nice, huh?" She heard the nasty bite in her voice, as though this was somehow Dev's fault. But the rational part of her had simply stepped aside to watch her fall apart. Perhaps she was losing her own soul.

Dev's brows drew together, but he didn't take the bait.

Rafe rescued Ione from herself. "Hamilton is obviously behind this. I should have killed him when I had the chance."

Ione couldn't disagree with the sentiment, but the timing of events was troubling. "We took away the source of his power."

Rafe nodded and shrugged. "Yes, I burned the bone relics he'd collected and released the shades he'd bound with them, but he's obviously enlisted Laurel to get him access to another. Isn't that why you had Phoebe following her?"

Ione felt the accusation in it, though Rafe hadn't said it with blame. Tears stung behind her eyes and she couldn't trust herself to speak.

"She meant the one we found yesterday," said Dev.

Rafe blinked. "The one…what?"

"We discovered a corpse in the basement of the temple. It seems Hamilton had unearthed it and was controlling the soul through its desecration. I believe the method he was using would have given the shade greater power to interact with the living while doing his bidding. It managed to communicate with a very lovely girl in Ione's coven who now believes she's an evocator." Dev glanced at Ione. "I didn't mention it when we interviewed her yesterday but I'm quite certain she's not. She would have encountered shades before now if that were the case."

It had certainly been true of Phoebe. Ione's heart twisted like a wet dishrag at the memory of all the times she'd criticized and belittled her kid sister for her remarkable skill instead of supporting her. *Please let me have a chance to make it up to her.*

Rafe ran his fingers through his unruly curls; they'd both foregone their product today. "Wait a minute. Slow down. Can we go back to the part where you found a *corpse* in the temple basement?"

"We laid it to rest," said Dev. "There were no missing extremities that he could have used to make a bone fetish. Hamilton shouldn't be able to maintain his control over it."

Ione glanced at Dev. "But I think we must have been wrong about that." She looked up at Rafe. "I think Rafe would have seen him if he was free."

Rafe paused with his hand at his nape. "Seen whom?"

"Matthew."

His hand dropped to his side and his face went white. "Matthew? But he—Hamilton never—he used the shades under his control to keep Matthew from making contact with Phoebe but he never controlled Matthew himself. He couldn't, not without bone. And like you said, Matthew's body was whole when they buried him."

"It seems," said Dev, "that Hamilton has upped his game. He's using more sophisticated necromancy. Perhaps he thought it would be impossible to get access to bones from behind bars so he devised another method."

"But why hasn't Rafe seen Matthew's shade if we freed him?" Ione insisted.

Dev scratched the stubble at his chin. "Something other than the corpse must be keeping his soul tied to Hamilton. And I'd be willing to bet that whatever method he's using is connected to what he's doing to Phoebe. If we can figure out what his hold is on one, we may be able to break his hold on the other."

Ione glanced at her sister, lying in the bed beside her like a stranger, someone she'd never seen before. A strand of hair was stuck to one cheek and Ione brushed it aside and stroked Phoebe's hair absently.

"Then we need to find out." She paused with Phoebe's hair clutched between her fingers. "Rafe, can I borrow your knife?"

"My knife?" Rafe unhooked the knife from the sheath on his belt. "What are you going to do?"

"I think Carter Hamilton is due another visit from his lawyer."

Chapter 24

Dev watched Ione preparing to march into the lion's den. With something concrete to do, the despair that had gripped her since Rafe's phone call had fallen away. This was the high priestess, strong and steady, ready to defend her own, propelled by righteous anger. There was a touch of wrathfulness in her expression, like a mother bear about to avenge her cub. He wouldn't want to be on the receiving end of that. Carter Hamilton had obviously picked the wrong witch to mess with.

He'd tried to talk Ione out of her plan, but when she asked what bright ideas he had instead, he had to admit he couldn't think of anything better.

"If you're doing this, I'm going with you," he insisted.

"There's no way they'll let you in with me. It's going to take my best acting to get them to let me in to see him a second time without giving advance notice."

"I'm his spiritual counsel."

Ione's expression was incredulous in the little mirror over the sink in the loo as she wove the lock of Phoebe's hair into her own. "You're what?"

Dev cleared his throat. "Mr. Hamilton has sent us a communication leading us to believe he means harm to himself. As his spiritual counsel, I've naturally contacted his solicitor to get me in to see him immediately to offer him guidance and moral support during this spiritual crisis."

Like a digital image glitch, Ione's eyes flickered from green to periwinkle blue as the glamour took effect. "That's not bad, actually. All right, you're in. But don't gloat," she warned, glaring at the pleased look he couldn't mask quickly enough.

Rafe sat watching them from the chair by Phoebe's bed. "If I could think of a way to get in there myself, I'd insist on going, as well. But I'm afraid I'd simply snap his neck, and then I'd be taking his place in prison."

Ione shook her head. "You need to be here to keep watch on Phoebe. You're the only one who'll see her shade if it starts to pull away from her. You have to keep her anchored."

They left for the town of Florence, southeast of Phoenix, once Ione's little sisters had arrived. Dev knew they'd been at Ione's place during his transformation but had no recollection of either of them. They clearly remembered him, however. The dark-haired one, Theia, was tongue-tied and awed by him, while the blonde with the unruly spikes commented with a saucy grin that his "skin condition" had improved.

"She's in good hands," Dev remarked as they drove out of the hospital car park. "They won't let anything happen to her."

"*I'm* not going to let anything happen to her." Ione was fierce. "It's my fault she's lying there half-alive. If I hadn't sent her after Laurel, none of this would have happened."

"You can't know that. Hamilton has been escalating his

campaign against you steadily since this Nemesis business began. He obviously has no qualms about taking a life."

"He hasn't taken a life yet." Ione's voice was sharp.

"No, of course. And he won't. I just mean that he was bound to try sooner or later. He's got a serious chip on his shoulder and he blames you for everything he's done to himself."

"When I get done with *him*, he's going to wish he'd never met me."

Dev believed it.

The "spiritual counsel" ruse managed to get them in to see Hamilton. He could have refused them, of course. The fact that he hadn't meant he was enjoying his little game of cat and mouse and believed he had the upper hand.

"Ah, here he is in the flesh." Carter gave Dev the once-over while Ione held the receiver between her and Dev so they could both hear. "Your little lapdog. Must like the taste of your blood, Ione, dear. I understand that's the only way to return the demon once he's gotten out. Also the only way to set him loose. Tell me, how did that happen the first time? Was Dev earning his crimson wings?"

Before Dev could make a guess at what that phrase probably meant, Ione pulled the receiver close to speak into it directly.

"Shut up, Carter. I didn't come here to listen to your impression of a twelve-year-old boy. I came here to warn you that you're playing with fire."

"Oh, am I?"

Kur's keen hearing and a bit of lip-reading allowed Dev to pick up Hamilton's reply despite the fact that Ione still held the receiver to her ear.

"I know you're behind what's happened to Phoebe."

Hamilton blinked innocently. “I’m so confused. I thought *you* were Phoebe.”

“Did you actually think you could go up against the quetzal?”

Hamilton’s expression remained amused, but there was a slight tic of tension in his jaw at the words.

“You weren’t man enough to take his power when you had him drugged and bound at your mercy.” She’d gone for the jugular. The fact that it turned Dev on was probably inappropriate right now. “What makes you think you can best him when you’re locked up and powerless? You don’t even have access to magic.”

Hamilton’s calmness didn’t bode well. “Your trouble, my dear, is that you overestimate your own. Did *you* actually think I hadn’t planned for the eventuality of someone finding my little stash of reserves in the basement?” He smiled as Ione’s face clouded with dismay. “I’m well aware that you returned my property to its original location. Surely you can’t have imagined I wouldn’t have a contingency plan in place. My acolytes had taken the necessary steps to anchor the shadow revenant in this plane—before you besmirched their good names in the eyes of the law and endangered their livelihoods.”

“Acolytes,” Ione scoffed. “You mean sexual predators. And how dare you refer to a human body as property?”

Hamilton rolled his eyes. “Spare me the PC feminist rant. People volunteer themselves as property in all sorts of ways. Prostitution, sadomasochistic power exchange—perhaps you’re familiar with that one—working for corporations…” He flicked his gaze toward Dev, obviously aware that Dev could hear every word he was saying. “*Familiars.* Call it what you will, but our dear Matthew, bless his soul, forfeited his autonomy to me. Rafael believed his apprentice was an innocent bystander in our little drama, but Matthew was eager to learn and impatient at having to go at the snail's pace of Covent practice. When Rafael's mentorship didn't offer what he needed, Matthew was more than happy to hitch his little sled to the sleigh of a mentor who would. So to speak."

"You're telling me Matthew bound his soul to you in exchange for a fast track to magical instruction?"

"I'm telling you that Matthew knew what he was getting into. He knew what the price would be if things went south. And while you and your little whelp were distracted by his corpse, my apprentice had already obtained what was necessary to uphold that contract. And was busy obtaining a little extra security from sweet Phoebe while you were digging in the dirt with Fido." Hamilton lifted his arm and waggled his wrist, revealing the dark brown braided bracelet tied around it. The fiber it was braided from appeared to be human hair.

Of course. Hair. The most easily portable source of DNA. And not something a prisoner would be forbidden to accept as a gift. Laurel had probably included it in an envelope with her correspondence as though sending her lover a lock of her own hair as a token of her devotion. Only it had been hair from Matthew Palacio's corpse. And now Laurel had obtained hair from Phoebe, as well, the base on which Hamilton had constructed his necromantic spells.

Hamilton was laughing softly at Ione's look of shock and hopelessness. "Really, it's almost too easy. I almost feel guilty for having a superior intellect. What fun is there in outsmarting a woman of, at best, average intelligence? And her faithful pooch?"

Dev had finally had enough of the dog references.

He grabbed the receiver out of Ione's hand against little resistance and leaned close to the glass to stare Hamilton in the eye. "You listen to me, you son of a bitch. You're going to leave Ione and the rest of the Carlisle sisters alone.

I'm prepared to swear to having personally witnessed your practice of necromancy in my report to the Covent elders. Your little game is over."

Hamilton snorted. "You're going to tell on me? I'm quaking in my boots. You can't touch me, Gideon. You'd think even a pup would have learned to recognize when he's licked."

"Really?" said Dev. "*You* haven't." He breathed in, mentally drawing on Kur's magic, and punched his right hand toward the barrier between them. Despite the inch-thick bulletproof glass, Hamilton flinched but didn't move, clearly expecting only the impact of Dev's fist against the glass. But Dev's body was no longer in phase with its matter as the demon shifted within him. He punched right through the relative insubstantiality of the glass, snatching the bracelet from Hamilton's wrist and yanking it free before pulling his hand back and letting the molecules of the glass reset themselves.

Dev held up the broken braid of hair in his hand. "How's that superior intellect working for you now?"

Hamilton's smug expression transformed into a black fury and, for a moment, he looked more inhuman than Kur ever had. He slammed his palm against the glass, causing the guard to step in and prod him up.

"Milk and Cookie Time with your lawyer is over, Hamilton. You know the rules. Let's go."

Hamilton still clung to the receiver as the guard hauled him out of his chair. "You've just signed your little sister's death warrant," he snarled before a second guard arrived and wrested the phone from his hand and hung it up.

Dev looked down at the braided strands of hair in his fist while Ione stared in speechless shock.

After a moment she found her voice and it was tight with alarm. "What did you do?"

Dev raised his head, crushed by the look on her face.

"I thought I was freeing their souls. This has to be how he was maintaining control over them."

"Why wouldn't he just have more? He could have dozens of the goddamn bracelets in his cell!"

Dev tried to calm her with reason. "There are only so many hair clippings you can take from a person before it becomes obvious. You've done it twice with Phoebe in the last few days. If Laurel took some, it couldn't have been more than this." He held out the fetish on his palm. "We would have noticed when we saw her in hospital."

"Would we?" Ione's glamour was slipping, the now-jade-green eyes rimmed with the red of despair. "Did we look that closely? She has cuts and abrasions on the side of her head, the stitches—there could be an entire bald patch under that bandage. That little monster Laurel could have yanked out a fistful."

Their escort opened the door to the visitation room and nodded toward the exit. "Come on, folks. This isn't a coffee lounge."

Ione swept past him and Dev followed, stuffing the bracelet in his pocket.

When he reached the car park, Ione was already on her mobile. "Rafe. How is she?"

Dev's heart broke for her as her face crumpled. Had he just killed Ione's sister with that stunt? "What's wrong? She's not…?"

Ione dropped the phone into her handbag, forgetting to end the call. "They've put her on a ventilator. She stopped breathing."

"God. I'm sorry, love." He reached for her to comfort her, but she hunched away from his grasp, her expression a stone mask.

"Get me back there before she's gone."

Chapter 25

Ione stared out the window at the brown, lifeless landscape speeding by. The desert seemed to be mocking her, more barren and empty than it had ever been, as if foreshadowing the empty landscape of the face she was driving to see. Rafe hadn't seen Phoebe's shade since the first appearance, but perhaps that was just because it had already been separated from her. Perhaps it was unanchored now, unable to return.

She held the bracelet of hair in her hand. Dev had given it to her without a word after they'd gotten into the car. The severed ends where he'd snapped it in two in taking it from Carter felt like Phoebe's bones, as if Dev had broken them. Even the fantastic moment of seeing Dev defy the laws of physics to take it couldn't penetrate Ione's hollowness. She could have kissed him in that moment—and then that infinitesimal instant of triumph had been snatched away.

It was after dark when they reached the hospital in Sedona. Phoebe was still hanging on, but if she'd seemed like a stranger before, now she was just a body and tubes. But that wasn't Phoebe. Phoebe was gone. Rafe looked like a shell of himself, as though Phoebe's shade had taken his with it. And the twins were as silent as Ione was, alternately sharing wordless hugs with her. No one needed language now. Language was useless.

Theia and Rhea had been too young to fully feel the loss of their parents. Ione had swept into that role, trying to make sure they never felt the lack. She'd finally failed in that impossible task of holding the family together. And why? Because another sister Ione hadn't even known existed had been too stupid to know she was being used by Carter Hamilton. Laurel Carpenter had done this to Phoebe as surely as Carter had. And Ione was going to make her pay. Before the night was over, Laurel Carpenter was going to understand the power of the Carlisle blood.

No one else needed to know what she was going to do. God knew Rafe would probably want to help her do it. But she wasn't taking any chances that one of them would try to stop her, to talk sense into her. She'd goddamn had it with sense.

"I need to be alone tonight," she told Dev after he'd driven her back to her place.

"Of course." He squeezed her hand but she couldn't feel it. She couldn't feel anything except hatred for Carter and Laurel. "You just call me if you need anything, love. I can be here in ten minutes." He walked her to the door and held her tight, pressing his lips to the top of her head. "Make sure your mobile is charged," he admonished, letting her go after her limbs didn't respond.

She nodded solemnly. She didn't want to miss the call when it came. The call that said she needed to be there immediately to say goodbye. Phoebe's doctors had said there was no imminent danger. The ventilator was merely a precaution in case she slipped deeper into herself. But the doctors didn't understand that there was no "self" left to slip into. Phoebe might lie there for years now, her flesh taking nourishment and oxygen through tubes, mindless cells obeying the code to regenerate themselves. But she wouldn't be Phoebe.

Ione waited until Dev had been gone long enough that he wouldn't see her bike on the road.

The message from Nemesis had appeared on her phone while Ione was still numb with despair.

The wages of sin is death. Come to the temple tonight. Your wages have come due—Nemesis.

She knew as soon as she read it that this was fate. Ione would face her alone and see that justice was done.

Perhaps it was a threat on Ione's life. She doubted it. Likely more games and more carcasses. But she no longer cared if Laurel was a danger to her. She would avenge Phoebe if it was the last thing she did.

Ione didn't even bother to wear her helmet, something she'd never neglected before. She wanted to feel the wind in her hair. Who gave a damn about rules anymore? Where had following rules gotten her? And who gave a damn about her hair?

She yanked the hair tie out and threw it on the ground as she dismounted the bike at Covent Temple. The wild hair, the hair of a madwoman—or a free woman—stood out on her shadow as she crossed under the lamplight before the entryway.

Ione opened both doors inside the atrium, drawing them outward and leaving them open, the wind following behind her, making the candle flames sputter on her way to the altar.

Laurel stood with her back to the door, a slight flinch of her spine acknowledging Ione's entrance. The altar had been lit for ritual and incense streamed in the breeze. Ione made the walk down the aisle in silence, stopping when she reached the front. Only then did Laurel turn to face her, surprisingly pallid, with a defenseless, fragile air, though her chin was raised defiantly.

Ione looked her up and down with cold hatred. "So here you are, you coward. Doing your master's dirty work."

Laurel's face flooded with color. "Oh, *I'm* the coward. You hide behind demon blood and the legitimacy of the Covent, as if the two were compatible."

"And you do the bidding of a necromancer."

"That's just another of your lies. Trying to twist what he does—and leaving him no recourse but to use magic that lies outside the accepted tenets of the Covent. He's never taken a life. He's merely had to call on the help of the souls who've passed because the living abandoned him."

Ione didn't know whether to laugh or cry at the audacity of it. "Whose body do you think you dug up the other night? You think he died of natural causes and Carter just happened to feel like feeding on the power of his soul by coincidence?"

"You're out of your mind. I didn't dig up any bodies."

"God, you're a pathological liar, just like he is."

Laurel folded her arms. "He said you'd say that."

This time Ione did laugh—if the sharp, humorless sound that burst from her lungs could be called laughter. "And what did he tell you about what you're doing to my sister? What twisted logic are you contorting to justify participating in soul murder?"

It was a slight move, barely noticeable, but Laurel

flinched. "Sometimes the ends have to justify the means. If you hadn't backed him into this position—"

"Oh, shut up." Ione stripped off her bike gloves and tossed them onto the bench beside her. "Let's just get this over with, shall we? Why don't you tell me why you brought me here while you still have the opportunity?"

Laurel backed up slightly against the altar, picking up a file folder from beside it. "Carter wanted me to be the one to tell you about the Covent's decision."

"What decision? How would he know anything about a decision?"

"The Covent has ruled on your offenses. You've been found guilty of oath-breaking and you're being formally expelled."

Ione blinked at her, utterly blindsided. "What are you talking about? You're lying. Dev hasn't even turned in his report."

"Dev…that's Assayer Dharamdev Gideon? Apparently he has. See for yourself."

Ione took the folder from her and opened it, her conviction shaken. There was Dev's signature at the bottom of the typed report.

> It is this assayer's opinion that Ms. Ione Carlisle has, with full knowledge, acted in a manner contrary to the laws of the Covent. Though it pains me to come to this conclusion, her continued recklessness with regard to her vendetta against Mr. Carter Hamilton cannot be ignored. Given Ms. Carlisle's willful participation in a conspiracy against Mr. Hamilton with former Covent member Rafael Diamante Jr. to force him to confess to the crime of necromancy, there is no doubt that she has used magic to harm another witch, and has thus broken her oath to this body.

A film of tears blurred her vision, quickly replaced with a blinding, red haze. He had promised not to do this, had promised his report would reflect the truth about Carter and about herself. He'd murmured those terms of endearment to her. And yet here in her hands was proof that he'd betrayed her, after all.

But Carter had fooled her before.

She blinked to clear her vision and focused on Laurel. "How do I know this isn't some kind of illusion? I'm sure the necromancer has all sorts of tricks up his sleeve."

Laurel almost looked sympathetic, the little monster. "I suppose Mr. Gideon didn't have much of a choice. The Covent knows all about the demon Kur. The Conclave ruled that he wasn't responsible for being bound to the demon but, in order to retain his membership in the Covent, he needed to demonstrate absolute loyalty. His objective report assured them of that."

It rang horribly true. Dev had kept his secret despite having revealed Ione's. His guilt over his condition had weighed on him for years, and Ione had heaped even more guilt on top of it by telling him the truth about what Rhea had seen of Kur's torment and Simon's betrayal.

But true or not, it was a distraction from what Laurel was really doing there. From the reason Ione had come.

Laurel raised a hand to brush her fingers through her hair—the same dark chestnut as Phoebe's and the twins' natural color—and Ione saw the bracelet slide toward Laurel's elbow and disappear into her sleeve.

Laurel seemed to notice Ione's glance. She dropped her hand away from her hair and covered the braided fetish with her other hand.

A spark of desperate hope erupted in the darkness.

Ione tossed the report onto the bench. "Is that how you're doing it?"

Laurel looked startled. "Doing what?"

"Don't play coy." Ione took a step closer. "That bracelet on your wrist. The one you're trying to hide. Where did you get it? What is it?"

Laurel had been fiddling with the place where it was tied and she pulled it away from her wrist, holding it up, no longer coy but defiant. "You mean this? It's your sister's hair. I took it from her while she lay unconscious in the dirt. Or, to be more precise, it's your sister's soul." She stepped up to the altar, holding the fetish near the candle. "On this Day of the Dead, I consign this soul to the flame, and she shall walk forever in the twilight between the worlds."

Ione clenched her fists in the air, a futile miming of the action of grabbing for it. She had to tread carefully. If there was a chance of saving Phoebe after all, she had to treat Laurel with kid gloves.

Ione spoke softly. "She's your sister, too."

Laurel's periwinkle eyes darkened. "You think I don't know? That the four of you got to grow up with my father's attention and affection? That the reason my mother had no money to buy us decent clothes was because all of it went to you? That all the advantages—and the *power*—of the Carlisle heritage went only to you?" Her voice dripped with vitriol as she spoke the word "power."

Ione was subdued for a moment by the palpable anger. "We didn't know about it at all. We only discovered it when we were trying to figure out who you were."

Laurel's fist clenched around the fetish. "Bullshit. My sisters contested the will." Her eyes narrowed in acknowledgment of the surprise on Ione's face. "Yes, I know about that. Even though I was living in foster care by then and it wouldn't have mattered to me. But your fancy lawyers made sure my sisters didn't get a penny."

"I knew someone contested it, but I didn't know the details. None of us had any idea that our father had a secret second family until a few days ago." She could see Laurel didn't believe her as she opened her fist and contemplated the fetish. Ione had to keep her from completing the ritual she'd obviously begun when she'd ambushed Phoebe last night. "You're wrong about the power, too. The blood you've been expressing such disgust for in your campaign for purity—you have it."

Laurel's face twisted in a bitter sneer. "I may have the recessive gene from my father, but you four got the magic combination. Two tainted parents. You're the abominations with your Lilith blood and your demonic gifts."

"No." Ione shook her head. "Your mother was a carrier. You have it."

Laurel flinched and stepped backward as if Ione had struck her. *"No."*

"As much as I hate to think it, I believe my father—our father—may have sought out our mothers deliberately." She moved slowly closer to Laurel as she spoke with patient calm. "Or maybe it wasn't deliberate. Maybe it was just predisposition drawing him to two women who shared his distant ancestry. But I think once he began to have children, he must have known what we were. I don't know what his endgame was."

She was telling herself the story as much as she was telling Laurel, trying to work it out as she pondered it. "Maybe he thought he could avoid some kind of fated destiny for his children by having a second family. But in the end, there were seven of us, all named for powerful Titanesses in one way or another. By the time you were born, he had to have known. He named you Laurel, for victory. For justice." Ione stopped just inches away from her. "For Themis."

Laurel's hand convulsed around the fetish. "Carter said you would try to confuse me, try to paint yourself as sympathetic and win my trust. It's not going to happen."

"What do you suppose he gains by keeping you feeling isolated and untrusting? If we're enemies, it gives him strength. It's not a coincidence that he chose you as his apprentice. He sought you out—to hurt me and to use your power."

"I don't have any power!" Laurel's shout filled the temple, utterly unlike her normally quiet demeanor.

"You must, Laurel." She managed to feel an actual touch of kindness toward the girl. "If you were powerless, he wouldn't want you."

Tears were streaming down Laurel's cheeks. "He does want me. He wants me for *me*, not some…some contaminated blood. Besides, I'd know if I had some kind of unnatural power." For the first time she seemed to be wavering, looking for something to believe.

"You've never had anything unusual happen to you? A feeling you couldn't explain? Each of our powers seems to correlate in some way to our namesakes'. Themis's power was the ability to foresee the future."

Something flickered in Laurel's eyes, a flash of recognition, accompanied by a spark of fear.

"You've seen things, haven't you?" Ione kept her manner gentle. "Tell me what you've seen."

"Everyone sees things. Like déjà vu, only…"

"Only something that hasn't happened yet, instead of something that feels like it's happened before? No, Laurel. Everyone doesn't. If you've seen things that have come true—"

"Stop trying to confuse me! You just want to stop me from protecting Carter. You want to destroy a good man."

It was all Ione could do not to launch herself at Laurel

with fury at the very idea of Carter being a good man. But there was something in Laurel's words that gave her hope.

"You've seen something about him, haven't you? You've seen other things that have come true, and now you're afraid that this thing you've seen is real, too."

"No. He wouldn't..."

"He wouldn't what? What did you see?"

Laurel opened her hand once more, staring at the braid of dark hair the same color as her own. "I have to trust him. Everything else is lies. The demon blood. Intrinsic magic. Rafael Diamante and Phoebe have taken advantage of the souls of the dead, manipulating them into possessing Carter to force him to tell lies about himself in court." She glanced up, her eyes dark. "I saw *that*, you know. That's why I sought him out. He didn't seek me. I saw Rafael use his quetzal power over the dead to make Carter confess to crimes he didn't commit. Are you going to deny that?" When Ione unconsciously bit her lip, a dark smile turned up the corner of Laurel's mouth. "You can't. Because you know it's true."

"No," Ione conceded. "I won't deny that Rafe used a shade to get Carter to confess."

Laurel's face was triumphant.

"But they were Carter's crimes. I know you don't want to believe that. *I* didn't want to believe it when my sisters told me what he was doing to the shades and to Rafe. But I saw it with my own eyes. After he'd cut Rafe's throat and stabbed Phoebe in the back, I saw Carter move in to finish them off. And he'll do the same to you if you keep giving him your power."

Something had hardened in Laurel's features. Ione was losing the argument. Confirming the one piece of truth Carter had used to build his lies had been a mistake.

"I have to stop them." Laurel seemed to be trying to

convince herself. “They brought this on themselves. You all did.”

As she moved her hand toward the flame once more, Ione did the only thing she could think of. Words weren’t going to cut it. Changing the perception of reality was her only hope. She concentrated on the flame, and the oxygen in the air around it, lifting her hand to draw the oxygen toward her, mentally encapsulating it in her fist. The flame wavered, almost going out, and Laurel made a sharp sound as if Ione had cut off her oxygen to do it.

Maybe she had. Was that how this worked? Was she really holding the oxygen she’d stolen from the air around the altar in her hand? There was something tempting in the idea of cutting off the source of what was feeding them both.

Laurel put her other hand to her throat, wheezing as if she was having an asthma attack. Ione started to open her hand, but the memory of Phoebe sucking in that same oxygen through a blue plastic tube, the realization that Phoebe would be lost forever if she let Laurel win, caused her to clench her fist with a vengeance.

Still trying to hold the fetish toward the flame, Laurel slid to her knees beside the altar, her face turning red.

“Ione, stop.” Dev’s voice came sharply from the open doors to the atrium.

Ione wavered but didn’t turn. “You don’t understand. She’s going to give him Phoebe’s soul. She’s going to kill my sister.”

“I know. But this isn’t the way.” His voice became louder as he approached the front of the temple. “You can’t use magic for harm.”

Ione spun to face him. “Now you’re quoting the Covent Rede at me? Is that the only thing that matters to you?

Following the rules, no matter whose life hangs in the balance?"

Dev's eyes sparkled like the dragon's in the low light of the candles. "I'm trying to stop you from making a mistake you'll regret for the rest of your life." He raised his eyes to the dais. "Just as I'm trying to stop Laurel from doing the same."

Ione had lost her concentration and she'd felt the loss of control over the element of air, the wind whispering like falling sand through her fingers. The weak flame on the altar candle flared brightly once more as she turned her attention back to it. Beside the altar, Laurel got to her feet, the fetish still clutched in her hand. She hadn't yet touched it to the flame.

"It's not supposed to kill her." Laurel looked shaken to her core. "He said we were stopping them from taking advantage of the dead."

Dev paused before the dais. "Stopping whom?"

But Laurel didn't seem to see him or to hear him. "He said the only way to stop her was to bind her soul. That it wouldn't hurt her."

Ione wanted to slap her. "You go take a look at her lying in that hospital with tubes jammed down her throat and tell me you haven't hurt her."

Laurel shuddered and focused at last on Ione. "He'll use her shade to control me. That's what I saw. He thinks he'll take the quetzal's power if he has my—" Her voice broke before she went on. "My demon blood." Laurel opened her hand and stared at it. "If you give this back to her, tie it around her wrist, her soul can be re-anchored." She lifted her palm and held it out toward Dev, who was closest to her, but a sudden gust of wind rushed through the temple and swept it from her hand into the flame.

Ione heard herself scream, moving in slow motion, the air

around her like the thickness of a dream as she tried to grab for the fetish before it burned completely. Dev was closer, but as he thrust out his hand to snuff out the candle, the wind seemed to strike him right beneath the ribs and shove him backward into a row of benches. At the same time the altar table tipped backward, taking the candle and the fetish with it as flames licked across the dais. Whatever spirit had plagued Phoebe the night of Carter's psychic attack—Matthew or something else—it was here, throwing things, affecting the physical plane. It was no simple shade.

Laurel looked on in horror as though frozen to the spot as flame began to surround her, and in the tumble of upended benches across from her, Dev was doubled over, trying to breathe, his diaphragm obviously locked in a spasm. It was up to Ione to make sure Phoebe's soul wasn't lost forever.

As she tried to get to the other side of the dais to rescue the fetish from among the overturned altar accoutrements, it dawned on her that Laurel wasn't just frozen with inaction. She was being held immobile by the same unseen force, and the flames were already licking up the sides of her jeans. Ione would have to choose between letting Phoebe's soul be torn from her body forever as the fetish was consumed or letting Laurel Carpenter burn to death in front of her eyes.

With a wail of despair, she scrambled across the wreckage of the altar and wrapped her arms around Laurel, tumbling with her onto the floor to roll out the flames. Both of them were coughing and choking as they tried to struggle to their hands and knees. Dev had recovered his breath, and he moved between them, taking each of them by the arm to haul them out of the temple before they succumbed to smoke inhalation.

Through the stained-glass windows they could see the

glow of the burning altar, the charm around the perpetually burning candles that lit the chamber keeping the fire from spreading any farther than the four-by-six-foot rectangle of the dais itself.

Dev headed back toward the doors.

"What are you doing?" Ione's throat was harsh with smoke as she shouted after him.

"There's a fire extinguisher just inside." He grabbed it from beside the inner set of doors and darted back into the smoky interior, foam spraying in front of him as he ran. In a moment the flames were out.

Several seconds passed while Ione felt her heart stop, convinced the smoke had gotten to him, but just when she made a move to go in after him, Dev returned.

His normally brilliant eyes were heavy, watering from the acrid smoke. "There was nothing left of it. I'm sorry, love."

Beside her, Laurel dropped to her knees on the asphalt and began to sob.

Chapter 26

The girl was inconsolable after realizing what Carter Hamilton had seduced her into doing, and it was clear she was no longer going to be giving them any trouble. Dev managed to convince Ione that the best thing for both her and Laurel at this point was rest.

With Laurel quietly weeping beside him in his rental, he followed Ione to her house, where she gave Laurel a Valium and put her to bed on the couch. It was disheartening, however, how readily Ione had agreed to his suggestion. The fire had gone out of her. And there was only one way to get it back. Phoebe's soul had to be rescued from Carter Hamilton.

The conviction that it could be done was best kept to himself. He couldn't bear to get her hopes up only to fail. Because the chances were high that he would.

Of paramount importance to his plan was that Phoebe's body remained in stasis, and Dev was relieved when he returned to the hospital to find her condition largely unchanged. As the doctors had predicted, she'd slipped deeper into the coma but remained stable on the ventilator. Diamante had stayed with her, looking empty and hollow, his eyes red from lack of sleep—or from crying—though he'd sent the twins home to Phoebe's place to get some rest.

He clasped Diamante's shoulder as the other man sat back down after Dev declined to take his seat. "Listen, Rafael—"

"It's Rafe. Only strangers call me Rafael."

Dev smiled. "Glad to know you don't consider me a stranger. Listen, I have to tell you something." Rafe's shoulder tightened beneath his grip. "But hear me out. I may have a solution. About an hour ago Laurel Carpenter...inadvertently completed Hamilton's ritual to bind Phoebe's soul to him."

"Oh, God." Rafe dropped his head forward, his face in his hands. "She's gone. I knew it. I felt something. I couldn't see her, but I felt her go."

"Maybe not," Dev reassured him, squeezing the shoulder. "Not permanently, at least."

Rafe lifted his head. "What do you mean?"

"As quetzal, you have a certain amount of contact with the unseen world, what some would call the netherworld—or hell, to be vulgar."

"It doesn't matter. I can't go there myself. I can't do anything to free her from Hamilton's control." He drew his shoulders up. "Except kill her and destroy her bones by fire." His face was set like cold stone. "That's what I have to do."

"No, no. Just wait. Please hear me out, and don't do anything rash. Not until I try what I have in mind. With your help."

The stony expression remained, as though Rafe had already made up his mind. "Which is?"

"The demon inside me—when it's dormant, or 'caged,' it returns to its natural realm, though trapped within my physical matter. When I've traded places with it, my consciousness has been severely depressed, but I've still been aware of being in that state, that realm. I believe if my body were temporarily incapacitated and rendered unresponsive—in essence, in the same state Phoebe is in now—that both Kur and I could move about within his realm unfettered. Once there, I could reach Phoebe's soul and bring her back with me. When you wake me."

Rafe's dark brows drew together. "Are you out of your mind? You want me to put you into a coma?"

"With all due respect, *your* plan is to smother and immolate your girlfriend. I think mine is better."

Rafe considered for an instant. "All right. What do I need to do to incapacitate you?"

Dev raised an eyebrow. "Under other circumstances, I might be a bit offended that you capitulated so quickly. But I think you've made the right choice. The comatose state will need to be magically induced so that you can bring me out of it."

He laid out his plan, based on the same magic Laurel herself had used. He'd had a moment to talk to the girl in private to get the details on the drive. Besides the incantations and the specific elements of the spell—namely, a lock of his hair collected to anchor his shade to Rafe—a sufficient blow to the head to induce what would otherwise be transitory unconsciousness was key. Whether Kur would cooperate once Dev had stepped out of his physical body remained to be seen. He ran the risk of setting the demon loose, but for Ione's sake, it was a risk he had to take.

Dev steeled himself, expecting Rafe to strike him with

the tire iron Dev had brought with him, but a blow to the side of his head from a bare fist and the recoil of the back of his head against the wall beside him did the trick.

He became aware once more as Rafe uttered the incantation and ordered him to come forth. Dev shivered as though cold—as if he could somehow feel the air flowing through his disembodied form. Looking back at his body slumped in the chair was unnerving.

"So now what?" Rafe, with the eyes and ears of the quetzal that allowed him to see and hear shades, spoke to him as if addressing Dev's shade was no different than addressing a living man. "How do I help you make contact?"

"I think you need to officially commend me to the netherworld."

"You *think*?"

"Laurel wasn't privy to how Hamilton was keeping Phoebe from coming to you, but it's the only explanation that makes sense to me. That he's keeping her in the realm of the dead when he's not…"

Rafe's eyes darkened. "Not what?"

"I was going to say, when he's not—using her." He hastened to continue as Rafe's eyes seemed to crackle with fire around the edges. "But I sincerely doubt he's doing anything approaching the more unsavory connotations of that word. Laurel said he intended to force Phoebe's shade into her body to control them both, and I believe his intentions were to use the catalyst of Laurel's demon blood to give him the power to come after you."

Rafe's mouth twisted with anger. "The catalyst that awakened the power of the quetzal was sex with Phoebe."

"Ah." Dev swallowed, though he had no true throat to swallow with—or saliva to swallow, or air to breathe, for that matter, all of which were equally unsettling. "Sorry, mate. I suppose we'd best get on with this, then, and bring her home."

Rafe nodded and clasped the wrist on which he wore Dev's fetish—also a tad unsettling—as he invoked his deities. "Mictlantecuhtli and Mictecacihuatl, Lord and Lady of the Underworld, I send you the soul of one who walks between the worlds. Grant him entry that he may seek the soul of Phoebe Carlisle within your domain."

Dev stepped back into his unconscious body to enter the virtual cage, the door through which he hoped Kur's currency as a denizen of the realm would buy him safe passage. In an instant the grayness of the cage's ordinary formlessness gave way to a cool, dark corridor. Perhaps his human mind simply supplied the form based on his concept of the netherworld, but it looked for all intents and purposes like a subterranean cave. And Kur was prowling beside him.

Dev nodded to the demon, his spine tingling slightly with apprehension. "Cheers, mate."

The demon returned a deep purr-like growl that seemed to be a greeting. At least, he hoped it was a greeting and not a threat.

"I don't suppose you know how to find Phoebe?"

The demon cocked its dragon head to one side.

"Ione's sister."

That seemed to do the trick. Raising his snout into the air and sniffing, Kur began to lumber forward. Dev followed, hoping the dragon hadn't simply scented dinner. Which begged the question, if the demon ate meat in the human realm, what did it feast on within its own? On second thought, Dev didn't really want to know.

They plodded through the dank passageway for what seemed like more than a mile before at last taking a turn that opened into a large, domed chamber. The earthen walls seemed to give off their own phosphorescence. Dev paused, his eyes adjusting to the relative light of the space after the darkness of the passage. At the far end, before a wall that trickled with water, a pair of thrones made of bone—with skulls for headrests—was occupied by a diminutive but somewhat stout couple whose faces, though flesh, revealed the skulls beneath them. Dark, beetle-like eyes gazed out at him from the sunken sockets.

Despite his experiences with Simon and his belief in magic within the practice of the Craft, Dev didn't subscribe to any religious tradition. But these two were clearly Rafe's Lord and Lady of the Underworld, the Aztec gods the other man had invoked.

Dev gave them a slight bow, uncertain what the proper protocol was here.

"You come seeking one who is not dead and yet not alive." Neither of their mouths had moved and Dev couldn't be sure who was addressing him.

"That's correct. I seek the soul of Phoebe Renée Carlisle. The mate of the quetzal."

"She has not come here of her own free will." Again, the mouths remained motionless. "Her soul is bound to another."

"Through trickery and deceit," said Dev.

"As you are bound to the demon beside you through trickery and deceit."

Dev glanced at Kur, who was crouched into a compact shape like a cat. "Yes, that's true."

"And you wish to take the soul of the woman, breaking the unnatural bond that holds her here, to return her to the world of the living." This time the female of the couple had spoken aloud, shifting on her throne in an uncannily life-like departure from the breathing statuary she'd seemed a moment before, the straight black hair on her translucent scalp sparkling in the phosphorescent glow as she moved.

Dev nodded. “Yes, ma’am. I do.”

Mictecacihuatl swept her arm outward. “Come forth, Phoebe Renée Carlisle, mate of the quetzal.”

Phoebe materialized before the throne, a chain around her neck, which the Lady of the Underworld held in her hand. Dev’s brow wrinkled at the costume Phoebe’s soul seemed to be wearing. He’d entered the realm in the clothes he’d had on when Rafe had knocked him out, but Phoebe was wearing some sort of bathing suit made of metal, like a skimpy suit of armor.

Dev felt the heat in his cheeks as he recognized it. She was curled up on her hip before the throne like Princess Leia in Jabba the Hutt’s lair. Whether this was another of his own mental inventions or whether Carter Hamilton had enslaved her soul with the Princess Leia slave-girl fantasy in mind, he wasn’t sure he wanted to examine. Whichever it was, he certainly wasn’t going to mention it to Rafe or Ione once he’d freed Phoebe’s soul.

“Phoebe.” He nodded to her, taking a step toward her.

“She cannot speak to you here.” The goddess toyed with the chain. “Not while she is bound. To break this bond, you must offer up your own in sacrifice.”

Dev squinted at her. “How’s that?”

“Give us the demon as our own.”

“Give you the—?” Dev glanced at Kur, whose dragon eyes were unreadable. “To do what with?”

“That is not your concern.” The god had spoken at last and his deathlike voice chilled Dev to the mental projection of his bones.

Dev cleared his throat, trying to keep the fear from affecting his speech. “Sorry, but it is my concern. I didn’t ask for this bond. And Kur bloody well didn’t ask for it.

But I'm responsible for his welfare as surely as I'm responsible for his actions within my realm."

"There must be an exchange," Mictlantecuhtli insisted in that bone-chilling voice. "One must stay if the other is to leave."

Dev glanced once more at the demon, still sitting stoically in its catlike position. "I will not leave Kur here to be enslaved. He's not my property to give. If Kur stays, I stay."

"So be it."

"Sorry? I'm not sure what you—"

But Mictlantecuhtli had clapped his hands, the echo against the stone walls nearly deafening. Dev ducked his head and put his hands to his ears.

When he looked up, Phoebe Carlisle was gone.

Chapter 27

Ione grabbed for the phone when it chimed beside her head. She'd slept with it on the pillow next to her, afraid she'd miss the summons to Phoebe's deathbed. She held it in her hand, letting it ring once more, not wanting to hear the news. What if she'd missed it, after all? What if Rafe was calling to tell her Phoebe was already gone?

She pressed the button. "This is Ione."

"Ione! There's someone here who wants to speak to you." Rafe sounded far more animated than she would have expected.

"What do you mean? Who?"

Another voice came on the line, one she'd never expected to hear again. "Hey, Di, it's me."

Ione nearly dropped the phone, clinging to it and holding it to her ear with both hands. "Phoebe? Oh, my God. *Phoebe*. Is that really you?"

"It's really me."

"What happened? I thought..." She couldn't say what she'd thought.

"It's kind of a long story. I'm fine but they won't let me leave yet, and...well, why don't you just come to the hospital so we can talk in person?"

"Of course! I'll be there in ten minutes."

Ione left Laurel sleeping and jumped on her bike to get there as fast as she could, so excited she forgot to take off her gloves and leave the helmet on the bike as she hurried to Phoebe's room.

And Phoebe was on her like a hawk. "*What* is that in your hand?"

Ione grinned, happy to see Phoebe sitting up in bed and looking like herself, if just a bit paler than usual. "This thing? It's my racecar-driver helmet."

"It is *not*. You're riding a motorcycle! When did you learn to ride a motorcycle?"

"When I was fifteen." Ione tossed the helmet into an empty chair and bent to hug Phoebe tight. The hug was probably more of a shock to Phoebe than the bike was. Ione had never been big on demonstrative affection. "I can't believe you're okay. When I saw the fetish burn I was sure we'd lost you." Ione pulled back to look her up and down. "*How* are you okay?"

Phoebe glanced at Rafe standing off to the side. "Maybe he'd better tell you."

Ione's smile wavered as she turned to Rafe. "Tell me what? Is something wrong with Phoebe?"

Rafe looked uncomfortable. "No, Phoebe's fine. It's just... I think I should show you." He was standing in front of the curtain drawn around the side of Phoebe's bed. Ione had noticed it as she entered the room but dismissed it in her eagerness to see Phoebe.

He pulled it aside to reveal Dev asleep in a chair. "Gideon brought her back."

"He did?" Ione smiled again, stepping toward him. With a lock of dark hair slipped out of his usually careful coiffure at the center of his forehead, Dev looked like a lovely fallen angel. "How?"

"It was his idea." Rafe sounded oddly defensive. "He asked me to perform a spell that would allow him to enter the netherworld from within himself."

"Within himself?" Ione turned to study Rafe. "What exactly did he do?"

"He said Kur's cage inside him was within the demon's realm, and he could access it if he was unconscious." Rafe glanced nervously at Phoebe. "And...he hasn't come back."

"What do you mean he hasn't come back?" Ione reached for Dev's hand to wake him, but his skin was abnormally cool to the touch. She whirled on Rafe. "What did you do?"

"He's in a...magically induced coma." Rafe hurried on as Ione gaped at him. "He should have woken when I unbound the fetish—"

"You made a *fetish* of Dev's soul? How did you even know this spell?" When Rafe didn't say anything, she knew the answer. "That little witch Laurel gave it to him. You performed one of Carter's spells on him."

"It was what he wanted to do. The alternative was..." Rafe glanced at Phoebe and, from the pain in his eyes, it was obvious what he'd been prepared to do to free her.

Phoebe pulled her knees up under the thermal hospital blanket. "I'm so grateful to him, Ione. You don't know what it was like."

Ione dropped onto the edge of the bed and took her hand. "Of course, sweetie. I'm sorry. I wouldn't wish you back there for the world."

"I remember him being there, but I couldn't understand what he was saying. I don't know why he stayed while I was allowed to return. But we can't let him stay there. I can't have him stuck there in my place. I couldn't live with myself."

"I think there may be a way to reach him." Rafe glanced up, as if at someone taller than himself. "Kur's shade is here."

The dragon had a shade?

Ione looked in the direction of the empty space where Rafe's eyes were focused. "What about Dev's shade?"

"That's what I can't figure out." Rafe nodded to Phoebe. "If Phoebe's willing, perhaps Kur can communicate with us."

"Absolutely," said Phoebe. "I'm in."

"Ione?" Rafe looked at her expectantly.

"You're asking my permission?"

"Kur is."

"Oh." For some reason it made her cheeks warm. "Okay. Tell him he's got it."

Rafe smiled. "He can hear you. In fact, he hangs on your every word."

Yeah, that didn't make her blush worse *at all.*

Phoebe inhaled deeply and closed her eyes, and in a moment, they shot open, her breath escaping in a rush.

A word escaped with it as she looked at Ione, her voice rough and inhuman. "Mistress."

Certain she'd turned an unprecedented shade of red, Ione tried to compose herself. "Kur. What's happened to Dev?"

"The man." Phoebe's voice was like rocks in a tumbler. "He protect Kur." The dragon seemed to have a better understanding of English now that it was in Phoebe's head.

"He protects you? From what?"

Phoebe glanced at Rafe, her foreign expression somewhat wary. "Snake's gods."

"Snake gods?"

"Snake's," said Rafe. "I think that means me. You mean Mictlantecuhtli and Mictecacihuatl? The Lord and Lady of the Underworld?"

Phoebe nodded. "Snake's gods say Kur stay. Man say no. If Kur stay, man stay."

"He wouldn't leave you." Ione glanced at Dev's motionless body, surprised that Dev had demonstrated such loyalty to the demon he'd barely acknowledged as a sentient being a day or two ago. She looked back at Phoebe, studying the unfamiliar expression on her face. "Do you want to stay there, Kur? It's your realm, isn't it? Wouldn't you be free of Dev if you stayed?"

Phoebe's shoulders lifted in a shrug that spoke of a much larger frame and of burdens Ione couldn't imagine. "Man protect Kur. Kur protect man. Kur stay with mistress."

Ione was unreasonably pleased at the implication.

Rafe was studying her. "Kur is bound to you?"

"Dev says he's my familiar." Ione scowled. "Actually, Carter said it, trying to insult him, but Dev said it rang true."

"Then Kur has to obey you."

"Well...yes, I suppose so. I've never really had a familiar before." She glanced at Phoebe-Kur. "Kind of like Phoebe with Puddleglum, I guess."

Disconcertingly, Phoebe laughed, the dragon's demeanor momentarily cast off. "Oh, there's no obeying going on there. Unless I'm *his* familiar."

But Rafe was focused on something. "Kur, if Dev has been forbidden to return without leaving you, what about you? Have the gods forbidden you from returning?"

Phoebe's brow wrinkled with confusion. "Kur *here*."

"So you're not technically within the Underworld. And if you step into Dev's body now, what happens?"

This, Kur didn't need to think about. "Kur go back in cage."

"Until someone releases you." Rafe looked at Ione.

Ione drew her bottom lip between her teeth. "You think if Kur's shade returns to Dev's body and I unlock the warding, his body will resume dragon form…"

"And then you order Kur's shade to return from the Underworld. He can't disobey you, so it should break whatever magical binding is keeping him under. With the dragon awake, when he returns to human form, Dev should be awake, as well."

"Should be. Are you sure these Underworld gods of yours are going to let him go?"

"The abode of the dead, as I understand it, is constructed of what one imagines it to be. It isn't a true realm with a single reality. Dev perceives the gods I invoked and is currently constrained by the rules of that construct. Once he's back in our realm, he's back. The realm he perceived can no longer impose its rules upon him."

"Or so you think."

Rafe inclined his head. "It's worth a try."

Ione glanced around the small hospital room. "We can't do it here."

"We could wheel him out to the parking lot." Rafe took out his phone and started texting. "I think I have some orderlies around here somewhere who'd be happy to lend a hand."

"Orderlies?"

Phoebe laughed. "Tweedledum and Tweedledee. Rafe sent them to the cafeteria because they were smothering me with their happiness at having me back, and he wanted some quiet to work this out." She paused and put her hand to her diaphragm, breathing out once more sharply. "Kur's gone."

"He's waiting by Dev," said Rafe. "You need to direct him, Ione."

Ione looked in the general direction of Rafe's gaze. "Kur, you need to return to your cage." She glanced at Rafe when there was no change in Dev's slack form.

Rafe nodded. "I can't see him anymore. He must be in."

And not a moment too soon, as Theia and Rhea, having gotten Rafe's text, barged into the room as though the entrance were an emergency room door, using a gurney they'd borrowed from somewhere. Theia was wearing a white lab coat and Rhea had managed to get her hands on a pair of scrubs.

"Where do you want him?" they said together.

With visiting hours over, the visitors' parking lot was relatively empty. Phoebe, grudgingly, had stayed in bed while Rafe and Ione got Dev onto the gurney and covered him with a sheet, and the twins had wheeled him out.

Rafe offered Ione his blade. "I think the same method you used to bring Dev back the last time should work to release the dragon."

The last time the dragon had been released, of course, she'd let it bite her and lick the blood from her hand, but she wasn't about to get technical with Rafe about that.

With his shirt off and quetzal wings outstretched, Rafe repeated his invocation of the gods of the Underworld as he'd done in Ione's living room, while Ione unbuttoned Dev's shirt to bare the tattoo and made the cut on her hand. Cutting Dev's flesh while he was unconscious was slightly more unsettling than cutting into the thick hide of the dragon had been. She was careful to cut just enough to draw blood.

Rafe nodded and waved the twins back, though Rhea gave him an impressive growl of her own when he tried to shoo her farther.

Ione pressed her bloodied hand over Dev's solar plexus, letting their blood mix. No words were necessary. Beneath the vibration that always moved between them, Dev's skin was boiling.

Ione jumped back. She'd never seen the transformation from this direction before. It was a bit horrifying to watch. And to hear. Bones seemed to be cracking and stretching inside him as his unconscious body contorted. The clothes tore as his musculature changed, green, scaly flesh bursting through it. Ione should have undressed him. Then again, with the twins ogling him, it was just as well she hadn't.

The unconscious weight of the dragon as it fully emerged snapped the metal legs of the gurney and Kur thudded to the ground.

Rhea nudged her twin and whispered in a voice that was impossible not to hear, "Which would you rather have? Feathered quetzal or this bad boy? Cuz I'm team Dev. All the way."

Theia rolled her eyes. "Shut up, Rhe."

Rafe pretended not to have heard. "Now give him the order, Ione. Tell him to return from the Underworld."

Ione took a deep breath. "Kur, I command you to return to your physical form in this plane." Nothing happened. She tried again. "I command you, Kur, to come back to me from the Underworld." Still nothing.

Ione's shoulders slumped. "It's not working."

Rafe scratched his head, the iridescent quetzal wings still extended behind him. "Maybe you're not using the right terminology. Maybe he doesn't consider it the Underworld."

"Or maybe it just doesn't work," she snapped. But there was no point in taking out her frazzled nerves and disappointment on Rafe. "Sorry. I just..." She shook her head, staring at the dragon sprawled on the ground. "How are we going to explain an unconscious dragon in the parking lot?"

"Just breathe, Ione. Try again."

Ione closed her eyes, centering herself. "Kur, I order you to return to the earthly plane, to the realm of the living." She opened her eyes. Again, nothing. "Goddammit, Kur!" Tears of frustration stung behind her eyes and the cut on her hand was also stinging. She'd forgotten Rafe's earlier advice to keep the cut away from the center of her palm. Ione covered her face with her hands, unable to contain a moan of despair.

While she stood, trying to calm her breathing, she felt Theia and Rhea step up beside her, each putting a hand on one of her shoulders in encouragement. She dropped her hands and offered them to her sisters, taking strength from them. Maybe more of the Lilith blood magic—the "Lilith bond" as Theia had dubbed it—was what was needed.

"In the name of the ancient Lady Lilith whose blood runs in my veins, I order you to come back, Kur. Come back to me. Please." Her voice cracked. "Bring Dev back."

Wind from the valley whooshed in and lifted their hair, and Ione could feel the Lilith blood like a wave pulsing through them—trough and crest, trough and crest. And on the asphalt before them, the great beast began to stir.

The twins let go and stepped back instinctively as Ione stepped forward. Kur lumbered groggily to his clawed feet, tail whipping out behind him and thumping against the asphalt, sinewy wings outstretched. Ione was afraid for a moment that the dragon was about to leap into flight as it had before. But as the amber eyes cleared and focused on her, Kur closed his wings against his body and lowered his head as though bowing to her. The long snout nudged forward and snuffled against her palm, and Ione realized it was seeking the blood still dripping from the cut.

She held out her hand but Kur raised his head, blinking his sparkling eyes at her, and with his prickly outstretched tongue between his sharp fangs, he licked her face. Ione was frozen in surprise before remembering she'd pressed her bleeding hand to her cheek a moment ago. The dragon cleaned the blood from her face and then shuddered as the transformation overtook it once more, seemingly as difficult on Kur as it had been on Dev. In a moment the warm brown skin of the man had returned and Dev collapsed onto the pavement in a heap.

Ione went down on her knees beside him. "Dev?" She brushed the damp hair across his forehead, but there was no response. "It didn't work." She tried to keep the despair out of her voice. "He's still in the coma."

Rafe crouched beside her and pulled back one of Dev's eyelids. "No, I saw his shade return. I think he's just wiped out from going dragon and back so quickly." He squeezed her hand in reassurance then released it as she winced at the sting of the open cut. "Sorry. My bad. But your man's good. He just needs some sleep." Rafe smiled. "No worries."

Across from them, Rhea nudged Theia. This time, both of them waggled their eyebrows at each other in unspoken appreciation of Dev's sleeping form. Ione glared and yanked the sheet up over him. But she had to admit, it was one hell of a form.

Chapter 28

When Ione arrived home in the wee hours of the morning after entrusting Dev to Rafe's care, Laurel was gone. Ione couldn't bring herself to be sorry about it. Laurel might have finally come to her senses about Carter Hamilton, but Ione was a long way from forgiving her or trying to form any kind of familial bond over their half-blood connection. Even if that blood happened to be Lilith blood.

As Ione reached into her jacket pocket to take out the bike keys and hang them on their hook in the garage, she felt something soft against the lining: the fetish Dev had taken from Carter at the prison. She examined it in her hand. If it was Phoebe's hair that had formed the fetish Laurel had intended to burn, this one was Matthew's. She saw now that it didn't have the subtle chestnut undertones in the light. If this had given Carter his power over Matthew, where was Matthew's shade now?

She remembered the force at the temple upending the

altar like Jesus with the money changers' tables—the force that had punched Dev in the gut and held Laurel in place. The fire might have cost them Phoebe, but it had stopped Laurel from being the instrument of that deed, from committing an act so heinous that she would have forfeited her autonomy to Carter. Just as Carter claimed Matthew had. Maybe Matthew had done evil in life, after all, as unfathomable as it was for Ione to believe.

During his attempt to take Rafe's power, Carter had revealed a vision to Rafe of Matthew's last hours, wanting Rafe to see how he'd corrupted his apprentice. After using Barbara Fisher to seduce Matthew, Carter had directed a shade to possess him, using Matthew's hands to strangle her. Caught up in Carter's persuasive half-truths, perhaps Matthew had let the shade in willingly to take her life—just as Laurel had been about to take Phoebe's—an act that had bound him to Carter forever.

And Matthew's shade-turned-jumbee, freed from Carter, had tried to stop Laurel from making the same mistake, the only way he could. Whatever else Matthew had done, it seemed he'd acted, in the end, with good intentions. Ione could at least see to it that his soul was finally allowed to rest.

At the outdoor altar, she performed an unbinding spell, unbraiding the fetish and cutting each strand in two before burning them individually with an exhortation to be free. She threw in a Memorare prayer, just in case. Ione might not be welcome in the church any longer, but she wasn't quite ready to give up the traditions of her childhood entirely. She was a daughter of Lilith and a child of God.

Too wound up to go back to bed afterward, she made herself some tea and watched the sun rise over the side deck before going out to putter in her garden—which had been trampled by a dragon not long ago and by Rafe's work crew shortly after that. Most of what she'd planted was native to the region, but there were a few perennials that needed cutting back before the first frost.

Ione was on her hands and knees pruning her lantana bushes when the crunch of boots on the gravel walk made her look up.

Dev smiled down at her, dressed with uncharacteristic casualness in a pair of black jeans and an oatmeal-gray thermal undershirt. She realized the clothes must be Rafe's. Though they fit him extremely well.

Dev slipped his hands into the back pockets. "Good morning. Hope I'm not intruding."

Ione got to her feet and brushed dirt from her knees, feeling strangely self-conscious after all they'd been through. "Of course not. I'm glad to see you looking… more yourself."

"I understand I have you to thank for that. Again."

Ione tucked a flyaway strand of frizz behind her ear with a shrug, realizing she hadn't done anything with her hair since yesterday except tie it back. "I understand I have you to thank for getting Phoebe back. Honestly, I don't know *how* to thank you for what you did for her. I don't really know how I can *ever* thank you—"

Her awkward ramble was cut off as Dev stepped in and cupped her face in his hands and kissed her. His touch set off the familiar tingling vibration in her skin until it spiraled around her from head to toe, a fairy godmother's magic wand spinning its transformation before the ball, setting every nerve ending on fire. When he separated their mouths, Ione swayed against him.

"You smell delicious," she murmured, feeling slightly drunk.

"Like toasted marshmallows?" he offered, and Ione

laughed. "Listen, I came to tell you that I've filed my report with the Conclave." That sobered her up.

Ione stepped back, rubbing her forearm where the thorns of the lantana had scraped the skin. "I know."

"You know?" Dev cocked his head, invoking Kur's demeanor.

"Laurel showed it to me. And I suppose you had to do what you felt was right, no matter—"

"Wait, how would Laurel have had a copy? I just filed it this morning."

Ione wanted to believe he was telling the truth, but he'd echoed the words in the report when he'd come to stop her from avenging Phoebe. "I saw your signature."

Dev's brow wrinkled. "And what did this report conclude?"

"That I'd broken my oath."

His golden-brown eyes were troubled. "You believed I would write that?"

"I… She said the Covent had learned of Kur and that it was your only option if you wanted to keep your position." The stray hair had blown back into her eyes and Ione reached to tuck it back again, but Dev did it for her.

His hand lingered at her cheek. "I see. I suppose I can't blame you for believing I'd do that, but I assure you, love, that's not what my report says."

Ione's heartbeat quickened at that little word. "What… what does it say?"

"They do know about Kur. Because I told them. And I informed them that, following an exhaustive investigation, which has been an utter waste of the Covent's money and a political witch hunt against an outstanding and unimpeachably honorable high priestess, I've concluded you were completely blameless in your actions regarding the necromancer Carter Hamilton. And I resigned my commission as assayer."

"You...what?"

"I figured as assayer I'd be shipped off immediately to the next investigation, which might be anywhere in the world. And I don't want to be anywhere in the world. I want to be right here. With you. Always."

Ione blinked up at him, finding the chatoyant gold of his eyes mesmerizing. "Oh."

Dev slipped his arms around her waist and drew her to him. "Is that all right with you?"

She managed to nod, her toes beginning to go numb as every inch of her awareness became focused on the firm insistence of his desire where she pressed against him. "Mmm-hmm."

"You okay, love?"

That tiny little word made the tingling vibrate on its own frequency, and Ione let out a soft, moaning hum in reply. She'd been a fool to doubt him—and to doubt her own feelings.

Dev studied her with amusement. "You seem to have become monosyllabic. If not downright preverbal."

Ione slipped her arms around his neck, reveling in the vibration between them and in the sheer relief of giving in to the pull of need and desire, fated or not. "Mmm...hmm."

Dev's lips teased her neck. "As long as you're preverbal, shall I take you upstairs and render you completely insensible?"

Ione couldn't suppress a grin, though she still had her face buried in his chest. "You have a way with words, Mr. Gideon," she murmured. "How can I possibly refuse?"

Dev clucked his tongue in disapproval. "I see we're back to square one with complete sentences." He tipped her chin up to look her in the eyes as he began working through the buttons on the front of her shirt. “Perhaps I can find something under here to keep you quiet.” He slipped off her sleeves and dropped the shirt to the ground, and then tugged on the front of her bra. “I think I might be able to make this work.”

As he reached behind her to undo the clasp, Ione caught movement out of the corner of her eye. Her nosy neighbor stood in front of her driveway across the street looking scandalized. Ione held the cups of the bra in place as the clasp came away.

Dev followed Ione’s gaze with a little lift of his eyebrows. Before Ione could stop him, he’d whisked the undergarment from her hands and was waving it in the air in greeting at her horrified neighbor.

“Lovely day for it!”

Ione covered her mouth with her hands, trying not to laugh out loud at the look on “Gladys Kravitz’s” face, but it only got worse when Ione realized she was covering the wrong bits. “Lovely day for what?” she managed to gasp.

Dev slipped the straps of the bra onto a twig of dead lantana. “A marshmallow roast, of course.” He winked and tossed the twig bearing the two padded white cups into the waning embers in the fire pit.

Ione lost all pretense at composure, laughing so hard she could barely stay upright as her neighbor stalked into her house in righteous indignation. Still laughing uncontrollably, she found herself being whisked off her feet and carried into the living room through the open glass door.

Dev deposited her onto the couch. “I don’t know what’s so funny.” He shook his head at her as he unzipped her jeans and began working them down. “It *is* a lovely day for it. Your neighbor’s just going to have to get used to it, because I expect there will be a great many lovely days for it from here on out. In case you didn’t know, witches’ familiars mate for life." Dev dropped the jeans to the floor and peeled back her panties. "Ah, now *there's* my warm, gooey, sweet treat."

The last of Ione's laughter died away into a delicious moan.

* * * * *